EARLY MORNING

My landline was ringing, and the digital alarm read seven o'clock. I closed my eyes and pulled the pillow over my head, hoping the caller would go away, and waited for the voice mail to kick in.

"Dodie? It's Lola." Her voice cracked as if she'd been crying.

My hand searched for the receiver and I lifted it off the base. "Lola? Are you okay?"

"I'm sorry to call this early. There's been some . . . trouble at the theater."

"What's going on?"

"Oh, Dodie, I don't know how to tell you. . . ."

"Just say it quickly."

"Jerome is dead." She started to cry. "I went home at midnight, but Walter stayed to finish casting the play, you know. . . ."

"And so?" I desperately wanted to believe that her story was a nightmare that I would wake from.

"He said he left at one."

"When did they . . . ?"

"It was horrible. The garbage men came to empty the Dumpster on the loading dock this morning . . . and found him."

I could hear her breathing deeply and I felt my eyes tear up. Jerome was only a Windjammer acquaintance, but I felt like I'd gotten to know him.

"What was Jerome doing on the loading dock? Was it a heart attack or something?"

"Dodie, Jerome was murdered. . . ."

Show Time

Suzanne Trauth

LYRICAL UNDERGROUND
Kensington Publishing Corp.
www.kensingtonbooks.com

LYRICAL UNDERGROUND BOOKS are published by

Kensington Publishing Corp.
119 West 40th Street
New York, NY 10018

All Kensington titles, imprints, and distributed lines are available at special quantity discounts for bulk purchases for sales promotion, premiums, fund-raising, educational, or institutional use.

Special book excerpts or customized printings can also be created to fit specific needs. For details, write or phone the office of the Kensington Sales Manager: Kensington Publishing Corp., 119 West 40th Street, New York, NY 10018. Attn. Sales Department. Phone: 1-800-221-2647.

First Electronic Edition: July 2016
eISBN-13: 978-1-60183-719-6
eISBN-10: 1-60183-719-4

First Print Edition: July 2016
ISBN-13: 978-1-60183-720-2
ISBN-10: 1-60183-720-8

Printed in the United States of America

For Elaine, my first and last reader . . . and creative ATM.

ACKNOWLEDGMENTS

Thanks to everyone who generously supported this project from the beginning by reading early sections of the book: Lisa Romeo, the Book Doctors, Judith Lindbergh at The Writers Circle, and Jordan Baker-Kilner. I am particularly indebted to Paul Dinas, whose editing and encouragement have made all the difference, and to Toni's Kitchen, whose staff provided inspiration for the restaurant business. A special thanks to John Scognamiglio and the folks at Kensington Books.

Chapter 1

There is no such thing as *a* Jersey girl. For example, if you lived below the Driscoll Bridge and were a citizen of the Jersey Shore, as I had been for most of my life, you were not necessarily defined by certain hairstyles and a particular accent. You were more likely to have a six-month tan and a strong penchant for boardwalk fries and fresh oysters. So I was a Jersey *Shore* girl.

Until Hurricane Sandy graced us with her presence. I watched the angry, churning water and crashing waves chew up the boardwalk like a hungry beast. Bigelow's, the restaurant that I managed, sat right on the beach. But then Bigelow's was destroyed, along with every other business in the vicinity. And so was my job. I turned in my keys, took one last look at my beloved ocean, packed my 2000 Chevy Metro, and stepped on the accelerator.

I was headed for Etonville, a quaint little community nestled in the shadow of New York City with a history that dated from Revolutionary War days. Etonville was intended to be a pit stop on my way to New York, somewhere I could live just long enough to save some money and make plans for my future. My former boss had a cousin who owned the Windjammer, a casual, family-style restaurant in Etonville that supposedly needed managing badly. I found an apartment on Craigslist and ended up renting a preWorld War II bungalow in the south end of town, five comfortable rooms all painted the same shade of optimistic yellow.

I settled in to get the Windjammer in shape. I'd been at it eighteen months.

The lunch rush was over. Henry, the owner/chef, and sous chef Enrico were working on prep for dinner, while bartender Benny restocked the bar and part-time server Carmen, Enrico's wife, cleaned tables. Our primary waitress, Gillian, was texting her boyfriend. I usually slipped out for a break at three o'clock.

"Be right back, Benny. Hold down the fort." I headed out the front door. It was a cool, breezy April day. New Jersey in spring. The weather could swing wildly this time of the year—hot, cold, or somewhere in between. I'd even seen a few late winter blizzards in April.

I zipped up my jacket, closed my eyes, and stopped to inhale. It was a favorite habit of mine down the shore, taking the time to smell the salt air and listen to the wheeling seagulls. This time of the day, the gulls would be coming in for a quick landing to scarf up all the edible debris on the boardwalk—

"I was just coming to see you."

It was Lola Tripper.

Lola and I had met the first day I started at the Windjammer. I had been a little harried—Gillian had called in sick and Henry had been barking at me to pick up orders. I'd stumbled out the kitchen door, tripped on my own feet, and plopped a chef salad onto Lola's lap. I'd apologized profusely, but she'd just laughed. I'd loved her instantly. She'd been my go-to confidante ever since. Despite our slight age gap—she was forty-four to my thirty-four—we had become fast friends: Broadway shows and the occasional trip to Atlantic City to play the slots.

Lola had become a widow a decade ago. Since her daughter was away at college in Chicago, Lola was left alone. Alone, but wealthy, thanks to a generous insurance policy. Three years ago, she retired early from the science department at Etonville High and made the time to pursue her passions, one of which was the Etonville Little Theatre, a community theater group with an all-volunteer membership.

"Hi, Lola. How's pre-production going?"

The ELT was getting ready to audition for *Romeo and Juliet*.

"Doing Shakespeare is more complicated than we thought. It's our biggest show yet. We need a broader casting pool. Are you interested?"

My theater experience was limited to a grammar school production, in which I had been an apple in an orchard of dying trees, and one semester of acting, taken as a lark with my college roommate, that had required us to work on productions. I'd painted backdrops and built a few props, and when a spear carrier caught the flu during the run of the show, I'd stepped in because the costume fit. But I had no greasepaint in my blood.

"Sorry. Acting's not for me. I thought most of the regulars would be cast."

"They probably will." Lola frowned. "It's just that most of them have never spoken blank verse before."

I wasn't sure the ELT was ready for the challenge of Shakespeare. I'd seen all of their productions, and they did a good job with musicals and comedies. They'd even gone to a couple of community theater conferences and won prizes. But iambic pentameter?

"Walter thinks we are up to the challenge," she said as if she could read my mind.

Walter was Walter Zeitzman, the general factotum of the theater part-time, real estate agent full-time. He'd been running the ELT for fifteen years after a middling career as an off-off Broadway director in New York. His primary responsibility was getting the shows up on schedule. For the last year, he'd had to pay more attention to the competition in neighboring Creston, where an upstart theater had just opened. He'd even toyed with the notion of bringing in professional guest artists from the city. *Romeo and Juliet* was his attempt to solidify the ELT's reputation as the premier theatrical entertainment venue in the area.

"If you want to do Shakespeare, why not start with a comedy? People love to laugh. How about *Midsummer Night's Dream*? You could get kids from the high school to play the fairies and frankly, I might have a better shot at our dinner theater package. Summer, picnics . . . we could do a barbecue outside," I said.

There were exactly three eating establishments in Etonville: Coffee Heaven, an old-fashioned, great-for-breakfast Jersey diner; the Windjammer; and recently opened upscale bistro La Famiglia. Henry's regulars were beginning to sample the new Italian cuisine. Desperate to maintain his position as Etonville's gastronomic king, he was willing to let me think outside the box—which I've always been good at. I had a brainstorm. With the ELT conveniently situated next door, I suggested we begin a dinner-then-theater package, coordinating the menu with theme specials and offering discounts. Of course, the whole thing had taken some finessing. The artistic director had been resistant, and the ELT season had consisted of only four plays, a couple of music events, and a night of Irish step dancing in March. Still, it was a start.

But now I was stumped. The obvious choice was Italian, but with La Famiglia dishing up fettuccine alfredo and shrimp fra diavolo, we needed another theme and I needed inspiration.

"Walter thinks we need a show with 'gravitas,'" Lola said. "Something that will really knock the socks off Etonville."

"*Romeo and Juliet* certainly has gravitas."

"Walter has ideas about the Jets and the Sharks."

"That was *West Side Story*."

Lola flipped her blond hair off her shoulders. "Of course. But Walter wants to create contemporary resonance. So the audience will relate to the story of two lovers separated by gangs."

"But we don't have gangs in Etonville." Unless you counted the senior citizens center and the pickle ball club. They squared off once a year for a bocce ball tournament.

"Everyone loves a good romance," said Lola.

"True," I said. Which made me think about the state of my own romantic life. But that's another story.

"Walter's going to play Lord Capulet, and I'm pretty sure I'm playing Lady Capulet." She smiled serenely and assumed a regal pose.

I knew she'd been spending more time than usual at board meetings. Good for her. Walter was fiftyish, a good-looking guy with brown hair, dark eyes, and a full beard. He'd recently become single as a result of a rather messy divorce that had been discussed ad nauseam at the Snippets Salon.

"It's all so overwhelming for him. Directing and playing a lead role. Could you help out with auditions next Tuesday?"

"I'm not sure what Henry—"

"Dodie, we need your managerial skills! Penny will be stage managing, of course, but, well, you know Penny."

Enough said. Penny Ossining meant well, but if there was a complicated way to do things, she'd find it. Walter was loyal to her since she had been one of the first volunteers at the ELT when the doors opened twenty-five years ago.

"I'll have to check the work schedule." Monday was my day off so Tuesday was spent catching up. But Benny and I shared closing duties so some nights I took off after the dinner rush.

"Thanks, Dodie. And do you think Henry would mind putting

these near the cash register?" Lola held up a stack of full-color flyers advertising auditions for *Romeo and Juliet*. "We already put an ad in the *Etonville Standard*."

I took the flyers. "Sure. You guys are going all out this time."

"Well, it's a big deal." She checked her watch. "Oops. I've got an appointment with Carol in fifteen minutes." Carol was the owner of Snippets, the local salon.

I lifted my auburn hair off my neck and pulled it into a ponytail. "I think I need a trim, too. I'll meet you there. I need some ideas on theme food for *R and J*. And Carol is such a great cook."

"I'll start thinking." Lola waved good-bye and hurried down the street to her car.

I had about an hour and a half before I was back on duty for dinner. I headed in the opposite direction and climbed into my red Metro.

Chapter 2

In the town center, I found a parking spot on a side street and glanced at my watch. Just enough time to get a haircut before the dinner crowd arrived. I pushed open the door of the salon and was greeted by a swoosh of sound: dueling hair dryers, a ringing phone, and Carol, laughing loudly with Lola, who was in the process of getting shampooed. Carol had a booming, joyful, infectious laugh that could lighten up even the gloomiest days. It was the first thing I noticed about her. Whenever I needed more funny in my life, she was my go-to person.

I waved from the receptionist's desk, and Carol motioned for me to join them. Snippets had garnered a reputation for great service and reasonable prices. I walked down the middle of the salon, through two parallel rows of cutting and color stations, to the back wall, where silver side-by-side sinks were occupied by Lola and another Etonville patron. The woman on the right stood and wrapped a towel around her head and walked to a cutting station.

"Busy today?" I asked Carol.

"As a one-armed paperhanger."

"Can you fit me in? I just need a half-inch taken off," I said.

"Lola, can you wait a few minutes?" Carol asked.

"Sure. I told Walter I was going home after I was finished here anyway."

I plopped down into the vacant chair. Carol's curly salt-and-pepper head bobbed as she whipped out a cape, snapping it open and around my neck in one motion. Carol was a firmly grounded, forty-year-old Sicilian beauty. After Lola, Carol was my other BFF.

"Speaking of Walter . . ." Carol said.

Lola sat up straighter. "Have you heard something?"

Carol lowered her voice. "I hear his ex has been carrying on." She arched an eyebrow.

"About what?" I asked.

While she shampooed my hair, rinsed out the suds, and brushed some conditioner through it, Carol divulged the latest on Walter's divorce. We didn't call Snippets gossip central for no reason. I was just generally interested in catching up with the small-town goings-on. Lola had a more personal stake in Walter's marital status. We settled into her cutting station.

"Annie Walsh. Remember her?" Carol asked.

Lola frowned. "Is she the one who used to own the bake shop on Anderson Street before it became Georgette's?"

Georgette's was a pastry shop *par excellence* that provided all of the Windjammer's desserts.

"That's the one. Well, she was in here yesterday, and *she* said that Walter's *ex* said that he was holding out on her alimony."

"What does that mean?" Lola was a tad defensive.

Carol shrugged. "Something about his having money in other accounts that he didn't fess up to during the divorce proceedings."

"I find that hard to believe," Lola said and opened a magazine.

Carol and I exchanged glances. I'd picked up a little scuttlebutt about Walter's shaky finances from some theater folks one night at the Windjammer.

"What are we doing?" Carol brandished the scissors and frowned at my shoulder-length locks.

"Just clip off the split ends." I swiveled my chair to see the other side of my head in the mirror facing me and looked beyond the sinks to the very rear of the salon. "Is that Pauli?"

He looked up and gave the three of us a solemn wave. Carol stomped on the hydraulic foot rest with authority, and the chair dropped several inches. She glanced over her shoulder to see her seventeen-year-old son, Pauli, seated on a carton of shampoo bottles, securely wedged between a portable hair dryer on wheels and a rolling service tray. His head was bent over a laptop, with an iPod for company.

"I told him he could use the receptionist's desk. I think he's a little self-conscious being in a salon with all these women around."

"What's he doing?" Lola squinted at him.

"Creating a website for Snippets," Carol said.

"Wow. Good for him." Pauli's father was a tech guy who worked in the city. *Like father, like son*, I thought. Pauli was a bright kid, but a little quiet. Whenever I visited Carol's home and he happened to be visible, it was usually with his face buried in a computer game on his laptop or cell phone, or on Carol's iPad.

Carol combed and clipped and combed and clipped vigorously. "Yeah, I'm proud of him. He wants to start a business doing websites. Can you imagine?"

"His dad must be pleased."

"He is, but I worry," she said.

I noticed Pauli texting, his thumbs moving so quickly they were like appendages of his brain.

"I wish he'd get out more. You know. With girls."

"He doesn't date?"

"He has this group of boys he hangs out with. All of them like him—glued to the computer and video games. He has no social life."

"I think if you're seventeen that is a social life these days. That and Facebook and Instagram."

Lola folded her magazine open and held it up in front of my face. "Look at this. It's a recipe for strawberries dipped in chocolate and covered with fresh cream. Yummy *and* romantic." Lola's eyes lit up.

"Are you looking for dessert recipes?" Carol stopped mid-snip.

"I'm working on the theme food for *Romeo and Juliet* and drawing a blank. I've ruled out Italian," I said.

"Too bad. I could give you my meatball recipe." Her husband's chubby physique was a testament to Carol's cooking.

Henry had inaugurated the dinner-then-theater with corned beef and cabbage to celebrate St. Patrick's Day—and the step dancing—and folks had been a little slow to come aboard. But things picked up with a French farce accompanied by beef Bourguignon, and Etonville was eating up the new idea. By the time the ELT produced *Dames at Sea* and I had devised a seafood buffet, patrons were getting used to dining early and darting next door to the show. It was a marriage made in culinary heaven.

"Something romantic might work."

"I remember a dinner *al fresco* years ago . . . oysters, cheeses, avocados, champagne. . . . It was luscious." Lola sighed.

"Maybe we should look into an outdoor café," I said, as Carol blow-dried my hair, giving it a fluff now and then. "Lola thinks I should audition for *R and J*."

"We need all the potential actors we can get," Lola trilled, still flipping through the magazine.

"Why don't you audition?" I said to Carol, looking at her in the mirror.

"When would I have time to rehearse a play? Not to mention that I can't act."

"Ditto," I said. "Are you helping with the hair and makeup?"

"Yes, she is," Lola volunteered. "Walter needs her expertise."

"If I can get the shop covered." She gelled her hands and patted my hair to pacify the frizzies.

Without our realizing it, Pauli had abandoned his nest in the back of the salon and ambled over to Carol's station.

"Mom?"

Carol looked up and smiled. "Honey, say hi to Lola and Dodie."

He brushed a hunk of dark hair off his pimply forehead. "Hey."

"Are you hungry?" Carol asked.

"I can wait." He was smart *and* considerate.

"After I do Lola, I'll drive you home."

I stood up and grabbed my bag from the floor. "How's the website going?"

Pauli hesitated. "Okay, I guess."

"Better than okay. Show Dodie what you've done." Carol nudged him.

He pretended to be reluctant to demonstrate his computer prowess, but I could read his face. He was thrilled to walk me through the various pages and links. It was impressive.

"Maybe we can hire you to do one for the Windjammer. I've been on Henry's case to move into the twenty-first century. I'll let you know."

Pauli just nodded, trying to hide his enthusiasm.

My cell binged: a text from Henry, wanting to know where I was. "See you all later."

At ten-thirty p.m., I took a break in my favorite booth with a bowl of black bean soup—Henry was famous for his homemade soups—and mulled over the idea of an *R and J* amorous dinner theme. I was just getting lost in the romantic possibilities of various entrees when I heard, "Thought I'd find you here."

"Hi, Jerome," I said to the elderly gentleman who sat down across from me. "Want something to eat? Kitchen's open for about twenty more minutes."

He shook his head. "Just a drink."

I waved to Benny and pointed to Jerome Angleton. Benny nodded. Jerome was a regular. He drank a double Scotch, Chivas Regal, neat, no more, no less, almost every night that the Windjammer was open. Often, he exited the Etonville Little Theatre, walked next door, and sat at the bar. But when I wasn't busy, he liked to sit with me. I enjoyed his company.

Long retired from Etonville High as an English teacher, Jerome—seventyish, tall, and lanky with thinning hair and a lot of energy—was a fixture at the theater. He supervised the box office, ushered, did some backstage work, and once in a while assumed a role on stage. His big break had been Sergeant Trotter in *The Mousetrap* last year. I had no idea what he did when he wasn't at the ELT. But he was friendly, had taken a liking to me—if I was twenty years older, or he was twenty years younger, we might be hitting on each other—and he shared my love of mysteries and thrillers.

He pulled a paperback out of his jacket pocket. "Got the new Cindy Collins mystery."

"Yeah? Let me see." I eyeballed the cover art. An angry slash of red broken up by crisscrossing lines of a picket fence, the title in bold type. *Murder One and a Half.*

"You can have it when I'm finished," he said as Benny set his drink on a coaster.

"Here you go, Jerome." Benny smiled at the older man and sauntered back to the bar.

Jerome took a long swallow. He looked frazzled.

"Tough day in show business?" I asked.

"It's Walter. He's been on everybody's case. Especially mine."

"He's probably just anxious about auditions next week. Shakespeare . . . you know?"

"Maybe, but I think there's something going on."

"Oh?"

Jerome lowered his voice. "Money's been disappearing from the safe."

"Seriously?"

"Whenever I've been in the safe, I leave an accounting of what I take out for petty cash for the costume shop or whatever. Lately there've been some . . . irregularities."

I knew about the business practices at the ELT from Lola. My Accounting 101 professor would have yanked the few stray hairs on his head out by the roots. Walter kept Post-its scattered around his desk with notes on bank deposits and withdrawals and the petty cash account in the safe. I had hinted to Lola more than once that Walter needed to keep a better eye on the financial status of the theater. She agreed, but said Walter was testy about management suggestions. He liked to run all aspects of the show his way.

My management mind was racing to create a to-do list for Jerome: talk to theater folks to see if anyone else was in the safe; check all of the Post-it notes for an accounting error; confirm who had keys to the theater and knew the combination to the safe.

"Have you approached him with it?"

Jerome nodded. "In a roundabout way."

"And?"

"He said that I was the one responsible for petty cash accounting."

"Is he accusing you of stealing from the theater? He can't think you would do such a thing. What are we talking here, fifty bucks? A hundred?"

Jerome emptied his glass and returned it carefully to the coaster. "More. Lots more."

"Like how much more?" I asked carefully.

"Over the past month or so, more like a thousand."

My jaw hung loosely on its hinge, my mouth forming an O. "In cash?"

Jerome nodded.

"No wonder Walter's on edge. Did he call the police?"

"I told him he should, but he just waved me away." Jerome took a swipe at the air in imitation of Walter's dismissive gesture.

Funny that Lola hadn't mentioned anything about this. Did she know? It seemed that she and Walter were getting closer these days, but maybe—

"Don't tell anyone I told you, okay? Walter is short-tempered enough, and I wouldn't want to aggravate him further."

"No problem."

"Take care, Dodie," Jerome said and saluted. It was his standard way of saying good-night.

"'Night, Jerome. And don't let this get you down. I'm sure it will all work out."

I knew better than that. Walter was a smooth operator in front of an audience or when hosting post-show wine and cheese parties. But I'd had occasion to see his wrath in full bloom when the dinner-then-theater program hit a few bumps. There were two sides to his personality.

A thousand dollars, I mused. Walter was the one having some post-marital financial difficulties at the moment.

"Go home. I'll finish up," I called to Benny, who was about to take a wet mop to the tile floor. He nodded with appreciation. Benny had a four-year-old daughter, a working wife, and a mortgage. Besides waiting tables at the Windjammer, he drove a UPS delivery truck part-time and always looked tired.

"Thanks." He practically ran out the door.

By eleven-thirty, I had shooed Henry out the door, too. I could close up more efficiently by myself; straightening up the dining room, closing out the register, doing a last bar inventory and freezer check to see what needed to be ordered for the weekend. Henry had gussied up the menu with a few "spring changes." La Famiglia had already printed its spring menu in the *Etonville Standard*. The competition was really getting to him.

I stepped outside, breathed in the nippy night air, and looked upward at a dark sky with a smattering of white specks. Not bad for north Jersey. Of course, it couldn't compare to the wide expanse of the night over the ocean. I was still getting used to the idea that I lived inland.

I took the long way home as I drove slowly through Etonville; it was one of my favorite times of day. People were off the streets, a certain quiet had descended, and I felt as if the town were all mine. Population 3,284. Home to a park, an art gallery, an antique shop, one bank, two churches, a post office, and a Saturday farmer's market, Etonville was a placid, close-knit place, small enough to feel cozy but large enough to need its own police department. Etonville had its own personality.

I passed Snippets, the Etonville Public Library, and my personal favorite hangout, Coffee Heaven—five booths, a soda fountain, a counter that seated eight, and a stack of local and national newspapers by the door, free for the reading. The Etonville literary society met in its back room once a month. Its only concession to modern times was the addition of a few fancy drink options to the standard menu. Caramel macchiato was my obsession.

As I turned into my driveway, it occurred to me that I would have loved to curl up with a good man instead of a good book tonight. But that ship had sailed for me. Literally. The month before Hurricane Sandy struck, I broke up with my boyfriend of three years. Or, more accurately, we agreed to put things on hiatus. Jackson owned a charter fishing boat and had experienced great years and not-so-great years. When he received an offer to join his brother selling farm equipment, he decided to chuck the boat business and head back to Iowa. He wanted me to come with him. But I couldn't leave the shore. At least that was the excuse I'd given Jackson. When Hurricane Sandy gave me the perfect opportunity to bail on New Jersey and join him, I opted to head north instead of west and held my breath as I crossed over the Driscoll Bridge, uncertain about a new life away from the sun and sand and saltwater taffy. North Jersey felt different from the shore: it knew where it was going and had only a short time to get there.

I suppose I was admitting the truth about Jackson and me. He had been the longest, most serious relationship of my life, not counting a high school crush that lasted on and off through college days. I had begun to think that we might settle down, buy a little shore cottage, open our own restaurant. . . . Now I knew those were pipe dreams. Despite his foray into the boat charter business, he was tied to the Midwest while I had always wanted to be within spitting distance of the shoreline. True love was like a good pair of socks. It took two, and they had to match.

I missed him for the first few months. We emailed and texted a few times, but we sort of fell out of touch. I turned the key in the lock of my front door and switched on the lights. The good book was calling me.

Chapter 3

I had assured Lola I would be at the auditions for *Romeo and Juliet* by six-thirty since it was Benny's night to close. Henry was in a foul mood: too much lemon in his chicken soup and the seafood supplier ran out of flounder. He had been forced to improvise, which he hated. It was a good night to vanish.

I raced home to my unfussy but comfy home, large enough for me to have a decent-sized dining room and a guest bedroom, small enough for me to keep tidy on a regular basis. I showered and flung open the closet door, tugged on a black skirt and a black V-neck sweater, and studied myself in the mirror. I was Irish on both sides of my family, and my dark red, wavy hair came straight from my maternal grandmother. The green eyes were compliments of my father. I was lucky I'd inherited his build and metabolism as well. I could usually eat just about anything, watch someone else exercise, and still maintain a decent weight and shape. Right now, I was feeling okay with my reflection.

It had been rainy throughout the day, but the sky had cleared, leaving a blanket of blue overhead. I found my usual parking space in front of the Windjammer—I deliberately avoided glancing in the front window—and strode into the theater. I was greeted with a barrage of nervous babbling in the lobby. Two dozen folding chairs lined the walls, occupied by prospective cast members—including some folks I recognized from the Windjammer—filling out audition sheets. I remembered the first time I'd seen *Romeo and Juliet* on stage. The most vivid part of the production had not been the sword-play, or the murders, or the potions, but the old, funny, gentle Nurse. When she'd held Juliet in her arms, I'd cried. She had reminded me of my grandmother. Did the ELT have someone to play the Nurse? Depended on the depth of the talent auditioning, I thought.

Penny, a pencil jammed into her short black hair, stuck her head out of the theater door and knocked a pen against her clipboard. "Lola said you might be stopping by to help out," she said guardedly. Penny straightened up to her full five-feet-two inches. She was built like a fireplug: short and squat. When not "managing" the Etonville Little Theatre, her day job was post office clerk. Her inefficiency wasn't a problem there. . . .

I glanced around the lobby. It was still twenty minutes before the auditions began. "She thought you might be inundated with hopefuls." No need to intentionally offend Penny by commenting on her managerial skills. "You want to show me the ropes?"

Penny frowned, cracked her gum, and looked me over carefully. She jerked her head in the direction of the theater. "Let's go."

Walter's office was to the right and the box office to the left; the theater was wedged between them.

A few more folks appeared in the lobby. "People are here early."

"Walter likes everyone to be on time."

I looked at my watch. "It's not even six-forty-five," I said.

Penny took on a condescending let-me-explain-myself-to-you tone. "There's life time and then there's theater time. On time in theater time means fifteen minutes early."

"Oh. So they're all early in life time but just on time in theater time. Got it."

Penny groaned.

I followed her into the house, and she deposited me midway down the aisle before charging back out into the lobby. Walter was seated in Row H, head bent over his script—probably praying, if he had any sense—and Lola was leaning casually against the edge of the stage.

"Hi, Dodie!" She smiled with relief and ran up the aisle.

Walter did a three-sixty in his seat. "Dodie, are you auditioning?" The tinge of hope in his voice told me all I needed to know about the upcoming tryouts.

"No. I'm just here to help out."

Walter stood up and studied me, his eyes grazing my face, chest, and hips. He looked startled, as if shocked I had legs. Come to think of it, he had probably only seen me in work clothes—black slacks and variously colored tops. "Are you sure?"

"Walter, I asked Dodie to help Penny keep us on track tonight," Lola murmured and put an arm around my shoulders.

Walter nodded. He brushed a hand through his barely graying hair, which would no doubt be grayer by opening night. "We are taking on quite a challenge here, you know." His shoulders slumped which made his stomach protrude. Poor guy. He'd lost his usual *joie de vivre.*

"I can see that," I agreed a little too strongly.

Penny charged back into the house. "Walter, are we ready to start?"

"You haven't given out the sides."

Sides?

"Uh . . ." Penny hesitated. "No, but I have the list of who's—"

Walter handed her a stack of Xeroxed sheets. "Give these scenes out, and be sure to note who is reading what with whom."

Aha. Sides were scenes. Theater lingo.

"Dodie, you can collect the audition forms," he said.

"Right."

Penny and I headed back to the lobby, and I waited while Penny blew a whistle—causing people to hold their ears—and yelled "Listen up." Most of the auditionees were familiar with the ELT and knew Penny and her ways. Newcomers were alarmed at the shrill blast. While I collected forms, Penny handed out sides, using her theatrical judgment to determine who should read what by accosting every other person who walked in the door. "What part do you want to read?" she asked and invariably got "Whatever Walter thinks is right for me." Some major sucking up going on.

Unless it was terribly obvious. A cute guy with wavy dark hair and big brown eyes strolled in. *Romeo?* I mouthed to Penny. She pretended to consider my suggestion before agreeing. It was a no-brainer.

We lined folks up, sending in twosomes and threesomes, and sometimes groups of people who were going to be considered for extras. "Walter is casting Ladies-in-Waiting, Citizens of Verona, and young guys who fight in the square," Penny informed them.

I was trying to keep everything straight—forms collected, names checked off the list, partners assigned, actors moving in a steady stream into the theater—and not step on Penny's toes. I looked around. She was making notes on her clipboard or jawing with friends; they all assumed she was second in command to Walter. Big mistake. Penny was a catastrophe, and if I didn't keep things rolling, we'd all be here until midnight.

Halfway through the evening, Abby Henderson crept up to Penny to make sure her name was on the list. I knew Abby from the Windjammer, where she tended to sit in a corner booth and enjoy a few drinks with Jim Albright, a big loveable bear of a guy. He was a security guard at the box factory in the next town over. She was the manager of the Valley View Shooting Range and a bit past her prime. They seemed perfect for each other.

"Hi, Dodie. Are you auditioning?" Abby nervously twisted the pages of script until they were limp.

"Me? Oh no. I'm just here to keep things . . ." I saw Penny out of the corner of my eye.

"To help Penny keep things moving."

Abby edged closer to me. "Do you think I'm right for Juliet?"

I looked into her hopeful eyes and lied. "Well, sure." I compared my image of the virginal, teenage Juliet to Abby: late thirties, chubby, and in need of a serious makeover. "Good luck."

Penny appeared at my elbow. "Some roles are already cast."

"Yeah?"

"Walter is Capulet, and Lola," Penny said dryly with a big wink, "is Lady Capulet."

"I know."

At that moment, Jerome walked in the door. We had gotten behind and now were auditioning the eight-thirty group at nine o'clock.

"Hi, Jerome. I've been waiting for you."

He observed Penny yukking it up loudly with two young guys, then shushing everyone else in the lobby, and grinned. "I guess you're running things?"

"Just assisting."

"That's a good thing." He jammed his Cindy Collins paperback into his coat pocket and bounced up and down on his sneakers like a pogo stick. He seemed anxious.

"Is everything okay with . . . you know."

"Dodie, forget what I said about Walter and the missing money, okay? It really doesn't matter much anymore."

I handed him a scene with the Prince of Verona—the most logical choice for him. "You seemed pretty upset the other night." I studied his face. Jerome was clearly elated about something.

"Things have changed." He leaned in to me and I could smell liquor on his breath. "In fact, I wanted to tell you—"

Walter burst out the lobby door. "Penny! Where is the next Juliet?"

Everyone froze and Penny looked stricken. She glanced at her clipboard, then at me, then at Walter. "Uh . . . okay . . . uh . . . Abby?"

Walter gestured to me. "Dodie, can you stand inside the door and monitor the flow?" he asked quietly.

"Sure." I gave Jerome a pat on the shoulder. "We can talk later if you want."

He nodded and walked off to the other side of the lobby.

A chastened Penny handed me copies of the scene between Juliet and Lady Capulet, and I trailed Walter into the house. I leaned against the heavy wooden door and watched Abby take the stage next to Lola, who was getting quite the workout tonight. Walter offered some pointers to the two women. Lady Capulet was alerting Juliet that she would be marrying Paris on the "morrow" and she'd better stop her sniveling. It reminded me of many adolescent scenes in my own household, without the marriage.

Lola and Abby faced each other and began to read. Lola looked especially attractive this evening—hair piled on top of her head, dark crimson sweater gliding over her curvy hips. Though I'd seen her in several ELT plays, I was amazed at Lola's facility with the language. She spoke the lines naturally, peering into Abby's face to glean some reaction. Abby, unfortunately, was baffled, the verse beyond her. Her only recourse was to carry on. She screamed her displeasure with her mother and broke down in fake sobs, falling to her knees. Shakespeare was, no doubt, cringing and regretting the day he'd set pen to paper.

Walter sat stone-faced, not pleased.

"He's in trouble," Penny said at my side.

"What are you doing in here? You're supposed to be in the lobby handing out scenes," I said.

Penny shrugged the world-weary shrug of the stage manager at the Etonville Little Theatre. "I need those blank sign-up forms." She grabbed my stack of papers. "He's got a few really hot Romeos, but he's sucking wind when it comes to Juliet."

"Next Juliet, please," Walter called out.

Abby looked distraught as she wiped her tears—real this time—and moved off the stage.

Penny scrambled to the lobby and I followed, looking for Abby's replacement.

As the next victim climbed the steps to the stage, Lola whispered encouragingly, "Just speak as honestly as you can. Try not to get too caught up in the rhythm."

God bless Lola. If this all came off, it would be due in no small part to her talent and good sense. Walter was fortunate to have her in the ELT, in more ways than one. The next Juliet, a petite blond beauty whom I'd seen in *Dames at Sea*, started the scene with Lola, tripping over every other word. But Lola looked her in the eye and took her arm, answering as any mother would. They were having a mother-daughter argument—in poetry, of course, but the lines began to sound like real-life dialogue and I could feel Walter relax.

He might have found at least one star-crossed lover.

By 11 PM, we had auditioned nearly sixty people, most of whom had some tie to the ELT. Walter was breathing easier since he had some options for most roles, and my feet were killing me so I collapsed on a lobby bench. Penny and I had collected discarded scenes and stacked folding chairs. She'd gotten over Walter's reprimand and was the old Penny: a little full of herself, trying to take charge while tripping over her own feet and making notes on her clipboard.

"Dodie, could you give the sign-up forms to Walter? We need to keep track of who came out tonight." She scooted her glasses up her nose.

"Sure." I dragged my tired body to a standing position, grabbed the forms and my bag, and walked into the theater.

Walter and Lola had their heads close together. Lola was really an assistant artistic director without the title. She'd been anointed its reigning diva whenever a play called for a statuesque blonde, which was usually every one. She sat on a rotating board of directors, which at the present time also included the mayor, the proprietress of Coffee Heaven, Walter, and JC from JC's Hardware. She even sewed a costume or two. Without Lola, the ELT might have to close up its proscenium and go home. It was Lola who had greased the wheels that made the dinner-then-theater happen. She had a way of making events materialize where the ELT was concerned.

I handed the forms to Walter.

"Oh, Dodie, thanks for coming tonight. We needed you, didn't we, Walter?" Lola gently poked him and he looked up from his script.

"Huh? Yes, right. Thanks."

Walter would never receive a prize for courtesy and gratitude.

"Happy to help." I hesitated. "I'm great with numbers, just in case you'd like someone to help out with the books, too."

Walter studied me carefully. "I'm perfectly capable of managing the finances of this company. Thank you very much."

I wondered about that. I felt sorry for Jerome, and it didn't seem as though he would have the chutzpah to confront Walter himself.

"Just a thought. I know you and Jerome have your hands full."

"I'll take it under advisement." He put a somewhat possessive hand on Lola's arm.

Chapter 4

I slept fitfully, waking every hour until I finally passed out around 2 AM. Then I awoke with a start. My landline was ringing and the digital alarm read seven o'clock. I closed my eyes and pulled the pillow over my head, hoping the caller would go away, and waited for the voice mail to kick in.

"Dodie? It's Lola." Her voice cracked as if she'd been crying.

I was wide awake now. My hand searched for the receiver and I lifted it off the base. "Lola? Are you okay?" I said, an octave lower than I would speak in an hour.

"I'm sorry to call this early. There's been some . . . trouble at the theater."

"What's going on?"

"The police are here."

"What happened?"

"Oh, Dodie, I don't know how to tell you. . . ."

"Just say it quickly."

"Jerome is dead."

"Oh my God. How? Where?"

She started to cry. "I went home at midnight, but Walter stayed to finish casting the play, you know. . . ."

"And so?" I desperately wanted to believe that her story was a nightmare that I would awaken from.

"He said he left at one."

"When did they . . . ?"

"It was horrible. The garbage men came to empty the Dumpster on the loading dock this morning . . . and found him."

I could hear her breathing deeply and I felt my eyes tear up. Jerome was only a Windjammer acquaintance, but I felt like I'd gotten to know him. Besides, he was such a nice guy.

"What was Jerome doing on the loading dock? Was it a heart attack or something?"

"Dodie, Jerome was murdered."

I elicited a bit more information from Lola before she broke down completely. According to Walter, who had gotten it from the garbage guys, Jerome had been lying face down on the cement. They'd thought he had fallen asleep out there at first, but when they'd seen a patch of dried blood on the left side of his torso, they'd called the police, who had notified Walter, who had called Lola for moral support.

I pulled on a pair of jeans and my Irish knit sweater, grabbed a hoodie and car keys, and sped out the door. A glimmer of sunlight peeked tentatively from a layer of clouds, as if asking permission to shine. I drove to the theater and considered my last conversation with Jerome. Who in the world would want to hurt him? Jerome was a real gentleman, in the old-fashioned sense.

I stopped my Metro a few doors down from the theater as the spaces in front were occupied: two Etonville black-and-white police vehicles, a police van, and an ambulance. A small group of townspeople had gathered to check out the excitement. I made my way through the crowd and approached an officer who was working security.

"I need to go in," I said.

"Sorry. This is a crime scene," Officer Suki Shung said, putting up one hand to prevent me from entering the theater. I knew Suki was new, the first woman to join the force.

"I spoke with him last night. I saw him a few days ago." I gulped fresh air. "I was a friend of his. I'm part of the theater group."

She studied me some more, asked me my name, then spoke into a walkie-talkie. Within seconds, Lola burst out the front door and threw her arms around my neck. We hugged tightly.

"Dodie knew Jerome. She needs to speak to the chief."

Officer Shung's walkie-talkie crackled, and she turned her back on us. She listened, then nodded. "Go ahead."

We scuttled past her, opened the door to the theater, and had barely taken a step into the building when we were accosted by Penny. "Can you believe it? Jerome? "I'll be in the theater if anybody needs me."

"How did Penny get here so soon?" I asked as she scooted away. Penny had a way of always being where the action was, like a GPS system that tracked trouble.

"Walter must have called her."

I knocked on Walter's office door, and we slowly pushed it open.

Two desks, piled high with papers, scripts, assorted props, and a few costumes, sat facing each other like boxers squaring off for a match. One was Walter's; the other was generally occupied by Penny or Lola. A fax machine hummed, then spat out a sheet of paper. Birds' nattering floated in through an open window, but otherwise, stillness.

Lola joined Walter on the sofa, next to a box of Kleenex. His head was in his hands as he faced an officer, apparently answering questions.

"Excuse me. Officer Shung told me it was okay—"

The officer pulled out a desk chair and offered me a seat. "Chief Thompson," he said abruptly.

Chief Bill Thompson was new to Etonville, having arrived only three months ago. I'd met him briefly when he'd stopped by the Windjammer a few times for lunch. His predecessor, Chief Angus "Bull" Bennett, had died with his boots on—literally. At sixty-eight, he had dropped over dead while fishing, knee deep in waders, in the old Ridgewood Reservoir. Bull had been well-loved. Of course, the worst things he'd had to handle were wrangling a few rowdy kids from the high school on Saturday night as they trolled through town looking for fun or keeping Etonville's two meter maids from killing each other over territorial disputes or investigating the odd accident down on the highway.

"She said you knew the victim, Ms. O'Donnell, right?"

"O'Dell. Yes, I did."

I sized up the new chief: a ruddy complexion with a golden brush cut and tight-fitting uniform. He was attractive and built like a running back. In fact, I'd heard that he had had a short-lived career as a professional football player before he entered law enforcement in Philadelphia.

"We all did." Lola nodded. Walter was now resting his head on the back of the sofa, eyes closed.

"I understand he was here last night at auditions. Can you tell me what time he came and when he left?" His deep blue eyes looked right through me. I had to blink a few times.

Penny's explanation of theater time versus life time sprang into my head. "He arrived a little late, about eight-thirty. I didn't see him leave."

"Did he speak to you?"

"Briefly. I gave him a scene to take a look at. He read for the Prince of Verona. . . ."

"Uh-huh," he said and jotted a note in a pad he was holding. Was it significant that Jerome would have probably been cast as the aristocratic head of the Italian state? "How did he seem? Was he disturbed? Agitated?" Chief Thompson asked.

"Not really. Well, maybe a little." I glanced at Lola, who was holding Walter's hand, and shrugged. "Jerome was . . . pleasant. Gentle." I paused and remembered our conversation that night at the Windjammer. "We both liked mysteries and thrillers. We traded books back and forth. In fact, he brought me the latest—"

"Agitated how?" the chief asked, getting back to last night.

I had to tell the truth. I related as many details as I could recollect from that night before at the Windjammer. Walter looked guilty and nervous. Chief Thompson fixed his steely eyes on him and stated firmly that he should have filed a police report if he hadn't found the money within twenty-four hours.

Walter shifted from guilty to sheepish. "I understand. We have these kinds of bookkeeping issues periodically. I'll search one final time and come by the station if I don't find anything today." He smiled weakly.

Lola crossed her arms and watched an early spring fly that was zooming around the office looking for a way out. Probably how Walter felt.

"I'll need you to stop by anyway to go over a few details," the chief said.

"I could get together a list of people who were here to audition," I offered. "We have sheets on—"

"Thanks, but I'll have one of my officers follow up with Walter." He frowned at his notebook. "I guess that's it for now."

I let myself into the Windjammer, put on the coffee, and plunked down into my "office," the back booth by the kitchen door. It was 9 AM. The restaurant wouldn't be open for two hours yet; the staff wouldn't even show up for another half hour or so. I was grateful for the quiet time alone. Jerome. My eyes welled up. It was the first time since Lola's call woke me that I could actually sit and contemplate the enormity of the morning's events. It was all so shocking.

I sipped from the scalding mug and closed my eyes. I could see Jerome's face, strangely lit up, as he confided that he was not all that concerned about the missing money.

My cell clanged and I jumped. I checked the caller ID. "Hi, Carol."

"Oh, Dodie, it's just terrible. Poor man," she said.

Word traveled faster than the speed of light in Etonville. "I guess you heard from Lola?"

"Lola? No. Snippets is buzzing with the news. I heard Bill Thompson interrogated you."

I could hear the hum of hair dryers in the background. "Well, he asked me a few questions."

Carol lowered her voice. "Do they have any suspects? You know there hasn't been a murder in Etonville since..." She paused to think. "Maybe 1980, '81?"

I'd heard about that one. A hold-up gone awry and the owner of the gas station on the edge of town bludgeoned to death. A pretty grisly affair. "I know. It's just hard to imagine who would want to hurt Jerome."

Silence on the line for a moment.

"I didn't know him. According to the gals in Snippets, no one really knew much about him. He never married. He had a great reputation as a teacher."

"He always wore sneakers. Weird for a man his age," I said.

"Okay..."

"That's not much background. He liked Chivas Regal...and mysteries," I said.

Was that all I knew about him? We'd spent hours talking about books and writers, but nothing else.

"Is Lola okay? She must be devastated."

"She's pretty upset. Walter is too."

The front door opened. "Carol, Henry's here. Got to run."

She paused. "Did you get a chance to ask Henry about the website? Pauli's ready when you are."

"Not yet."

"He's really terrific on this website stuff. It forces him to talk to people."

Not the nerd herd he usually runs with, I thought.

"I'll have to get back to you. Bye." I clicked off and I took a breath before easing out of the booth.

Henry stood by the bar and took a ball cap off his bald head. "Heard about Jerome. Bad business," he said.

That was as demonstrative as Henry was going to get. Unlike Etonville.

Jerome's murder was all anyone in the Windjammer could talk about. Benny hopped from the bar to tables to back up our server Gillian, and I rode shotgun on the kitchen to keep the crowd from getting testy. In between, I picked up strands of conversation:

". . . he was shot three times . . ."

". . . he was robbed of hundreds of dollars . . ."

". . . he was found lying on top of the Dumpster . . ."

The rumors were bouncing off the walls like bumper cars at the state fair. So many rumors it was impossible to take them all in. I gave up even thinking of trying and focused on today's specials: grilled Caesar salad, meatloaf, and mashed potatoes. I hated to admit it, but Jerome's murder was good for business: everyone was out and about and, apparently, hungry.

"Dodie, we heard you were the first person Chief Thompson interrogated," a lady said and speared a chunk of meat loaf. I recognized her as one half of the elderly Banger sisters duo. I knew their reputation for being a little dotty and Etonville's most enthusiastic gossipmongers.

"Well, I wasn't really the first—"

"I heard Jerome was drunk," her sister whispered.

Who in the world was spreading that bit of gossip?

"Do you think it had anything to do with the casting of *Romeo and Juliet*? After all, the competition was fierce," the first sister said. The other nodded and both of them looked at me expectantly.

I gritted my teeth. "I'm pretty sure the play had nothing to do with Jerome's death."

* * *

I was worn down to a nub by the end of lunch, tired of fending off ridiculous theories on Jerome's murder, tired of soothing Henry's ruffled feathers when a patron sent his meat loaf back to the kitchen because it was too salty. In addition to helping organize the menu and managing staff, I also made sure Henry stayed away from customers on his grumpy days.

Henry planned to serve French onion soup for dinner. I knew he had a dentist's appointment—he'd been complaining about a toothache all week—so I offered to help Enrico with the prep work and sent him off to seek a cure. Benny had the dining room in hand so I wrapped myself in one of Henry's aprons, picked up his prized tool—an eight-inch chef's knife—and faced a mound of red onions. Normally, I never lifted a utensil in the kitchen, but this wasn't a normal day. I began to peel and chop, and before too long, streams of water coursed down my cheeks. I stopped to blow my dripping nose and wipe my eyes, but the tears were undeterred, running down my chin and dropping onto my neck. Unexpectedly, I began to feel really bad, sad for Jerome, sad for my loss, and I cried—not just because of the onions, but because I had lost a friend. Enrico glanced my way discreetly and then went back to marinating chicken.

After about twenty minutes of crying and mincing, I calmed down. All of Etonville's theories on Jerome's death got me thinking. What if the missing box-office money was connected to Jerome's murder? Could he have discovered the culprit, who then killed him to keep him quiet? Did any of it involve Walter? I wondered. I was beginning to discover that Jerome's death was like a gnat bite that required scratching.

Chapter 5

Between Jerome's murder and the casting for *Romeo and Juliet,* the anxiety level at the ELT was off the charts. Walter had promised everyone that the list would be posted by early afternoon—online and in the theater lobby for those who refused to do e-business.

I took a break from the Windjammer at three after the lunch rush had died down and went to see Lola. I now sat carefully on her pristine couch, wary of dropping crumbs from my cinnamon coffee cake onto her Persian rug. Lola was particular about her living room and its furnishings—antique end tables, a baby grand piano, and brown leather sofas. The décor was spare, stylish, and dominated by earth tones. What my Irish father would have called artsy. I would have preferred the kitchen table, but Lola liked to entertain in here.

"I couldn't sleep at all last night. Every time I closed my eyes, I saw Jerome's body lying on the loading dock." Lola downed two aspirins with a swallow of black coffee.

I studied her blond hair as it cascaded loosely around the nape of her neck and partially covered her face. She could easily be taken for a thirty-year-old. To the world, Lola was a figure of poise and elegance with posture to die for and perfect timing. But the woman in front of me in a bathrobe and slippers was neither poised nor elegant; her eyes were rimmed in red, face devoid of makeup, her head propped up on her right hand.

"It's like Etonville has suddenly become . . . I don't know . . . dangerous."

In her lap, the front page of the *Etonville Standard* blared its headline: MAN MURDERED—NO SUSPECTS. The paper had published a special afternoon edition and the story was brief—an indication of the lack of evidence surrounding the case—and referred to a single bullet wound in Jerome's chest. There was a mention of Jerome's unmarried state and a summary of his years teaching English at the high school. Former students were quoted remarking on his enthusiasm, generosity, and love of literature. I could have said as much and I'd never stepped foot in his classroom. The sub-heading of the article included "member of Etonville Little Theatre." There were two pictures. One was from the Etonville High School yearbook and the other was a picture of Jerome, Walter, and a third man I didn't recognize, all in formal wear. Walter would love that.

I picked up the paper and pointed to the photo. "Who is this?"

"That's Elliot Schenk."

"I've never seen him around the theater."

"You wouldn't have. He left town very suddenly just before you arrived," she said and polished off the rest of her coffee. "Elliot was a star in the ELT firmament and ran the box office. Jerome was in the chorus a couple of times and had a role in *The Mousetrap*, but he mostly ushered and worked backstage doing props until Elliot left. Then he took over the box office."

"When was this taken? The three of them look very fancy."

Lola studied the picture. "This was the fundraiser for the theater several years back. Walter decided we needed a dash of elegance."

The yearly fundraiser, in addition to box office receipts, comprised the bulk of the theater's income. Fortunately, the town was generous, and donations of furniture, props, and clothing often made up for holes in the budget.

"Handsome dudes. Did you raise any money?"

"Yes, but then we overspent that season. Walter and money . . ." She groaned.

Which of course made me remember Jerome and the missing ELT funds.

She stood up. "I have to get ready to go to the theater. Walter needs to post the cast list."

"Right. Before sixty auditionees commit hari-kari."

Lola laughed, then stopped herself.

"I know. Tough to be light-hearted when Jerome . . ."

She nodded.

"I didn't get a chance to tell you, but you made a terrific Lady Capulet," I said. "Where'd you learn to speak blank verse? Not teaching high school biology."

I had a sudden flash back to my ninth-grade biology class. If I'd had to coerce thirty bored kids to stick their fingers into a formaldehyde-reeking frog's innards and stab at muscle tissue, I'd have retired early, too.

Lola headed out to the kitchen, and I followed her, newspaper, plate, and mug in hand. "I did lots of plays in college. I wanted to major in theater, but my parents thought it was too risky a career."

And monitoring thirty kids with dissection knives in a lab wasn't risky?

"I did a couple of plays in New York. Nothing much. Just some off-off stuff."

"Like Walter?"

Lola nodded. "That's where I first met him. In fact, I was responsible for getting him to apply for artistic director. I hope I don't live to regret that," she said and frowned.

"He's done a lot of good work for the ELT."

"True. Anyway, my car's in the shop. Can you drop me off?" she asked.

"Sure. I don't need to be back to work for another hour."

I waited in the kitchen while Lola went upstairs to dress. I studied the picture in the newspaper. Jerome had his arm around Elliot Schenk. Walter had adopted a degree of decorum—I knew Walter never really drank beyond a glass of champagne at openings—but the other two had drinks in their hands and were having a grand old time.

Lola reappeared, having transformed herself via white silk blouse and tan, pressed trousers, all trace of the morning's angst having vanished.

"Were Jerome and Elliot good friends? I mean they look like drinking buddies in this picture."

She snickered. "Oh, yes. The two of them were always into mischief. When Elliot was on the stage crew, he and Jerome used to sneak out between the opening and intermission. Penny would have to call Jerome's cell phone to get them back here for scene changes. They even took trips to Atlantic City every so often."

"Jerome?"

"I think he mostly walked on the boardwalk and played a few slot machines. Elliot was a high-stakes poker guy—who tended to lose."

"Two retired buddies on the prowl," I said softly.

"Elliot wasn't retired. He worked on Wall Street."

"Why did he leave so suddenly?" I asked.

"No one really knows." She shrugged. "Maybe Jerome knew, but he never said anything. They did stay in touch though. Jerome mentioned that he had spoken to Elliot a few times in the last month. But there was speculation."

"Such as?"

"That Elliot had gotten into some financial trouble and had to skip town. Or that he had a drinking problem and had to go into a rehab center. Or that he had a long-lost child who showed up one day." Lola smiled. "It was all quite a mystery."

"It's nice that Jerome had someone he could hang out with."

"They laughed a lot together," Lola said; then little frown lines appeared. "The only time I heard them argue was one night after they returned from a weekend in Atlantic City. It had to do with Elliot borrowing money from Jerome and not paying him back when he said he would. But it all blew over quickly."

"Jerome in Atlantic City. Something I never knew," I said, as we walked out the door.

We climbed into my red Metro, still chugging along at ninety thousand miles. Lola was used to her new Lexus and allowed only the faintest traces of distaste to cross her face at having to ride in my pre-owned Chevy.

"What's that odor?" she asked.

"Take-out garlic balls from La Famiglia. But don't tell Henry I was patronizing his competitor."

Lola tactfully held her hand to her face.

I dropped Lola off at the Etonville Little Theatre and cruised down the block to find parking. My regular spot in front of the Windjammer was occupied so I pulled into a metered space and searched my car—the ashtray, around the seats, in the upholstery—for money. The town meter maids were known to be crafty and appear out of nowhere. The result was a thirty-dollar ticket.

"Hi, Dodie."

I was stuck between the steering wheel and the console, one arm flung over my head into the passenger seat, the other wedged under the driver's seat. I looked up into Abby's eyes. "Hi, Abby. How's it going?"

"You need help?"

"Just looking for some spare change for the meter."

"Here." She dug into her pocket and withdrew a fistful of coins. "Take what you need."

"Thanks." I disengaged myself from park.

"Do you think Walter will post the cast list soon?" She checked her watch.

"I think so." I squinted into the glaze of sun that formed a halo around Abby's dishwater-blond hair. "You know there are a lot of good parts in *Romeo and Juliet* besides Romeo and Juliet." I wanted to let her down easy. "Like the Ladies-in-Waiting."

Abby tossed her head and sniffed. "I would never stoop to being one of them," she said haughtily.

"But you want to be in the show, right?"

She hesitated only a fraction of a second. "I have seniority at the Etonville Little Theatre."

Whatever that meant. She waved good-bye and flounced off.

I caught up with Lola outside the theater. She clicked off her cell. "I have ten messages from ELT actors," she said warily.

"Uh-oh."

In the lobby, we could hear yelling. Alarmed, Lola opened the door of the house and we went inside. Walter was toe-to-toe with a forty-year-old guy a head shorter and twenty pounds lighter.

Penny chewed gum and tapped her clipboard.

"A Servant!" the man shouted.

"Also a Watchman, a Guard, and a Citizen of Verona," Penny added, all business.

"Are you kidding me?" He backed up too quickly, lost his balance, and tripped over the leg of a table, knocking over a chair and landing smack on his backside. Lola rushed in and offered her hand, which he rejected. Irregular breathing was all that was left of the argument.

"I'm outta here," he said and limped off stage and through the house.

"Walter, are you okay?" Lola asked sympathetically.

"I guess the cast list has been posted?" I said as innocently as possible. Penny nodded.

Walter gathered a handful of papers together haphazardly, stuck them in a file, and tugged on his beard. "If anyone asks for me, I am gone for the day."

"But, Walter, we need to discuss the budget—" Lola said.

He icily raised a hand to curtail her reminder and stalked off the stage. She followed after him.

I righted the chair the Servant had toppled over. I picked up the cast list. Sure enough, the little blond was Juliet and the tall, dark kid I remembered from auditions was Romeo.

"People have been emailing and calling—" Penny said.

"You too?"

"—and then Leonard showed up . . ."

"Let me guess. . . . He wanted to be Romeo?"

"They all want to be Romeo or Juliet. I've never seen ELT casting like this before. Some of the regulars are fine with a contemporary play but Shakespeare? No way. And they just can't accept it." Penny paused. "Well, that's show biz," she said with authority.

I wondered how Abby would take the news. I was praying she and Jim didn't decide to spend the evening at the Windjammer. I was fed up with histrionics—both onstage and off.

"Penny, tell Lola to call me if she needs a ride home."

As I helped Gillian set up the dining room for the dinner service, and reminded her to remove her nose ring, I couldn't help thinking about Jerome. Seeing his picture in the newspaper and hearing about his friendship with Elliot made me remember our last conversation the night of auditions, the night he was murdered. He'd seemed to be trying to tell me something about his situation, but we had been interrupted. Had it been related to the missing money, or had it been something more urgent?

Then I saw them. Jim and Abby, heading straight for their favorite booth. Jim raised a hand and signaled to Benny to bring the usual: a couple of tall White Russians with extra ice.

I watched Benny set the drinks on their table—most folks knew to come to the bar during happy hour for the discount, but Abby and Jim made up for it by tipping big time and Benny benefitted from their generosity. I debated whether to escape to the kitchen when they entered. That path would require me to pass dangerously close to their booth and to Abby's grappling with her future at the Etonville Little

Theatre. Maybe I could pretend to have a call on my cell and just nod as I—

"Hi, Dodie!" Abby had spotted me and waved her arm.

I waved back and walked briskly to their table, definitely on my way to the kitchen.

"Did you hear the news?" Jim asked and downed the rest of his drink.

"What news?" I asked.

Jim tucked Abby into his shoulder. "Abby here's going to play Juliet. Isn't that great?"

"Understudy, Jim. I might *understudy* Juliet," Abby added.

Had Walter lost his mind?

"I'm so proud of my honeybunch," Jim said and planted a smooch on her mouth.

"Congratulations, Abby. I'm happy for you." I took my cell phone out of my pocket and waggled it in their direction. "Gotta' make a call."

"Wait 'til you see my costume," Abby said and patted Jim's arm.

I smiled and dashed into the kitchen. Walter had better pray that the cute, blond Juliet didn't break a leg, or something else, and force an understudy to take the stage.

Watching Enrico massage raw eggs into minced zucchini, onions, and parsley for the dinner frittata reminded me that I still needed the theme food for *R and J*. Given my mood, I was ready to forget the love and focus on the tragic. Something blood red? I shook off the morbid thoughts and picked up my inventory clipboard.

Henry's frittata experiment was a resounding success. Just as dinner was winding down, Carol and Pauli walked in the door. I motioned for them to follow me to my back booth, where we could yak.

They settled in, ordered drinks—red wine for Carol, a Coke for Pauli—and looked at me expectantly: the website. OMG. I had meant to confer with Henry today but forgot. I made an executive decision.

"So, Pauli, when do you want to get together and talk about the website?"

Carol looked like she could have kissed me, and Pauli stopped sipping and beamed.

"How about tomorrow?" Carol nudged Pauli gently. She'd make a great agent.

"Fine. Come by after school, okay?"

He nodded and gulped down the rest of his Coke. "Can I go?"

Carol nodded. "Don't be home too late, honey."

I sipped a seltzer and watched his baggy jeans exit the front door.

Carol dropped her voice. "Big hubbub in the shop today."

"Really?" I said, and stifled a yawn. It had been a long day.

"Jerome." Carol raised one eyebrow knowingly.

I snapped to attention. "What about him?"

"Well, one of the shampoo girls—"

"The one with the blue hair?"

"No the other one. Rita. She has a tattoo on her. . . ."

"Right."

"She said she heard from her cousin that Jerome had a female visitor." Carol paused to gauge my response.

"How did she know that?"

"Well, Rita's cousin lives on Ellison—"

"Jerome's street."

"Yes, and last month she was hanging out on her front porch, and she saw this car stop in front of Jerome's place—"

"She's Jerome's neighbor?"

"I guess so. Anyway, she saw this woman enter the house, and then fifteen minutes later she left. With Jerome in tow."

"He never mentioned anyone to me. Who was this someone?"

"She had no idea."

My imagination kicked into high gear. Was this mystery woman somehow connected to Jerome's agitated state the night he was murdered?

"Did she notice anything else?"

"They got into a car. That's all she said."

"This is important, Carol. Maybe we should tell Chief Thompson. . . ."

"He's a real hunk. You know he's single? And apparently unattached, according to Annie Walsh—"

"Who?"

"She owned the bake shop—"

"—before Georgette. Right."

"Uh-huh. Did you know he played for the Buffalo Bills? Until he tore his whatchamacallit?" She rolled her shoulders.

"Rotator cuff."

"That's it. He's a welcome change from Chief Bull in more ways than one." Carol looked to Benny and lifted her empty wineglass.

I had the feeling there might be as much information flowing in and out of Snippets as there was at the Etonville Police Department.

"Could you ask Rita if I could speak with her cousin? I need a few more details before going to Chief Thompson."

"Sure. She's a customer. I think she's due for a color and cut. I'll let you know."

"Thanks."

Her eyes twinkled. "You can count on me."

It was nearly nine by the time Carol left. I spent the next hour filling out inventory sheets and thinking about our conversation. Who was Jerome's visitor? What was their relationship? Why had he never mentioned her?

" 'Night, Benny," I said as he disappeared out the door. Henry was long gone, and I needed a few more minutes to finish closing up: prepare today's deposit, turn out the lights, and lock the doors. I was justifiably pleased with the progress we were making at the Windjammer. Profits were up, empty tables were down, and Henry appeared satisfied, though he'd never admit it.

I drove around the block to drop the cash bag in the night depository at the Valley Savings Bank. Driving around town with a thousand dollars in cash and credit card receipts could be a little nerve-wracking since Jerome's death. But I didn't think Jerome's murder was a random killing, despite what the newspaper implied. Benny offered to make the deposit for me, but as manager it was part of the job so I declined. I pulled out of the drive-thru lane at the bank and retraced my path down Amber and onto Main.

Cruising around town the week I arrived in Etonville, I'd noticed that the north end was slightly more upscale. Houses were either brick buildings still standing from the early 1800s or gingerbread Victorians in bright colors that dated from the late nineteenth century. They sat in dignified repose on well-manicured lawns. The south end, with homes constructed in the nineteen-thirties and forties, was middle-class and practical. Houses looked lived in, autos looked used, and folks mowed their own grass. The ambience at both ends of town seemed cheerful and friendly. All of which had been attractive after the chaos and devastation of Hurricane Sandy.

When the light changed at Fairfield Street, I could have turned right and crawled a few blocks to my place on Ames in the south end of Etonville. Instead, I headed in the direction of Ellison. I had driven Jerome home once after a post-show party—he had broken his one-drink rule and I hadn't thought he should be behind the wheel—so I was generally familiar with the neighborhood. I passed the Episcopal church, next door to a card and gift shop, both dark, as were most of the houses on the street.

Homes were as modest as those on my end of Fairfield. Some were cottage-sized residences built for a family of no more than four. Some were shotgun houses with small patches of grass for front yards and the occasional early spring flower bed outlining a porch. A handful of parked cars lined the street on both sides. I wondered which house belonged to Rita's cousin.

I crept down Ellison until a large, two-story house came into view—the place where Jerome had lived. It was the only one with a light on, in an upper room that faced the street. A car was parked in the driveway next to a sign: ROOM FOR RENT. The landlord hadn't lost any time looking for a tenant. Pretty ghoulish considering Jerome wasn't even buried yet.

I inched forward and switched off my headlights so that I could turn around in someone's driveway and not disturb the inhabitants. I was about to swing my Metro in a wide arc when the rumble of an engine behind me caused me to check the rearview mirror. I saw a dark SUV—an Escalade, from the look of it—stop directly across the street from Jerome's place. It switched off its headlights, too. I felt little shivers run down my spine. What were the odds that another car just happened to be driving down Ellison this time of night? Checking out Jerome's residence? I completed the turn, and drove home.

Chapter 6

"Look okay?" the delivery kid said and thrust a clipboard at me. I checked off the cartons of food that had been stacked inside the walk-in refrigerator. Enrico was assisting Henry as he concocted his secret-recipe herb-crusted pork loin—I knew about the paprika, basil, and parsley, but there was something else in the coating I could only guess at. Henry was tight-lipped about most of his specials—La Famiglia had definitely made him paranoid.

"Except for the missing twenty pounds of flounder." I frowned and signed the sheet. The seafood order was shorted again; I needed to find another wholesaler. Couldn't be that hard in this part of the state and—

Benny stuck his head in the kitchen. "Dodie. Got a visitor."

I walked out the swinging doors. Pauli sat at the bar drinking a Big Gulp Slurpee and texting. Pauli! I'd been so busy today I'd forgotten we had a meeting. "Hi."

"Hey, Mrs. O'Dell."

A polite kid, even if he did have my marital status screwed up. "Dodie. You can call me Dodie."

"Okay." It came out a croak: Pauli's voice deciding whether or not to change.

"So your mom says you are quite the entrepreneur?"

Pauli slid his eyes in my direction to see if I was making a joke.

"Your business is growing?" I poured myself a seltzer and sat down next to him.

"I guess," he said and jabbed his straw into the Slurpee.

"So how do we start?" I studied a thatch of brown hair falling into his eyes, the spatter pattern of acne across his cheeks, the gangly arms poking out of his hoodie sleeves. "I don't have a website. I don't know much about putting one together."

"Piece of cake," he said and opened his laptop. "First, we have to get a domain name . . . like from GoDaddy or something." He sat up straighter on his bar stool. "Like windjammer.com?"

"Makes sense."

"Yeah and then get a Web host and figure out like what you want on each page." His face was a question mark. "You know what you want on each page?"

"I'm sure I can figure it out. I'll check out some other restaurant websites and put some copy together."

"Uh-huh and you'll need, like, some pictures. Like of the inside here." He looked around, appraising the Web-worthiness of the Windjammer's dining room.

The restaurant dated from eighteen-ninety-eight, when a sea captain had given up his fishing business and settled in Etonville, naming the eatery after his whaling vessel. According to town lore, the poor guy had lost his ship in a poker game and been forced to resort to the life of a landlubber by his furious wife. Maybe to spite her, or because he was still in love with the fishing business, the captain had constructed the interior to remind him of his life upon the sea: two beams in the middle of the room resembled the masts on a whaler, the floor was laid with planking, and a figurehead of a woman's bust soared majestically over the entrance. Henry had kept the nautical theme when he'd purchased the restaurant in 2002. So now there were life preservers on the walls, linked by ropes and knots, and photographs of sailing ships from the seventeen and eighteen hundreds.

"Maybe we need to have some photos of dishes."

"Yeah, and people eating," he added enthusiastically. "And a menu and maybe, like, the times you're open." He stopped to inhale. "And the address and phone number for reservations."

"You really know what you're doing, Pauli."

He grinned bashfully. "I guess."

He was cute in a seventeen-year-old nerdy fashion; but he'd need some work if he was going to find a date for the prom, which was Carol's primary mission.

Pauli pulled up various restaurant websites while I kept one eye on the dining room and made notes of things I thought we could use for the Windjammer website.

"Uh . . . Mrs. . . . uh . . . Dodie, what do you think of this one?" He'd located the site for a very high-end New York restaurant, all muted lighting, intimate booths, and exotic flowers.

We both inspected the interior of the Windjammer. "Well, maybe," I said trying to be encouraging. "But it seems a bit too fancy."

Pauli nodded wisely and clicked a few keys. "Here's something more local." Up popped La Famiglia.

Pretty perceptive kid, I thought. I studied the home page. I'd stood at the cash register once, waiting for my take-out garlic knots. But it had been late afternoon and the place had been mostly empty. The website featured a photo that showed stucco and brick walls, an open wine rack, a central oven and cooking area, and a parquet tile floor. The dozen café tables were full.

"Dodie," Henry bellowed, halfway out the kitchen door. "What happened to the flounder?"

Perfect timing. "Henry, I want you to meet Pauli. He's the son of a friend and a real computer whiz."

"Hi," he said grudgingly. "We really need to finalize the menu. . . ."

"Take a look at this," I said and turned the laptop around.

Henry's eyes widened. "La Famiglia?"

"Pauli's got plans for a Windjammer website that will knock your socks off."

Henry seemed interested. "Okay, but right now we've got work to do."

"I can put some stuff together and get back to you," Pauli said quickly.

"Sounds like a plan. How about it Henry?"

He nodded. "Make sure you give me an idea of what it will cost."

"Yes, sir. Thanks." He shut his laptop, jammed it into his backpack, and slid off the stool. "I'd better be getting home."

I had a sudden urge to brush his forehead clear of that brown hank of hair. "Say hello to your mom for me," I said, and followed Henry into the kitchen.

* * *

Gillian had finished the set up for dinner, Benny had restocked the bar, and a few customers had begun to trickle in as I settled into my back booth. I was fantasizing about letting Benny close up and heading home for a glass of wine, a hot bath, and a Cindy Collins mystery. But Cindy Collins reminded me that Jerome had offered to lend me her latest book. I kept replaying last night's drive by his house, wondering who might have been in that SUV.

I had just shifted my focus back to the stack of bills in front of me when I heard a familiar voice. "Dodie, hi," Lola said. She sounded upset.

"Hi. What's up?"

Lola scooted into the booth. "Dodie, we're in trouble."

"What are you talking about?" I said.

"You know how Walter told Chief Thompson he'd report the missing money if he hadn't found it in twenty-four hours?"

I remembered. "Did he find the money?"

"No." Lola flipped her blond locks behind her shoulder. "I was in the box office straightening up. No one has cleaned up in there since Jerome died. There were food wrappers and Xeroxes of scenes from *Romeo and Juliet* . . . probably Penny hanging out."

"And . . ."

Lola hesitated. "I threw out the trash and opened the top drawer under the counter by the ticket window. Just to see if it needed to be cleaned out, too. Jerome spent so much time in front of house that he just thought of the box office as his personal space. He kept some things in the drawers. Like a tie he wore opening nights and paperback novels and . . . things."

"Lola?"

"I found a small ledger in the drawer that had an accounting of ELT income and expenses for the last six months. Most of it was pretty straightforward. Costume and scenery purchases. But every so often, Jerome made a notation. WZ. And next to the initials were amounts of money." She withdrew a black, five-by-seven notebook from her bag.

"Walter was borrowing from the box office?"

"And Jerome was keeping track of it."

I opened the book and scanned the pages. The last notation was

made the fourteenth. The day before auditions. After he and I had
had our conversation in the Windjammer.

"Oh, Dodie, if the board hears about this . . . Walter has a real
problem."

"Especially since, according to Jerome's notes, it adds up to a
thousand dollars. That's grand theft."

Lola put her elbows on the table, her head in her hands. "I know
Walter isn't always the most considerate person, but I thought he was
honest. The divorce has changed him."

I didn't agree. I'd always thought he was a pain in the neck. I
thumbed through the ledger again. Walter's initials first appeared the
previous December, just about the time he was in the throes of his
chaotic divorce. Jerome's accounting ended half-way through the
book. The rest of the pages were blank, but on the last page, someone, presumably Jerome, had written *MR* and a date: *4/16*.

"Did you see this?" I pushed the book across the table.

Lola stared at the writing and shook her head. "What does that
mean?"

"I don't know. The sixteenth was the morning Jerome was found.
This looks like a planned meeting. I wonder why Jerome made a note
in the ledger in the box office? Is there someone with these initials
connected to the theater?"

She thought a minute. "I don't think so. What should we do with it?"

"Let's save it for now. Maybe we could find out who or what
MR is?"

"How would we do that?" She handed me the ledger as if for safekeeping.

"I'll think of something," I said and patted her hand. I had no idea
how I was going to get this information.

Lola leaned in closer. "Dodie, we need help at the ELT. Things
are in an uproar. With Jerome gone, there's no one to run the box office, and Penny is more disorganized than ever with the murder investigation and the press. I don't know how she's going to get us
through rehearsals. And Walter is so preoccupied. You have to help
us," she pleaded.

"Me? I have a restaurant to manage."

"You did such a great job at auditions. It would only be a few
nights a week just to make sure everything is running smoothly. To

keep an eye on rehearsals, check the box office on nights of the show. And if there is an emergency, you'll be right next door." She paused. "As a favor to me? Just to get through *Romeo and Juliet*," she added sadly.

I did want to find out more about Jerome's death. Having access to the theater and its members might be helpful.

"Let me speak with Henry. You know he likes me to be available even on my days off."

"It's just for a few weeks. Walter has delayed the first rehearsal until after Jerome's funeral. And I'll help in any way I can," Lola said.

"I'll see what I can do. Benny might like to take on a few extra night shifts," I said.

"Thanks. By the way, did you hear about Jerome's funeral?"

I shook my head.

"Apparently Jerome has . . . uh, had a sister-in-law someplace in the Midwest. She called Walter today and offered to pay for everything, but she can't make it out here for the service. She asked if we could take care of the details."

"He never mentioned any family."

"I know. Walter is so overwhelmed with everything he can't really take on one more responsibility. So I offered to help."

The dinner special was a huge success: patrons gobbled up the pork loin—which made Henry ecstatic. I made a mental note to speak to him in the morning about my dropping in at the ELT a few nights a week in addition to my days off. Once dinner was nearly concluded, unless there was a crisis, I could slip out and leave Benny in charge. But I'd have to have Carmen in place for those nights as well. I was making my to-do list for tomorrow and watching Gillian clear the last of the tables when my cell clanged.

"Hello?"

"Dodie? It's Carol."

"Hi. What's happening?"

"When I got home tonight, I had an email from Monica Jenkins."

"Who's that?"

"Rita's cousin. The shampoo girl."

I sat up straighter. "What did she want?"

"An appointment to get her hair colored and trimmed. I talked her into coming by tomorrow morning. I figured the sooner, the better, and maybe you could stop by to see her before the Windjammer opened."

"Carol, that's great. When?"

"How's nine?"

"Perfect. That'll give me plenty of time. Good work." I could hear her smile through the phone line.

Chapter 7

The salon was a cacophony of sound, as usual: telephone ringing, dryers whirring, laughter rising and falling, and Carol, talking over it all to a customer getting her hair colored. She motioned to me to join her.

"Dodie, this is Monica Jenkins. Rita's cousin." Carol daubed a brownish mixture on Monica's roots and around her hairline. She must be graying early. She couldn't be more than late thirties.

"Hello," I said politely.

"She lives on Ellison," Carol said.

"So you're Jerome Angleton's neighbor?"

Monica squinted and held her glasses to her face, careful to avoid the hair dye on her forehead as she stared at me through the mirror. *"Was."* Her voice was raspy. A current or former smoker.

"Right. He was a friend of mine." I paused. "Did you know him well?"

"I only lived on Ellison for the last year. But I saw him come and go." She shifted her attention to Carol. "Don't forget that spot on the top of my head."

Carol nodded patiently.

"I miss him."

"I didn't know him well enough to miss him. Said hi now and then." Monica dropped her glasses into her lap.

"Carol mentioned that your cousin"—we all turned to see Rita massaging the scalp of a customer, lather up her arms—"said you'd seen a woman visiting Jerome last month."

"That's right."

"You were on your porch?" I asked.

"That's right. I get home from work about five. This was probably . . . five-thirty or six. I like to have a beer and sit in my swing at the end of the day."

"Uh-huh. And you saw this woman arrive?"

"Pulled up in her car and went into the house."

"Can you tell me anything about her? Had you ever seen her visiting Jerome before? What did she look like?"

"Nope. Average."

Hard to believe Monica lived in Etonville, where everyone had something to say about everything.

"Can you describe her?"

"I'd say seventy, gray hair, done up in a . . ." She made a swirl with one hand.

"A bun?"

"No, higher up her head."

"A French twist?" Carol said.

"Yep, that's it. With glasses around her neck."

I supposed that could describe quite a few folks in Etonville.

"Kind of like a librarian," Monica said.

"And you hadn't seen her before?"

"Just that once."

"What kind of car was she driving? Did they leave together?"

"Dark. Maybe . . . black or blue. I don't pay much attention to brands."

I smiled. "Me neither. My car's nine years old."

"She was in Jerome's place for maybe ten minutes. Then they came out and got in the car and left." Monica picked up a *People* magazine.

Then it occurred to me that Jerome was a renter. "Did you know Jerome's landlord?"

Monica looked up from a two page spread on Lady Gaga. "Landlady. Betty Everly. Kind of a pill. But her father's a friendly old guy. Waves hello in the morning when he picks up the newspaper. He spends the whole day staring out the front window while his daughter's working."

"Well, thanks for the information."

Carol scraped the last drops from the dye container, and Monica rotated in her seat to face me directly. "Know what I think? There's a new element moving into Etonville. I think maybe it was a gang member from New York who committed the murder," she said.

"Really?" I loved this town, but sometimes it was just too wacky for words. "Well, that's a theory."

I hustled to get to the Windjammer. Business was booming so I helped Benny cover the bar and seated folks and answered the phone for take-out orders.

By one-thirty there was a lull in the traffic and I hid in the kitchen to grab a bite to eat and get a break from customers. Today's lunch special was Henry's secret burger: one part barbecue sauce, one part avocado and cilantro, and one part who-knew-what. It was delicious.

I put my hand on the door to the dining room and peeked out the tiny window. At the bar was Chief Thompson, taking off his cap and running a hand over his bristly brush cut. He smiled as he gave an order to Gillian, who tilted her spiky streaked head and leaned provocatively across the bar in response. *Geez.*

I pushed open the door with authority.

"Chief Thompson," I said brightly, though businesslike.

"Ms. O'Dell. Nice to see you again."

"Get you anything to drink?" I put one hand possessively on the beer tap.

He shook his head. "On duty," he said ruefully. "I'll take a club soda."

"Coming right up." I handed him his drink and watched him take a sip.

"So how goes the investigation?" I asked.

"Nothing new to report so far," he said evasively.

"I hear they're planning a funeral service soon. Lola Tripper at the ELT is arranging it."

His eyes narrowed. "Thanks. I hadn't heard."

Henry stuck his head out the kitchen door, plate in hand.

"I'll get it," I said to Gillian.

I placed Bill's secret burger carefully in front of him, edging his club soda to one side. "There you go," I said and noticed that he had no rings on his fingers. The girls at Snippets were probably right: no attachments.

"Thanks." He positioned his napkin on his lap.

"Good idea. They're a little bit sloppy."

He nodded and took a bite.

"But tasty. Let me know if you need anything else." I started to head to the kitchen.

"Listen, I know you were friends with Mr. Angleton. I'd appreciate it if you could clue me in on any personal information you might hear. It could shed some light on the case." He fixed those laser-like eyes on my flushed face and stretchy knit top.

My heart skipped a beat, and a warm sphere glowed in my chest. I debated. Was now the time to share what I'd learned? "Well, now that you mention it, I have been hearing a few things. . . ."

"Oh?" He studied my face. "Why don't you stop by the office later today. What time do you get off?"

Was he making a date or setting up a business meeting? "I take a break around three. How's that sound?"

"I'll be there."

At three o'clock, I coasted down Amber Street and stopped in front of a one-story red brick building dating from the late 1700s, tucked between JC's Hardware and Betty's Boutique, which featured high-end women's lingerie. It was a mini version of Victoria's Secret, minus leopard-skin thongs and red lace bustiers. The RESERVED FOR CHIEF parking space was occupied.

I swung my bag over my shoulder and opened the front door of the Municipal Building, coming face-to-face with Etonville's Hall of Fame: a wall of photos, trophies, and certificates honoring past and present citizens for memorable feats. There were statuettes for the town's winning softball teams and certificates of merit from the state police, and in the middle was an eleven-by-seventeen of Chief Bull Bennett, smiling from ear to ear and showing off a thirty-pound bass that he had reeled in at Elmwood Lake.

"I guess he was quite the character."

I whipped around. "Oh, h-hi," I stuttered as though caught in an illicit activity

One side of Chief Thompson's mouth ticked upward in a crooked grin. Those eyes were mesmerizing.

"Let's go to my office," he said, and strode off.

To our left was a hallway that led to the town clerk's office, which dispensed everything from dog tags and yard sale permits to marriage and fishing licenses. I followed the chief to the right, past the dispatcher's window.

"Hi, Dodie," dispatcher Edna May called out. Being responsible for 911 calls, she knew everything and everyone in Etonville. "I hear you're going to be running rehearsals. Good thing. Penny is the most—"

"I'm not really—"

"You know, I'm a Lady-in-Waiting," she said, pleased.

"Congratulations."

"No lines yet, but Walter said, 'Wait and see.'"

Whatever that meant.

"What's Henry's special tonight?" She shoved a pencil into the brownish bun perched atop her head. Edna was downright skinny and had an appetite that was legend. Half the women in Etonville were jealous of her. She had been the most efficient aspect of the police department under Bull's watch. But I had the feeling things were a little different around here now.

"It's a surprise," I answered and kept Chief Thompson's frame in sight: broad shoulders, slim hips, and a uniform that fit like a glove. We entered the outer office of the department, where an officer sat at a computer terminal, head bent over a keyboard that was surrounded by three monitors. Floors gleamed and Lysol freshened the air.

"Suki, bring in that file on Jerome Angleton, please," he said, and a young Asian woman lifted her head. I recognized her from the crime scene. Suki Shung.

I nodded and smiled at her. She responded with an enigmatic expression that cut off any attempt at pleasantries. The atmosphere had changed noticeably at the station. No trace of Bull's bonhomie and good-natured clutter.

We entered the chief's inner office and he indicated that I should sit in a chair opposite his desk, which was as neatly arranged as Suki's. "So . . . you've been hearing some things? About Jerome Angleton?"

A knock at the door. "Enter," he said.

Suki appeared, file in hand. She silently placed the folder on Bill's desk and turned to leave. "Thanks. Let me know when Ralph returns."

She nodded and quietly closed the door.

"A woman of few words," I said lightly. "Almost . . . serene."

"She's a Buddhist."

"A Buddhist cop. Wow."

"Also a martial arts black belt. Suki's a solid professional."

Unlike Etonville's other full-time officer. Ralph had been Bull's fishing buddy, drinking partner, and poker pal. His attitude was laissez-faire and his work habits less than professional, but he was an agreeable guy.

"I can see that," I said.

"We worked together before."

I waited for him to continue, but he sat back in the desk chair and crossed his arms. "So, Jerome?"

"Right. Well, you know small-town life."

"I'm beginning to," he chuckled.

"It turns out that one of the shampoo girls at Snippets—that's a hair salon . . ."

"Got it."

"She has a cousin who lives on Ellison Street. A few doors down from the place where Jerome lived."

He nodded politely so I filled him in: Monica Jenkins on the front porch swing drinking a beer and a mystery woman dropping by to pick Jerome up. I couldn't offer much by way of description of either the woman or the car. But Chief Thompson frowned as I spoke, nodding occasionally. When I finished, he wrote down Monica's name.

"Do you think finding this woman might help the investigation?" I asked.

"Maybe," he said.

"I drove by his house the other night."

He raised an eyebrow.

"I'm not sure why."

Chief Thompson opened Jerome's file and studied its contents. "You were close to him?" he asked softly.

When he looked up again, after a minute, my eyes were full. "Just a good friend. I don't want to get in the way, but I'd like to help. If I can."

The chief tapped his index finger against the file, then carefully closed it. "Okay. Thanks for stopping in. Let me know if you hear anything else."

As an afterthought, I added, "The other night when I drove by, another car also drove down Ellison and stopped near Jerome's place. It was an SUV. A big one."

Chief Thompson made a note.

"Maybe it was just a coincidence."

He nodded and I pulled my bag onto my shoulder and walked to the door. At least I *thought* it was the entrance to the hallway. I entered a tiny room that had served as Bull's office kitchen; I'd delivered dinner here once and it had been chock-full of pastry boxes, take-out containers from fast-food joints on the highway, and dirty dishes. And Ralph stuffing his mouth. But all hints of Bull's epicurean excesses had been replaced with neat piles of stationery, a fax machine, and evidence cartons.

"Oops," I said and backed away from the door.

"Been a few changes around here," the chief said. I could hear, rather than see, the corner of his mouth sneak upward again.

I shut the office door behind me.

On my days off, I liked to sleep in, do my laundry, catch up with errands, and maybe get in a chapter or two of my latest thriller. But today I decided to clean house and invite Carol and Lola—and Pauli, who was dropping by after school to show me his ideas for the Windjammer website—for an early dinner.

By five o'clock, I was facing Pauli and his laptop at my dining room table. "Wow. Looking good. I like what you've done with the menus." I perused various pages while he basked in the glow of my praise.

The doorbell rang. "That must be your mom."

Carol bustled in the door. "I hope you're hungry," she announced. "I made lasagna." She went to work heating up the food and scrounged around in my refrigerator for the makings of a salad while I set the dining room table with my great aunt Maureen's silver and my most elegant paper napkins.

"How's the website coming?" Carol asked in a whisper.

"Pauli's quite the tech expert. He's doing great."

Carol smiled, fairly bursting with appreciation as Lola showed up bearing chocolate chip cookies.

We all sat at my dining room table scraping the last bits of cheese and pasta from Carol's casserole dish. "Ummm, this is so good," Lola said. "If I'm not careful, I won't fit into Lady C's costume." Her mauve top hugged her in all the right places.

Pauli asked to be excused, pushed at the hank of hair flopped over his forehead, and sauntered into my living room with his laptop.

"I heard you visited Chief Thompson." Carol winked and nibbled on a cookie. "Lucky you."

"Word gets around fast."

"Did it have something to do with the murder?" asked Lola.

"I told him about Rita's cousin and the woman visiting Jerome," I said.

"You did?" Carol sat up straighter.

"What woman?" Lola asked.

Carol and I proceeded to fill Lola in on Monica Jenkins. "Who do you think she is?" I asked. "Could she be someone connected to the ELT?"

Lola frowned. "I don't think so. I would have known about it."

"Do you think anyone else at the theater might know who she is? I mean, where else would he meet her? He seemed to spend most of his time there."

The three of us sat at the table munching on cookies, thinking.

"Online? It's very popular these days. I even tried it," Lola said.

"You did? You never told me."

"Match.com," Lola said. "I was kind of nervous about it."

"Jerome would need an email account." Carol brushed crumbs off the front of her sweater.

"I'm pretty sure he had an account, because most of the ELT communication is done via email."

"Well, if Jerome had access to a computer and wanted to find some-one, it wouldn't be a challenge. A guy his age, still in great shape? Not a problem," I said. "But if he had a computer, Chief Thompson must have it. If he didn't, where could he borrow computer time? The the-ater?"

"There's one in Walter's office, but no one touches it except Wal-ter. And sometimes Penny." Lola finished her coffee and wiped her mouth. "There's always the library."

"What?"

"There are computers at the library. I took a workshop there a couple of years ago on using Internet databases, searching the Web, things like that. It was full of people Jerome's age."

"Great idea." I thought about Jerome's reading habits. It was likely he'd spent some time at the Etonville Public Library.

Lola glanced at the wall clock, its hands registering six-thirty. "Board meeting tonight. I told Walter I'd stop by a little early. Did you speak with Henry about getting some time off?" She was so hopeful, I was touched.

"As long as I can cover the dinner rush, I'll be able to sneak away around eight a couple of nights a week."

"Oh, Dodie, that's perfect. We don't usually get started until seven or seven-thirty by the time everyone gets there anyway. I'm so glad you'll be on the scene."

"Penny will be up in arms."

"It's for a good cause."

"I've got to go back to the salon for an hour. I'll drop you off at home, Pauli," Carol said and cleared the table.

We loaded the dishwasher and left the casserole dish in the sink to soak, and Carol and Lola hurried off in separate directions.

Chapter 8

I proceeded down Main Street to Amber and stopped at the red light. To my left, I could see the entrance to the police station, and that made me think of Chief Thompson. The little buzz I got from remembering his eyes and hair and muscled arms made me wonder about my love life. On the corner of Belvidere and Amber, I pulled into the parking lot of the Etonville Public Library. The April air was brittle, and a brisk wind had picked up overnight. I turned the collar of my jacket up around my ears. The morning sunlight was fierce—not as fierce as it would be glinting off the ocean, but still intense. I missed this time of day down the shore, especially in the spring. No summer crowds yet, few people on the boardwalk, the gulls not as aggressive as they would be in a month or two. I used to meander in the sand and feel the wet granules squish between my toes. That was another life.

The lobby of the library was bustling for eight-thirty in the morning. Directly ahead was the main circulation desk. Off to the right side, a small group of senior citizens, each toting a book, chattered animatedly and filed into a conference room. I recognized a few from the ELT. On the left, a patient young man ushered exuberant tots into a reading room filled with kiddie chairs. Behind the circulation desk, Mildred Tower multitasked, the phone at her ear while she stamped the cards attached to the flyleaves of half a dozen volumes. Mildred and her husband ate dinner at the Windjammer at least once a week, always ordering the soup of the day, salad, and dessert. Rarely ever the entrée. You don't forget patrons with that pattern. The two of them were on a perpetual diet that seemed to have little impact.

I loved the smell of libraries, the dust and floor polish and aging paper. It did something to my insides. Immediately I relaxed and regretted the fact that I had never stepped foot into the Etonville Public

Library until today. The campus library had been the best part of my college experience.

Mildred nodded at me, her round face a grin from ear to ear, and held up a finger to "hold on." I nodded back and looked around.

She replaced the phone in its cradle. "Hi, Dodie. May I help you?"

"Yes, please. I'm wondering if the library has a computer lab."

"Of course." She slipped out the half-door that separated the oval reception area from the rest of the lobby. Despite her size, she practically sprinted to the back of the foyer and turned left, moving down a corridor that had a series of rooms on either side. I saw a foursome playing cards, and one of the players looked up as I passed the open door.

"Hi, Dodie."

"Hey, Chrystal. Getting ready for *Romeo and Juliet*?" I asked the ELT's costumer.

She looked at me over the rim of her reading glasses and giggled. "Walter has us working on codpieces, dontcha know."

Shakespearean costume history was not my strength, but even I knew that covers for the men's crotches were an Elizabethan custom. I'd seen leather versions on heavy-metal rockers; I couldn't wait to view the ELT variety. "Sounds like fun."

I waved at Chrystal and quick-stepped to catch up with Mildred. I passed large multicolored murals with cartoonish characters grinning crazily. Someone's version of a nightmare.

At the end of the hall, Mildred paused beside an open door and waited for me to enter. There were four computer stations. Only one was being used. "Feel free to stay as long as you like." She cocked her head to one side. "Do you have an email address, or do you need to set up an account?"

"I have an address. But how would I set up a new one?"

Mildred placed a plump hand on the top of the console. "It's very simple." She touched the mouse and clicked on an item. "You begin here and need only follow the prompts. They will lead you through the process to create a new account and password."

I nodded my appreciation.

"I imagine a young woman like you will have no problem finding her way. It's mostly the older gentlemen and women who aren't acquainted with the Internet."

"Do you have many seniors using the computers?"

"Oh yes. Our computer room is very popular. Everyone these days needs to email. Well, let me know if you need any help. I'll be at the front desk until four."

"Thanks. By the way, did you know Jerome Angleton?"

She put a hand to her mouth. "Poor Jerome. So terrible what happened to him."

"Yes." I allowed a proper beat. "Did he use this lab?"

"Oh, he was a frequent visitor," she said. "To the computer lab, to our Friday morning non-fiction book club . . ."

Jerome read other things besides mysteries and thrillers?

". . . and our special collections," Mildred added.

"The special collections?" I asked.

"In the basement. It's where we keep our rare books and papers." She glanced at the wall clock. "I'm sorry, but I need to get back to the circulation desk," she said contritely.

"No problem. Thanks for your help."

As long as I was here, I might as well see exactly what Jerome would have had to do to get an email account. I clicked on the first prompt. I was able to set up an email address and password with a minimum of effort. If Jerome was surfing the Internet, it would be simple enough to come here for a few hours and check out various dating websites.

I decided to stop by the basement area before I headed to the Windjammer. Downstairs was the media room, with a checkout desk in front of rows of metal shelves covered with old VHS tapes, CDs, and DVDs. To the left were the small listening rooms with CD players and headsets. Directly across from the desk was a locked door with SPECIAL COLLECTIONS stamped on a frosted window. I looked around; the floor was empty. Since there was no one to talk to, I retraced my steps to the lobby, waved good-bye to Mildred, and walked out into the sunshine.

Henry's cream of asparagus soup and grilled three-cheese sandwich killed during lunch. It took all hands on deck to handle the crunch of customers. But Henry was happy, and that made me happy. While my feet were running from the phone to the tables to the bar, my mind was slowly sifting through everything I knew about Jerome's life and death. It wasn't much.

I wanted to chat with Chief Thompson about the possibilities generated by the appearance of the mystery woman; but what could I add that I hadn't mentioned to him two days ago? There had to be something or someone else that could shed some light.

By three o'clock, I'd made up my mind. My break provided enough time to visit Ellison Street and hopefully get a look at Jerome's living space. And by going during the afternoon, I stood a better chance of dealing with the "friendly old man" instead of the "pill of a landlady."

I stepped outside the Windjammer. The late-afternoon sun had reached its zenith and begun to drift toward setting. It was going to be a lovely evening, high sixties and a beautiful sunset. Of course, nothing could compare to the sun over the ocean. Though I loved Etonville, I missed the pounding waves and thin film of foam that lapped at the sand as the tide rolled in.

After a short ride, I pulled down Ellison Street, which seemed as quiet by day as it did by night. I checked out the houses across the street from Jerome's residence. No sign of Monica Jenkins on a front porch. There was plenty of street parking so I eased my Metro to the curb and switched off the motor.

In the mystery novels I'd read, I'd learned that when gathering evidence, adopting a low profile was often more productive than entering with guns blazing. My plan was to knock on the door, tell whoever answered that I was Jerome's friend, and ask, politely, to see Jerome's room.

I couldn't concoct some wild, cockamamie story in this town. Word traveled too fast. I needed to play it straight.

I walked to the front door, alert for any sign of landlady Betty Everly's father staring soulfully into the street. The living room windows were open, and classical music wafted through the sheer curtains. I rang the bell and the music softened. After a few moments, an elderly man opened the door, squinting into the late-day sunlight. He was probably late eighties, with thin wisps of white hair above his ears and around the back of his head. A noticeable paunch hung over a belt that kept corduroy pants and a flannel shirt in place. His light brown eyes were watery, his large nose lined with red threads.

"Yes?" he said and smiled cheerfully.

"Hello, is this the Everly residence?"

"Well, yes. My daughter is Betty Everly. I'm Charles Waters."

"Mr. Waters, my name is Dodie O'Dell, and I was a friend of Jerome Angleton."

His face crumpled and his mouth formed an O. He opened the door wider and stepped aside. "Please come in."

I'd been preparing myself to have to convince someone to let me in. This might not be as difficult as I had anticipated. I followed him into the foyer. The house smelled like a combination of furniture polish and freshly baked cookies.

"So sad," he said.

"Yes. He rented a room here?" I asked.

"That's right."

"Did you know him well?"

"We played checkers on Sundays. I think he always let me win." He stood helplessly at the foot of a staircase and gazed up the steps, as if he expected Jerome to appear and walk down them.

I never saw Jerome on Sundays. The Windjammer was closed, and the ELT rarely rehearsed on weekends unless a show was about to open. "That sounds like him."

Charles wrung his hands helplessly. "I miss him."

"Me too," I said. "Do you think I could take a look at his room? I thought maybe I could find something to send to his family." It was only a little lie.

Charles looked at me blankly as if the thought that Jerome had a family was completely unexpected.

"Well, you know the police were here. . . ." As his voice trailed off, Charles jammed his hands in his pants pockets and rocked backward on his bedroom slippers. "They took a few things."

"Uh-huh," I said and nodded. "That makes sense."

He closed his eyes as though he might nod off.

"I'll only be a few minutes."

"For what?" His eyes flew open.

"To see Jerome's room . . . ?"

Without another word, Charles turned, padded to the stairs, and ascended slowly, taking one step at a time.

We paused in a hallway dimly lit by a single window on the back wall. There were three doors, two on one side, one on the other. Charles opened the door to the second room on the left.

Somewhere downstairs, a phone rang.

"That's my daughter. She doesn't trust me home alone." He smiled again.

"I won't be long," I promised and scooted into the room. As Charles descended the stairs, I shut the door.

I wasn't at all sure what I was looking for, but I knew I had only a few minutes to scour the place. I allowed my gaze to work its way around the bedroom. Beige walls, a closet, a bed, a rocker, two watercolors of pastoral scenes, a small night table, and the bureau. No computer. I crossed to an old oak chest of drawers and noiselessly opened the top one. Boxer shorts, undershirts, men's handkerchiefs, and half a dozen pairs of socks. The next two drawers held folded shirts: short-sleeved, long-sleeved, and polo. The bottom drawer was nearly empty except for three pairs of pajamas still in their plastic wrap.

I spied the nightstand and slid open its single drawer. It held a Bible, a notepad and pen, and a well-thumbed copy of a Sherlock Holmes mystery, overdue at the Etonville Public Library.

I considered the room again. In the closet I found khakis, neatly pressed, two dark suits, some starched dress shirts, a cardigan sweater, and half a dozen empty hangers. Slippers and a pair of sneakers lay on the floor of the closet. I brushed the suits aside to see if I had neglected anything. No luck.

I moved to his bathroom and checked out the medicine cabinet. Just the usual. Cold and cough products, Vicks, lozenges, Advil, aspirin, and an out-of-date prescription for penicillin.

Surrounding the sink were an electric toothbrush, toothpaste, mint-flavored dental tape, deodorant, and disposable shavers in a ceramic cup. Under the sink, there were ten rolls of toilet paper, probably from Costco over in Crestmont, and a dozen bars of soap. A black men's travel kit held a worn toothbrush.

I crossed back into his bedroom, took a last look around, and was about to close the closet door when I remembered my mother teasingly reminding my father to check his pockets whenever he took off a suit coat, or she'd get to keep the valuables. There was always a treasure trove of fascinating stuff in his pockets—at least so it seemed to a ten-year-old—like lint, gum, and little slips of paper. Never any money.

I eased my hand into the first suit jacket and withdrew a fresh handkerchief. The other pocket was empty. In the second suit, I found an old pen and a matchbook. Then I slipped my hand into the inside breast pocket and withdrew a small velvet box. I flipped the lid and gasped. I was holding a diamond ring. Though modest in size, its clarity was undeniable. Jerome was getting engaged? I was dumbfounded. He'd never even hinted at having a girlfriend, much less a fiancée.

Usually when something bothered me, these little prickly hairs on the back of my neck stood at attention. I could feel myself shivering even though Jerome's room was stuffy and warm. I slipped the ring box into my jacket pocket and hurried down the stairs. I couldn't have been in Jerome's room more than fifteen minutes, but Charles was waiting for me at the foot of the staircase, tapping his fingers against the bannister.

"Thanks for letting me into his room. It made me feel . . . close to him."

"My daughter's on her way home," he said. "She left work early."

"Oh, uh, that's good. Um, well . . ." I needed to leave. I really had no desire to explain my visit all over again, especially with someone much less understanding than Charles.

"She's going to rent the room out."

So the sign out front was accurate. "I'm sorry you lost your checkers partner," I said softly.

He shrugged. "Jerome was leaving anyway."

"He was? I didn't know . . . ?"

Of course, he was also planning on getting married.

"Do you play checkers?" he asked hopefully.

I started to maneuver my way to the front door. "Uh, no . . . sorry. But maybe your daughter . . . ?" I slid out the front door. "Thanks again."

He looked so mournful, I couldn't help myself. I gave him a quick hug and scurried to my Metro. At the top of the street, a white, late-model sedan was barreling down Ellison. I took off.

Chapter 9

I brushed my teeth, slipped into a funeral-appropriate outfit, black skirt and sweater, and nibbled on a piece of toast—coffee would have to wait until after the service. Lola's Lexus turned into my driveway so I grabbed my purse and keys and flew out the door. A few fluffy clouds skidded across the deep blue sky: a beautiful day for a funeral. I shut the passenger-side door and had just barely clicked my seat belt when Lola passed me a Coffee Heaven take-out paper cup.

"Decaf caramel macchiato, hold the foam," she said, looking sophisticated and serene in her black suit and pearls.

"Lola, you are my hero." I popped up the lid and inhaled. "To what do I owe this generosity?"

"I just thought it might be nice to be nice."

I smiled at her. "What can we expect this morning?"

"Jerome's sister isn't springing for anything beyond the bare necessities. A simple service and coffee in the undercroft."

"I'm sure Jerome would have appreciated your efforts," I said.

"I did my best. Of course, Walter had a hand in everything. The pallbearers, the eulogy—"

"I went to Jerome's place yesterday." I took a sip of my coffee. "You're not going to believe what I found." I described my visit to Ellison Street, including Charles Waters's loss of his checkers partner and the diamond ring.

"An engagement ring! So Jerome *was* stepping out," Lola said, stunned.

"More than stepping out. According to Charles, he was planning on leaving soon. Maybe to get married."

"I don't understand. Why did none of us know about her?"

"Jerome wanted to keep things under wraps?"

Lola turned left into the parking lot. A sizeable crowd had gathered in the churchyard of St. Andrew's Episcopal Church—people Jerome had come to know over the years as a beloved high school teacher, along with the ELT folks and the local press. Organ music wafted out of the vestibule as the undertaker appeared and began to direct people into the church.

"Where's Walter?" I asked.

Lola craned her neck as we filed into a pew halfway down the aisle. "I'm sure he's in the vestibule with the other pallbearers," she said nervously.

"Is something the matter?" I asked.

"Just wait."

I'd read enough mysteries and thrillers to know that, next to stakeouts and surreptitious photography, a funeral was a good friend to an investigator: who came, who didn't come, who broke down. At the left rear of the church, Chief Thompson leaned against a pillar, a good position from which to inspect the assembled parties. Opposite him, on the right side of the nave, sat Officer Suki Shung. Both of them out of uniform, expressions neutral.

"Show time," a voice hissed in my ear, and I jumped.

"Penny," I said, my heart banging around in my chest. "You're going to kill me."

"I hear the police did a biopsy."

"You mean autopsy," I said.

"Whatever."

"I think that's standard procedure when someone dies a violent death," Lola said calmly.

"You're looking good, Lola. Walter's giving the eulogy, right? I mean, after all, the ELT was Jerome's home," Penny said.

Lola nodded. "Maybe you should get a seat, Penny. The service is probably going to start soon."

The organist began to play "Let All Mortal Flesh Keep Silence." It was my fondest wish.

Penny jerked her head over one shoulder and nodded. "Here he comes to take his final bow."

I turned in my seat and saw the pallbearers and coffin in place at the back of the church.

"OMG, Lola?"

"I know," she whispered hoarsely, staring straight ahead. "It was

Walter's idea. I tried to talk him out of it but he thought it was . . . appropriate?"

Aligned along both sides of the casket were six guys, all ELT members, and Walter. The six were dressed in Elizabethan garb: tights and capes and frilly shirts. Walter, in modified Elizabethan costume with just the shirt and cape, stood at the rear of the casket.

"How did he convince them to dress like that? To wear that stuff to a funeral?"

Lola shrugged. "They're actors."

The organist started the chorus again, and we all stood as Jerome was wheeled down the aisle. The undertaker led the processional, and Walter pushed from the back of the coffin. In between, the six actors steered the casket. I had to stifle laughter, like, no doubt, many of the pews' occupants.

The minister began the service. There were prayers for Jerome's soul and a few words about his kindness and generosity. Heads nodded throughout the church. And then Walter rose and somberly approached the pulpit. He flipped the ends of his cape over his shoulders and withdrew a sheet of paper from the inside of his flowing white shirt. He cut a surprisingly striking, if odd, figure: grave and somewhat timeless. He cleared his throat. "Out, out, brief candle! Life's but a walking shadow, a poor player that struts and frets his hour upon the stage and then is heard no more. It is a tale told by an idiot, full of sound and fury, signifying nothing."

Most of the crowd certainly recognized Shakespeare's hand in this. If Walter had ended there and just said a few words about Jerome and the theater, we could have called it a funeral. But this was a performance.

"Jerome was our friend, part of the Etonville Little Theatre family. It is therefore only fitting to remember him and his last role in our circle of light and to wonder what his future in the theater might have been had he . . ." Walter took a dramatic beat. ". . . lived. 'To be, or not to be: that is the question . . .'"

No one could confuse murder with suicide, including Walter, but the line was too good to pass up. He described Jerome's sense of humor and listed all of the various duties he had performed at the ELT. A baby started to wail, but Walter soldiered on, building to the climax of his oration. "Friends and mourners, lend me your ears, I come to bury Jerome, *and* to praise him."

His mashup of *Julius Caesar* and *Hamlet* had left the crowd totally confused. "And so I remind us all that 'tomorrow, and tomorrow, and tomorrow, creeps in this petty pace from day to day.'"

He ended to thunderous silence. Then some members of the ELT, forgetting this was a memorial for Jerome, started to applaud. Everyone else looked around as though searching for permission before joining in. Walter bowed slightly and the minister announced prayers in the church cemetery, followed by refreshments in the church basement.

Walter rejoined the pallbearers and they rolled Jerome down the aisle, all of us filing out of our pews behind him. When the organist started in on "The Strife Is O'er," I saw Chief Thompson and Suki Shung still with neutral expressions, probably in shock from the whole affair. As far as the investigation was concerned, the strife had just begun.

After the prayers, we left Jerome's casket in St. Andrew's cemetery and moved into the church for refreshments.

I brushed a bit of apple strudel off my sweater as I observed the crowd; some were huddled around the dessert table noodling over their options while others, in groups of twos and threes, chatted in hushed tones. Occasionally, someone would let out a honk of a laugh and the place would go silent for a few moments before the general level of noise would ratchet up again.

"Jerome had a lot of friends," Chief Thompson said at my back.

I spun around. He was even more handsome in a suit than in uniform, his pale blue shirt and matching tie accentuating his eyes. I had to pull myself away from his stare. "Yes, he was well-loved." Was now the time to mention the engagement ring?

"Dodie, I think I'm ready to leave." Lola turned to face me. "Hi, Chief Thompson."

"Hello. Mrs. Tripper, right?" he said.

"Yes. Lola please."

There was some commotion over near the dessert table. "What's going on over there?" Lola said.

"Probably a run on the pecan Danish," I said.

Lola turned away again and did a double take. "Oh my. No. It couldn't be. . . ."

"Lola?" I watched her, zombie-like, approach a cluster of ELT folks, insert herself into the center of the group, and fall into the arms of a man I'd seen before, in the *Etonville Standard* photo with Jerome and Walter.

"Who's that," the chief asked, suddenly alert.

"His name is Elliot Schenk. He was a member of the Etonville Little Theatre until he just up and disappeared two years ago. According to Lola, he and Jerome were best friends and had been in touch recently." Lola leaned comfortably into the arm he put around her shoulders.

He must have been about sixty, tall, with perfect white teeth, streaks of gray at the temples of his black hair, and prominent cheekbones. Elliot was a more dapper, less sunburned version of George Hamilton. The newspaper photo didn't begin to do him justice. "Now that is a handsome man," I said, probably a little more enthusiastically than I'd intended.

"I wonder how he heard about the funeral?" the chief said, ignoring my comment.

"Good question. Maybe you should—"

"—have a talk with him. I was thinking the same thing," he said wryly.

"Good idea."

"You're in the theater a lot?" he asked.

"I will be more than usual in the next few weeks, helping out."

"Do me a favor, okay?"

My heart did a loop-de-loop. He'd actually asked me to do him a favor?

"Keep an eye out over there."

"For what?"

He shrugged. "Anything that strikes you as suspicious. Anything out of the ordinary."

I'd been around the ELT long enough to know that much of what happened over there was out of the ordinary. "You think someone knows something?"

"Maybe. Maybe not."

"Will do."

Lola waved me over, and Chief Thompson followed.

"Dodie, I'd like to introduce you to Elliot." Beaming, Lola snaked her arm through his. "Dodie and Jerome were good friends."

"We shared reading habits," I said.

Elliot flashed a blinding smile. "It's so nice to meet you. I wish it were under other circumstances." He took my hand and shook it warmly.

"And this is our new police chief, Bill Thompson," Lola said.

Chief Thompson grasped Elliot's hand firmly. "Hello. Are you in town for long?"

Elliot gazed at Lola. "I'm not sure."

"Well, if you are, I'd appreciate five minutes of your time." He handed Elliot his card. "We're interviewing anyone who knew Mr. Angleton for the investigation."

Elliot nodded politely. "I understand. I'll give you a call."

"Thanks."

Elliot rejoined some theater folks, the chief said good-bye, and Lola had a final word with Walter.

"This way," I said to Lola when we reached the foyer, pointing to a side exit that would open directly onto the parking lot. "You didn't tell me that you and Elliot were . . . ?"

"Just friends," she said, her face flushed.

"I'd say pretty good friends."

Lola swatted me teasingly on the arm. "We went out a few times."

"What did Walter have to say about it?"

"Walter wasn't on my radar then," Lola said pointedly.

"Did Elliot tell you why he left town?"

"Something about a business opportunity. What's important is that he came back. For Jerome."

"No wife?"

"Divorced. Like Walter." She sighed. "Maybe it's my destiny."

We crossed the vestibule and pulled open the side exit door.

I almost bumped into someone who stood on the outside, a massive and thick-necked man with powerful shoulders.

I caught my breath. "Sorry. I didn't see you."

He brushed past us without a word.

The Windjammer was packed for lunch. Many folks simply trotted over to the restaurant from Jerome's funeral. Henry's homemade tomato basil soup sold out. I had one eye on the few remaining customers and one eye on my watch. Henry was busy in the kitchen experimenting with a parmesan cream sauce for the broccoli on the dinner menu, and it was nearing my three o'clock break. I had already decided how I was going to spend the next hour or so.

"Benny, I'll be back soon." I searched my purse for my car keys.

He looked up from behind the bar, where he was ensconced cleaning the fountain taps, and eyed me thoughtfully. "You're doing a lot of running around these days," he said. "You're not applying for other jobs, are you?" There was a hint of panic in his voice.

I laughed. "And leave you and Henry? Nah. It's like a marriage here. More trouble to get out of than to get into."

Benny nodded. "I know what you mean."

There had to be a way to find out whom Jerome was seeing, in whom he had invested a decent chunk of money. He was retired and, I assumed, living on a fixed income so where had he gotten the funds for a diamond ring? If I could speak with the person who'd sold him the ring, maybe he or she would remember something he'd said or done that would give me a clue. I intended to turn the ring over to Chief Thompson, but first I needed to satisfy my curiosity about its purchase.

The inside cover of the ring box was gold-stamped with *Sadlers Fine Jewelry*, which was located in Creston. Last year, I bought my mother birthstone earrings there, and she loved them. Creston was four miles away but seemed like a different universe. Population twenty thousand, it lacked the charm of Etonville but had all of the features that made it a necessity from time to time: a big-box store, doctors who specialized in various body parts, and fast food places.

I stepped on the gas pedal of my Metro and eased out onto State Route 53. On the seat next to me was the *Etonville Standard* with Jerome's picture on the front page. I hadn't gone a mile when large beads of rain, like teardrops, splashed down on my windshield. The beautiful morning had turned into a damp and depressing afternoon. I flipped on the wipers, and the monotonous *flap-flap* of their rhythm was soothing.

On the periphery of Creston, I slowed to twenty-five and turned onto the main drag. I dashed from my parking space to the sidewalk and shop awning to shop awning to keep dry. As I reached the entrance to Sadlers, a flash of lightning lit up the sky, followed by a crack of thunder. I scooted inside and brushed moisture off my jacket.

A clerk, thirtyish and very neat, wearing a dress shirt, creased jeans, and a rust-colored sweater tied around his shoulders, was busy with a customer, so I sauntered around sizing up earrings and necklaces and matching bracelets. Gold was going for nearly a thousand dollars an ounce these days, so trinkets were on the expensive side. I computed the cost of a diamond ring.

"Can I help you?" The clerk hovered at my elbow.

"I hope so. May I speak with the manager?"

"I'm the manager," he said.

I pulled the newspaper from my bag and produced the front page. "I'm trying to get some information about this man."

He examined the photo, then scanned the headlines. "I heard about this. Terrible," he said, genuinely concerned.

"Do you recognize him? He might have made a purchase here recently."

The manager took off his glasses and stared at the picture. "Yes. I've seen this man," he said cautiously.

"Jerome? You recognize Jerome?" I could feel an adrenaline rush. Never mind that that meant almost nothing, only that Jerome had bought the ring here.

He studied my outfit. "Are you from the police?"

I hesitated. "No. I'm not. But Jerome was a good friend and I just want to help find out what happened to him."

The manager studied me for a moment, then nodded. "I didn't identify him at first. But now I remember." He put his glasses back on. "It was maybe . . . a month or so ago."

"You're sure it was him?"

"Yes. It was him. I remember because he mentioned the theater and some play it was getting ready to do."

Must have been *Romeo and Juliet*. "Do you remember anything else about him? Anything he said or did that seemed strange? Or interesting?"

"He said his purchase was for someone special. He was very happy. Smiling a lot."

Oh, poor Jerome. "Did he mention a name?"

The manager shook his head. "No."

He must have realized there was no sale here because he moved toward a display case in the rear of the store.

"Do you have a receipt? Could you tell me what he paid for the ring? Some way I could confirm the date?" I thought I was skating on thin ice, but there was no harm in pushing the envelope a bit.

The manager stopped. "Customer purchases are confidential." He lowered his voice. "Anyway, he might have bought a ring here from another employee. But the day I met him, he purchased a gold bracelet. Fourteen karats."

Chapter 10

There was definitely someone in the picture and Jerome was wooing her with jewelry. Expensive jewelry, from the look of things. I wondered where he'd gotten the money and if Chief Thompson had sorted through Jerome's bank accounts and credit card statements yet.

I called Carol on my way back to Etonville. I offered to pick up Pauli at Snippets and bring him to the Windjammer and set him up in a back booth to work on the website, which reminded me I had to confirm a price with Pauli. But first I had one more stop to make.

As I described my visit to Jerome's home, Chief Thompson's expression conveyed surprise and suspicion. He rolled up the sleeves of his pale blue shirt and loosened the matching tie. Guess he'd come straight to the station from the funeral.

"It's not really a crime scene, right? There was no yellow tape and the landlady's father was very accommodating."

He ran his hand through his hair for the third time in fifteen minutes. "What did you find? I assume you found something or I wouldn't be hearing this."

I dug my hand into my purse and withdrew the velvet ring box.

"What the—?" He looked up at me, then down to my palm and tentatively reached out.

"Open it."

The little black ring case looked miniscule in the chief's muscular hand. He slipped a thumbnail in the opening, pushed gently, and let out a sound that wasn't quite an actual word.

"It's beautiful, isn't it?"

He snapped the box shut. "Where did you say you found this?"

"In the closet. In a suit jacket pocket." I waited for him to react. "I assume officers searched the room, but I guess they just missed—"

Bill laid the ring box on his desk. "It should have been Suki, but we were up to our eyeballs in paperwork so I sent—"

"Ralph."

"Yeah. He said there was nothing out of the ordinary, just clothes and bathroom toiletries." Bill gave me a cool appraisal. "Pretty clever of you, doing police detection. Got anything else planned?"

I blushed. This was the moment to tell him about the visit to Sadlers Jewelry store, but instinct made me stop. TMI for one visit?

"Not really."

"Okay. I'll have Officer Shung stop by Sadlers later," he said.

"Oh! Well . . ."

He eyed me suspiciously. "Something wrong?"

"No . . . uh . . . I . . . was just wondering if you were able to pinpoint the time of death?" I asked quickly.

"Why?" he asked warily.

"I was gone by eleven-thirty. Only Lola and Walter were still there. I just wondered . . ."

"Between about three a.m. and five a.m.," he said. "Anyway, sometime before six a.m."

"When the garbage men discovered his body," I said. "Chief Thompson, did the police take a computer out of Jerome's room?"

"No. Why?" he asked again.

"No reason."

"Sorry to cut this short, but I have an appointment." Chief Thompson rose and picked up his jacket. "You've been a big help."

"Thanks, Chief."

"Bill," he said.

"Oh, okay. Then it's Dodie."

"You'll let me know if you have any other ideas?" he said.

"Sure."

His lip turned up at one corner in what was becoming a recognizable facial tic. He wanted to smile but controlled himself. "I admire your ingenuity."

I wondered if he'd still feel the same way once Suki Shung had visited Sadlers.

* * *

In my back booth, Pauli was creating a menu page for the website, choosing fonts and graphics and arranging the layout. I set him up with a plate of nachos and a large Coke. He ate and typed and grinned at me from time to time. I envied the simplicity of Pauli's life. Of course, being a teenager was no piece of cake either. I remember battling my parents about my clothes and boyfriends and staying out past my curfew.

"Do you have a logo?" Pauli asked.

I popped up from behind the bar, where I was unpacking a carton of cabernet. "A logo for the restaurant? Do we need one?"

"Yeah, like something for the home page. A picture of something."

"How about a picture of the front of the restaurant? Would that do?"

Pauli nodded. "That works."

He ambled out the door, crossed the street in front of the Windjammer, and proceeded to take shot after shot on his digital camera.

"We're going to have a Web presence," Benny said and smiled as he watched Pauli, standing, kneeling, and catching the restaurant from different angles as though he were a fashion photographer.

"It's about time. Hey, have you checked the schedule for the weekend?" I had rearranged a few evening hours to accommodate my dropping in at the ELT.

"Yep. Looks good. I can cover Friday night. Hey, what are you going to do over there?" he asked.

"Not sure. Organize things once rehearsals start. The place could use some shaping up. "

"Jerome's murder probably doesn't help."

"Benny, let me ask you something. Did Jerome ever strike you as a flashy guy? You know, money to burn?"

"Jerome? No way. He told me he lived on a modest pension and Social Security. One time, he was invited to take a trip to Europe with a group from the theater and he couldn't afford it. I kind of felt sorry for him. I liked him."

"Me too."

Pauli loped back in the door. "Got some good ones," he said and brushed the hair off his face. "Hey, you know what you need?"

I shook my head.

"An email address so people can make reservations online."

"Great idea. The last place I worked had that capability."

"Okay. I can do that."

"Will we need a password?"

"Yeah, but I can set something up."

Those little dancing hairs started to tingle. The mystery woman might have contacted Jerome through email and it's probable he had an account—Lola said the ELT often sent out messages to its membership. Though no computer was found in his room, the library was available and he was known to have visited there. If I could find his email address . . .

"Pauli, how hard would it be to check someone's email?" I asked on impulse.

"No problem," he said and closed his laptop.

"What if you had an email address but not the password?"

"Why don't you have the password?"

"Because it belongs to someone . . . else."

"Can't you, like, ask him. Or her?"

I paused. "I wish I could, but he isn't around."

"Oh." He gawked at me. "Like to hack it?"

"Well, you know, just to check on things . . ." I tried for my most professional voice.

He gazed at me as if seeing me in a different light. "I could probably do it."

"You can find someone's password?" My heart thumped.

"It's not that hard." He reopened his laptop.

I put a hand on the lid and slowly closed it. "Not now. I'll let you know."

"Okay."

The restaurant was calming down for the night so I knew I could slip away for a bit. I stepped outside onto the sidewalk. The air was brisk, but low-hanging clouds threatened rain. I turned to face the theater. The lone light in Walter's office flicked off and I hurried to the entrance just in time to see Penny exit the building.

"Working late?" I knew Penny was often the last one standing. Doing who knew what.

Her head bobbed. "Been handling a reporter from the *Etonville Standard*—they're doing a follow-up, you know." She cracked her gum knowingly.

"On Jerome's murder, you mean?"

"Duh," she said and rolled her eyes. "Walter's falling to pieces, what with the rehearsals starting soon and the murder investigation."

"It's a lot to handle."

"Whatever. Too bad about the money."

"What . . . money?" I asked carefully.

"The missing box-office cash." Penny buttoned her jacket. "Walter told me. But I'm not buying it."

"Why?"

"Jerome wasn't the type," Penny said.

"Jerome? Walter thinks Jerome took the money?"

"Anyway, Walter loses things."

"Even money?" I asked.

"Especially money. We've had box-office cash go missing before. Sometimes he even borrows a little bit," she said confidentially.

"Penny, I wonder if you could do me a favor?" I asked amiably. She looked suspicious.

"I know you're on your way out, but I was wondering if you could take one more minute? I'd like to borrow the sign-up sheets from auditions. Just overnight?"

"Sorry. Walter doesn't let paperwork leave his office. Under lock and key. Good night." She started off.

"I could look them over in his office," I said.

Penny put her hands on her hips and squinted at me. "Why?"

"Well, there were a few folks who auditioned that I need contact information on."

"Why?" she asked again, planting herself squarely between me and the theater.

My mind ran through a catalog of possibilities before coming to rest on a surefire Penny-motivator. "Chief Thompson asked me get the names and addresses of anyone who left the theater after ten p.m." Did that even make sense? "Maybe you could help me? In case I don't remember who auditioned early and who stayed later."

The mention of the chief was like a shot of adrenaline for Penny. Before I could say anything more, she had the door open, lights on, and audition forms in a stack on Walter's desk.

We'd been at it for twenty minutes. I suggested she start with the women and I do the men; each audition form had the actor's name, address, phone numbers, and email.

"Some sheets aren't complete. They don't have cell numbers and email addresses," I said.

"Yeah. Some of the older actors are still living in the twentieth century," Penny chuckled. "Like Jerome. He just got an email account a few months ago."

I wrote down names and information and, when her back was turned, I stuffed Jerome's sheet in the pocket of my jacket.

Penny held up a form. "NOYL," she read from the paper. "Abby."

"Huh?"

"Not On Your Life."

I was so fixated on finding Jerome's sheet that I'd neglected to read Walter's handwritten comments on each actor's audition. I had noticed that he coded them with a plus, minus, star, double star, or a series of letters such as NOYL or HWFO—Hell Will Freeze Over, Penny had explained.

"I feel sorry for some of them." I was ready to call it a night.

"Hey, O'Dell, that's show biz." Penny grinned.

"I think we have all the names we need. Thanks for your help." I stretched and checked my watch. "I need to get back to the Windjammer."

"Go ahead. I'm almost done." She gathered my sheets and tucked them into her pile.

"Thanks, Penny."

"I'll run these names down to the station tomorrow. The chief can check—"

"I can deliver them," I said quickly.

Penny held the papers close to her chest. She was not going to surrender her authority easily.

"Okay. Bye," I said.

I'd created a potential problem. Bill would wonder why Penny was delivering a list of auditionees; of course, he might chalk it up to her general enthusiasm regarding Jerome's murder. I doubted she would mention me; she was saving all of the glory for herself. Meanwhile, I had exactly what I needed. Jerome's email address.

Chapter 11

I hadn't quite figured out exactly what all I would be doing during rehearsals for *Romeo and Juliet*, but I knew I could help Walter and Lola get the show up, and keep an eye out for anything out of the ordinary. And maybe I could talk with someone who might have been familiar with Jerome's love life.

Lola and I entered the theater and bumped into Penny.

"We were wondering where you were." She tapped her pencil against the clipboard.

Lola shrugged and set off to find Walter. I followed Penny down the right aisle. "I told Walter I didn't need an assistant, but I guess he figured you might stay on book and run lines with actors in a week or two." She adjusted her glasses.

"Sure. Anything I can do to help," I said.

The theater was full of actors. Half stood up, laughing and talking together; the other half, and I was willing to bet they were the scared-to-death ones, had their noses buried in scripts. I sat in the house, halfway back, on the aisle. Walter appeared from backstage, accompanied by Lola, who was arm in arm with Elliot Schenk. The theater grew quiet.

"He's the new Prince," Penny croaked in my ear.

There was a slight rumbling among the cast members, a few astonished expressions, and one clearly disgruntled elderly fellow.

"Guess everyone's not thrilled to have him in the cast."

Penny scampered through a row of seats to Walter's side.

"Where is Tybalt?" Walter was trying to get the reading started.

"In the john. Want me to get him?"

"No, Penny, I'm sure he can find his way back here."

Walter called all of the actors onstage and proceeded to have the cast introduce themselves so we could "all get to know one another. After all, the theater is like a family." Walter had clearly thought this whole thing out. Seats were arranged according to which characters were related, or had scenes together. The guy playing Romeo, six feet of muscle with slick black hair that definitely suited Bernardo in *West Side Story*, and Walter sat on either side of the petite blonde playing Juliet.

"Lola, would you scoot around here so Tybalt can sit next to you? After all, the two of you are related." He winked and Lola smiled, first at him and then at Elliot, who sat himself on Lola's other side. I wasn't sure the Prince cozying up to Lady Capulet was part of Walter's game plan, but he let it go.

Tybalt, with a cute smile, two big dimples, and a head of curly hair, returned from the men's room. He looked more like a Romeo to me.

"He was almost cast as Romeo," Penny whispered to me. "But he didn't have the emotional depth."

"Oh."

She tossed her head. "Anyway, he's wacko just like Tybalt."

"That sweet-looking guy?"

Penny rolled her eyes.

The rest of the cast—Nurse, Friar, Mercutio, Benvolio, Gentlemen, and Ladies-in-Waiting, including Edna, who waved jauntily, and Abby—was spread out around the ends of the table. I caught Abby's eye to say hello, but her dissatisfaction with the casting was evident. She looked pasty white with a frosty pout. Finally, Walter introduced Penny and she smirked smugly. I was left for last and referred to as "Penny's assistant." Elliot inclined his head graciously, as if to say, *Welcome*. Penny and I sat behind Walter; it was a great vantage point from which to scan the group.

Lola murmured something to Elliot while Romeo stared at her chest and flirted with Juliet.

"Isn't he cute?" Penny whispered in my ear.

"Well, in an oily sort of way."

Walter was clearing his throat, a sign that he was ready to begin. The cast started to read. Most of the major characters were new to Shakespeare and iambic pentameter. Occasionally, Walter would stop someone and have them reread a line while he pounded the table with his fist: short, long, short, long, short, long, short, long, until the actor's speech sounded like a ping-pong ball. Only Lola and Elliot were left alone to find their own ways through the text. They had such a natural sense of the language, meaning and meter melded together. Lola and Elliot were Lamborghinis in a cast full of Fords.

By the end of Act III, Walter had browbeaten the cast into iambic submission. Tybalt had been up and down five times, Romeo and Mercutio were texting back and forth like school kids, and the Ladies-in-Waiting appeared to be tired of waiting. We took a break and I followed Lola to the restroom.

"You are really good at this," I said to her back as she disappeared inside a stall.

"Thanks. I took a Shakespeare class in New York a couple of years ago."

She shut the door. I could hear a zipper, rustling of clothing, the creak of the seat.

"Interesting that Elliot is in the cast." I checked my face in the mirror: circles under my eyes. I needed sleep. I retouched my lipstick and ran a brush through my hair.

"It was a no-brainer. Walter needed an older man who could handle the text."

"So he's going to be in town for a while?"

"He's renting an apartment in Creston temporarily," she said.

"Is Walter happy about that? I mean, you know, you and Elliot . . ."

"Walter didn't have a choice. Elliot was a leading man here for years."

"Yeah?"

"Uh-huh. He played opposite me in Noel Coward's *Private Lives* and we were together in *Death of a Salesman* and some Tennessee Williams plays."

The outer door opened. "Break's over." Penny pushed her glasses up her face and banged the clipboard against her leg. "Lola, Walter wants to know if you'll lead the trust exercise after the reading."

"Sure." Lola emerged from the stall and washed her hands.

"What trust exercise?"

"Just something that Walter likes to use to prove 'we're all one happy theater family.'" She walked through the door and I followed.

Penny stopped me. "Walter wants you to work on the rehearsal schedule."

"Okay. I can do that."

"So can I," she said with the kind of fake smile that usually suppressed a scream. Her nose was out of joint.

"Penny, can I ask you a question?" I said.

She looked suspicious. "What?"

"Did you ever see Jerome with a woman around the theater, like a . . . girlfriend? Maybe an ELT member?"

"Jerome and a girlfriend?" Penny grunted. "No way."

"Why do you say that?" I asked, curious.

"First of all, Jerome was too busy with box-office stuff to be 'dating' an ELT member. And second, he wasn't the type. Jerome was more of a loner. Didn't hang out with female members of the ELT." She clapped her clipboard against her leg. "Let's go, O'Dell. Break's over."

Penny took off.

So Jerome's mystery woman was no part of the theater.

By ten-thirty, we had slogged our way through the play and listened to Walter lecture on Elizabethan manners, and I had sketched out a broad, tentative rehearsal schedule based on the character breakdown for each scene.

"It is time for us to take our leave"—Walter had begun to speak Shakespearean—"but before we depart, we must join hands and demonstrate our trust in the circle of light."

People seemed to know what he was talking about. They abruptly rose from their seats, moved to a clear space on the stage, and formed a circle. Lola motioned for me to join them and she stepped inside.

"Lady Capulet will demonstrate her trust in us." Walter smiled warmly at Lola.

The circle tightened and the cast raised their hands, palms facing inward. As if in slow motion, Lola fell backward as Walter and Tybalt stopped her fall with their outstretched arms. They nudged her forward and she pivoted slightly into the arms of the Nurse and Benvolio, then Romeo and a Lady. She bounced lightly from person to person, trusting that the cast would not let her down—literally.

After a few minutes, she came to rest in Walter's arms. "That was wonderful, Lola! Who's next?"

I was the last to slip into the center of the group. Closing my eyes, I adjusted my balance and before I knew it I was falling through the air into the arms of Mercutio and Tybalt. They pushed me forward and I rebounded into the Nurse and Lola. I moved quicker and quicker. Someone behind me giggled, but I ignored it. I was on a giant spring—boing, boing, boing. And then, out of the corner of my eye, I saw Romeo reach behind the Nurse and grab for a Lady. At that exact second, Abby and another Lady propelled me in Romeo's direction. He extended his arms too late. I slipped through his hands. He tried to break my fall by reaching for my waist. My weight must have been too much for him, because he went down and I went down on top of him, wrenching my upper body in one direction and my lower half in another.

There was stunned silence for a second. Then everyone seemed to go into action at once and half a dozen pairs of hands grasped at me. Tybalt and Walter pulled me to my feet.

"Do you need 911?" Edna asked efficiently. She'd switched from Lady-in-Waiting to emergency dispatcher in a heartbeat.

"This has never happened in the circle of light," said Walter frantically.

"Are you hurt?" asked Elliot. "Let me drive you home."

"I'm okay," I said and stretched my back tentatively.

"You took a pretty hard fall." He smiled sympathetically. "Let me at least follow you home." He flashed his startlingly white teeth, and I forgot he was at least twenty years older than me.

"Well . . . thanks."

I handed the rehearsal schedule to Walter, who looked stunned to see the timeline for the next week, and told him he should approve it and get Penny to post it online. I said good-bye to Lola and Elliot helped me make my way out of the theater.

He was unfailingly solicitous as he walked me to my Metro, opened the door, and waited until I was settled in.

"Thanks, Elliot. You really don't need to hang around. I'm only a couple of miles away." I pushed my lower back into the seat cushion.

He grinned. "Etonville's a small town, I know."

"I was surprised to see you at the reading," I said.

"I moved back to the area recently, and when I heard about Jerome . . . it just felt right to be back at the ELT." He paused. "I couldn't refuse Walter's request."

"You and Jerome were good friends?" I asked.

"We were theater friends. Didn't really see each other much outside the ELT."

"Anyway, it's great of you to take a role and help out," I said.

"My pleasure to do what I can. Shakespeare at the Etonville Little Theatre . . . Walter's taking on quite the challenge." He arched an eyebrow.

"You can say that again."

We both laughed companionably as if *we* were also theater friends. I cranked the engine and he patted the door and said good-bye.

I turned right onto Fairfield and left on Ames, Elliot's Honda Accord keeping pace right on my bumper. As I pulled in front of my house, I waved him off and he honked and drove on. I watched his taillights grow small and disappear into the distance just as a pair of headlights came toward me moving down Ames in the opposite direction. I turned into my driveway and flicked off the lights as the automobile cruised past my place. I glanced in the rearview mirror. I could swear it was the dark SUV I'd seen on Jerome's street. Those little hairs danced on my neck.

I awoke early, bothered by bizarre dreams of Jerome and me on a trip to the Bahamas. What was that about? I tossed and turned for an hour and had just drifted off when the alarm clock rang. I opened one eye: 7 AM. I'd forgotten to turn it off last night. My one bona fide day off this week—I'd switched days with Benny—and I was up at 7 AM. In frustration, I gritted my teeth and threw back the covers. Last night's fall into the circle of light had left some lingering soreness in my lower back. Over coffee and cereal, I thought about my part in the murder investigation. I'd shared my visit to Jerome's and the ring box with Bill, but not my visit to Sadlers. Once he discovered I'd beat Officer Shung to the jewelry store, he might not be so friendly. Should I even mention the SUV driving down my street last night? Maybe I owed him a visit. . . .

Since I was up so early, I treated myself to a relaxing bubble bath to ease my aching back. I lowered myself into the tub and closed my eyes. I pretended that I was in one of those sybaritic anti-stress chambers. I could have stayed submerged all morning. But I wanted to stop by the police station. I washed and conditioned my hair, dried off in the last of my clean Turkish towels, a gift from my mother when I set up housekeeping years ago, and studied my wardrobe. I settled on black jeans and a crisp cotton blouse. I brushed my hair, until it lay softly skimming the tops of my shoulders, applied a touch of mascara and a swipe of lipstick, and checked my image in the mirror. *Not bad*, I thought. I collected my leather jacket and headed downtown.

I wound my way from Ames to Fairfield and down Main to Amber. I drove past the station and parked on a side street. One last look in the rearview mirror and I was out of my Metro and bounding down the sidewalk.

I entered the Municipal Building and turned into the right hallway. I stopped at Edna's dispatch window.

"Hey, Edna."

She spoke into a headset. "Mrs. Parker, you just stay put. Officer Ostrowski is en route to the scene." Her radio crackled. "Ralph. That's right." There was a pause. "I know you want the chief, but he's out on a call so Ralph will get Missy out of the sewer pipe." She clicked off. "That woman calls 911 three times a week. It's either her dog or her cat or her husband. One of them is somewhere they shouldn't be."

"So the chief's not in?" I asked.

"Nope. It's a 594 over on Route 53. He had to take the call."

"594?"

"Malicious mischief. Some kids skipped school and were hitchhiking on the highway."

"Doesn't sound too malicious." I remembered some of my escapades in high school.

"Well, there's no code for truancy and the chief figured if they weren't up to mischief now, they would be soon."

"Oh. Okay." I considered my next move. "When do you expect the chief back?"

"Is it urgent? Officer Shung is inside." She jerked her thumb in the direction of the station's outer office.

"No, no," I said hurriedly. "It can wait."

The radio crackled again. "Ralph? Are you en route? You'd better get a move-on before Mrs. Parker calls in again. 10-4."

All dressed up and no place to go, I thought. The day was too beautiful to spend at home so I opted for a corner booth in Coffee Heaven.

"Here you go, hon." Jocelyn, my waitress, plopped my caramel macchiato and a warm cinnamon bun on the table in front of me. I was drowning my disappointment in sugar.

"Don't know if you read this rag, but just in case." She handed me the *Etonville Standard* and stepped to the booth behind me.

I sipped coffee between bites of the warm roll and opened the newspaper. I scanned the front page for anything new on Jerome's murder. Below the fold was a short piece that recapped the investigation and summarized the funeral—complete with references to the pallbearers and Walter's Shakespearean antics. Essentially, there was nothing new.

I flipped to page two. The Etonville High baseball team was going to the state championships, and pothole filling was scheduled for the north end of town.

"Were you looking for me?"

I glanced up, right into Bill's dazzling eyes. Hands on his hips, a pair of sunglasses perched atop his blond hair.

"The regular, Chief?" Jocelyn called out.

"Thanks. May I?" he asked. When I nodded, he slipped onto the bench across from me.

"You were out on a call. A 594 according to Edna," I said.

He accepted the steaming mug of black coffee and shook his head. "Edna likes her codes. It was a couple of kids fooling around on the highway." He watched me over the rim of his cup. "Did you want something?"

I'd felt so confident this morning when I'd decided to come clean with Bill about my trip to Sadlers and let him know about the SUV, but now I was a little gun-shy. How did he really feel about my participation in the search for Jerome's killer?

"I had some information I wanted to share with you."

His eyebrows shot up as he took a gulp of his coffee. "About the jewelry store in Creston?"

Uh-oh. "Sadlers. Yes."

Bill downed the rest of his coffee and stood up abruptly. He dropped a ten on the table and put on his sunglasses. "Come on."

I had to hurry to keep up. On the street Bill leaned against his black-and-white police cruiser, while I stood opposite him.

"I can't talk in public about the investigation," he said and looked up and down the empty sidewalk.

"Of course."

"Suki went to Sadlers yesterday," he said.

"She did?" I tried to keep my voice as bland as possible.

"But you already know that the manager recognized Jerome. . . ." He frowned.

"From the *Etonville Standard*. Right. That picture of Jerome and Elliot and Walter."

"And that he bought other jewelry there," Bill said.

"A gold bracelet," I said.

"Yeah."

Bill shifted his weight from one foot to the other.

"That gold bracelet was not cheap. Jerome lived on a fixed income. Maybe he was coming into money? I wonder what he had in his bank account. Or what he put on credit cards—"

"Look, Dodie, I appreciate your enthusiasm, but I had to pull Suki off other work to send her to Creston only to find out that you'd already 'interviewed' the manager. Who thought we should all be talking to one another as well as with him."

I gulped and brushed my bangs out of my eyes.

"I can't have you snooping around playing detective while my office is coordinating an official investigation."

"Sorry," I said.

He scratched his head. "I shouldn't even be talking with you about . . . everything."

"Oh."

"But you found the ring—"

"And the mystery woman," I added.

"You do have insights," he admitted.

"Thanks."

He hesitated. "And we are doing a forensic check on his finances."

"Okay." I paused. "Maybe he fell in love," I said.

"What?"

"The engagement ring. Jerome met someone and it became serious. At least on his end. We don't know about her."

Bill drummed his fingers on the hood of his car. "From what you told me about him, it doesn't sound right, especially at his age."

"Relationships will do that to you," I said.

"Maybe."

What did that mean? Had I hit a nerve? I could feel heat moving up my neck and flowing into my hairline. "Little warm today." I unzipped my jacket.

That corner of his mouth inched upward. "Feels kind of cool to me."

His radio crackled. "Chief?"

Bill reached into the vehicle and hit a button. "Go ahead, Edna."

"We got a 10-26 on Pinter Drive behind the Dumpster at Lacey's Market."

He sighed. "Thanks."

"10-4."

"I suppose you need to get back to work; 10-26 and all."

"A 10-26 is an abandoned bicycle."

I started to laugh, then caught myself: I shouldn't make fun of police codes. "This is new for you? Police chief in a small town?" I asked.

"I was a deputy chief in Philadelphia before I came here. I have an urban mentality."

"I did an internship in Philadelphia during college."

"Yeah?" he said." What in?"

"Business management. I—"

The radio sputtered again.

"What is it, Edna?"

"Ralph wants to take an early lunch."

"Okay but tell him to check the . . . 10-26 on his way." Bill slid his eyes in my direction.

"10-4," she said cheerily.

He opened the door and had one leg inside his cruiser.

"Did his autopsy reveal anything?" I asked.

Bill studied me, then made a decision. "He died from the gunshot to his chest. Saturday night special. .38 caliber, cheap and easy to purchase. Back in the day, on a hot summer night in North Philly's Strawberry Mansion neighborhood, I could take half a dozen of them off kids hanging on a street corner."

"Not much help, I guess," I said.

He shook his head. "Various bruises on his torso."

"Well, good luck tracking down the owner of the bicycle."

"Yeah," he said drily. And as an afterthought: "Any more ideas—"

"I know. Keep you in the loop."

Chapter 12

Bill's squad car was already down the block when I realized I had forgotten to mention the SUV. That would need to wait until later. I didn't want to overstay my welcome as far as the murder investigation was concerned. And, besides, I had arranged for Pauli to come by my place later to explore Jerome's password and email account.

"It's really not that hard," Pauli said. He sat down at the computer and cracked his knuckles as if attempting a safecracking gig.

Choosing a password for email was like a Rorschach test. It revealed one's personality, likes, dislikes, etc. I'd read an article a few months ago that listed the twenty-five most common email passwords. It warned readers to be vigilant lest hackers take advantage. I glanced at Pauli sitting at my kitchen table concentrating on the keyboard of his laptop. He didn't need me to run down the list for him—password, Seinfeld, qwerty, 123456. I was dealing with an experienced computer whiz.

He started with the obvious: Jerome's name, birth date, address, age—all compliments of his obituary in the *Etonville Standard*. Pauli's fingers flew across the keyboard. Nothing.

Pauli raised his head. "Did he have a job?"

"He was a retired English teacher. Etonville High, but before you enrolled. He spent a lot of time at the Etonville Little Theatre."

"Favorite colors?"

I frowned. "I don't know."

"Family?"

"Just his sister-in-law, but I don't know her name."

Pauli sat back in his chair and took a snack break; then he attacked the keyboard again, Toaster Strudel in mouth, Coke in hand.

"How about friends?" he asked.

There was Elliot, me, Lola, and who knows who else at the ELT or in town. Maybe old students? Maybe the mystery woman? Pauli tried variations on Elliot's name and we ran through a few more categories of connections to the theater. It had been an hour and a half, and I was afraid Pauli was stumped. "Maybe we should—"

He stuck one finger in the air. "Like what did he do for fun?"

I suggested his work with the Etonville Little Theatre and reading mysteries. I gave Pauli a list of authors and titles that Jerome and I had shared, but nothing popped there either.

"You know, like in the future, people won't have passwords," Pauli said.

"Why not? How will we protect our email?"

"Biometric security."

I stared blankly at him and Pauli nodded, his eyes gleamed. "Sensors that read your fingerprints. Facial recognition software," he said excitedly.

The kid was really into this computer stuff. "I guess you want to follow in your dad's footsteps?" I asked.

He frowned. "Sort of." There was a pregnant pause.

"Oh? You have something specific in mind?"

"Digital forensics," he said quickly.

"Wow, that sounds cool. What would you do?"

Pauli launched into his topic and attempted to school me on the differences among computer forensics, mobile device forensics, and network forensics. He lost me ten minutes into his lecture, but I was impressed by his apparent depth of knowledge and mature evaluation of potential career options. Did Carol have any idea about all of this?

My cell phone binged. It was Lola texting, wondering when I would be at rehearsal. According to the schedule I'd prepared, the cast would be focusing on Act I tonight. Meanwhile, I would be focusing on the cast. Who among them might have some information on Jerome's mystery woman?

"Dodie?"

I looked up at Enrico, who was smiling apologetically. "Yeah?"

"I think there is a problem with the delivery."

I followed the sous chef through the swinging doors.

Henry stood in the center of the kitchen surrounded by crates of broccoli, carrots, squash, and cucumbers. But no turnips. He was adamant about having roasted turnips on the menu tonight. I promised to make a call and dashed away. I heard him turn his attention to lecturing Enrico on Spanish versus Hungarian paprika for the roast chicken. Enrico, patient and attentive, nodded frequently.

This was the second foul-up of the food delivery in a week. The foodservice distributor—Cheney Brothers—was becoming a pain, what with late deliveries and incomplete orders. I wanted to change companies, but Henry hated change and simply wanted me to straighten them out. I phoned and gave them a mild tongue-lashing for mucking up the order again. I was assured that the turnips would be here first thing tomorrow morning. I broke the news to Henry and listened to him carry on about how he "couldn't change the menu on short notice" even though he'd done it any number of times.

It was three o'clock. "Benny, I'm taking my break."

"No problem."

Benny was happier of late. Extra evening hours a couple of nights a week meant a little more cash in his pocket and fewer hours driving the UPS truck.

When I called Bill and told him about the SUV that had cruised down my street two nights ago, he asked me to stop by so that we could talk. The day was overcast and cloudy, and a fine, intermittent mist sprinkled anyone who wandered the streets of Etonville. I could have jumped in my car and been at the Municipal Building in three minutes. But a walk in the light rain fit my contemplative mood and would take all of fifteen minutes. The sidewalk in front of the Wind-jammer was virtually empty; folks were staying in and avoiding the weather. I pulled the hood of my jacket over my head and tramped down Main and onto Amber. I mulled over my impending meeting with Bill. I was so preoccupied I walked right past my destination.

"Power walking in the rain?" a voice yelled to me.

It was Bill, negotiating his black-and-white into its assigned space. I stopped in my tracks and raised a hand in greeting. Even on a rainy day, his hair seemed to glint as if in golden sunshine. I jogged back to the Municipal Building. "Just deep in thought."

He slammed his door shut and grabbed my arm just as the skies opened. We ran to the cover of the overhang above the door. "Thanks for coming by."

I followed him past Edna's dispatch station. "Hey, Dodie. I meant to tell you. Great first rehearsal." She bobbed her head enthusiastically.

"I didn't really do—"

"You're in the play?" Bill's right lip curved slightly.

"Well, getting that rehearsal schedule on email? That was something." Edna announced.

I turned to Bill. "I'm helping Penny."

His left lip joined the right one. "I see."

"Listen, I've been in ELT shows for twenty years, and this is the first time I got a whole week's rehearsal schedule ahead of time. Well done, Dodie," Edna said.

"I'm impressed," Bill said, clearly amused.

"How's your back?" Edna asked.

"What's wrong with your back?" he asked.

"We were doing the circle of light at the first rehearsal—" Edna started in.

"The what?" Bill asked.

"—and somebody, *I won't say who*, slipped up and dropped Dodie." Edna was *not* amused.

"Are you okay?" he asked seriously.

I'd experienced a twinge or two today, but I'd just stretched and shaken it off. "I'm fine." The bubble bath helped.

Suki had silently left her inner office and joined us in the hallway. "I know a great doctor if you think you need to see someone," she said solemnly.

"Suki does Chinese medicine," clarified Edna.

"Oh, okay. Well . . . if it still hurts next week . . ."

Suki nodded, our interaction complete, and handed Bill a sheaf of papers.

His eyes ran down the top sheet and he nodded. "Thanks."

"See you at rehearsal, Dodie," Edna said.

I let my attention wander around Bill's office as he took a call. I mimed my offer to leave, but he shook his head. "Ralph, you need to follow up with Mrs. Parker. . . . Yeah, I know she's a little silly, but she's a citizen of the town and deserves our—well, Bull's no longer in this office. Yeah. Okay." He slammed the receiver into the cradle. "10-4 to you too," he grumbled.

I noticed a ball cap, with the Buffalo Bills insignia, peeking out of a gym bag, and I remembered the chatter about his NFL career.

"Two years," he said.

"You played for Buffalo? I'm impressed."

"Don't be. Before that, two years for the Browns and a year with Oakland."

"You moved around," I said.

"The last season, I was on the practice squad," he said.

"Why did you give it up?"

"Well, let's see. There was a broken tibia, a dislocated shoulder, and a rotator cuff that wouldn't even speak to me by the end."

"I heard you were a running back?"

"Yep. Undrafted free agent out of Temple. So I know from sore backs," he said sympathetically and tapped his pen on the sheet Suki had handed him. He shoved the cluster of papers into a folder. "So you saw the SUV again."

"Right. I was sitting in my driveway."

"What time was this?"

"About eleven. Elliot had just said good-bye and took off down the street and coming in the opposite direction was the SUV."

"That would be Elliot Schenk?"

"Yes."

"He seemed torn up about Jerome," he said.

"Yeah. I guess they were better friends than Jerome let on."

"As for the SUV . . . without a license plate number . . ."

"Sorry."

Bill shook his head. "There are a lot of unanswered questions in this investigation."

This would have been an opportune time to mention the date written on the inside of the ledger Lola had found. "Did you ever speak with Walter about the missing money?" I asked casually.

He blinked. "You mean the theater money?"

"Uh-huh."

"Walter claims he knew nothing about it. He was hinting that Jerome might have made an accounting error."

Nothing like besmirching the reputation of a dead man, I thought.

Bill cocked his head and leaned back in his desk chair. "Anyway I wanted to talk with you about the night of auditions."

"I think I told you everything I could remember."

"You said Jerome seemed excited."

"Right. Like he knew something great was about to happen." Like getting engaged to the mystery woman?

"But he didn't give you any hint about what it might be?" Bill asked.

"No. I just had the feeling he wanted to talk to me, and then we got interrupted."

"Okay. Let's say you are correct. What *might* he have needed to talk about? Family issues? Theater problems?"

"Sorry. I don't have any idea. Unless it had something to do with the engagement ring." We sat in silence for a minute. "It would help to know where he went after the auditions or why he was killed at the theater."

"I'm going to tell you something that I expect you to keep quiet," he warned. "Of course, in this town, between the gossip and the *Etonville Standard*, I'm surprised it hasn't leaked yet."

"Okay." I waited.

"Jerome wasn't killed at the theater," Bill said quietly. "Forensics said he was killed elsewhere and deposited on the loading dock."

"How do they know?" I asked.

"No significant amount of blood at the crime scene. When the heart stops, no more blood is pumped," he said matter-of-factly, as if investigating a murder were an everyday occurrence for him.

"But his car was still parked at the theater the morning he was found."

"We had it scrubbed. Nothing in it to help us." Bill ran a hand over his bristly hair. "There's just not a lot to go on. Could have been a robbery gone wrong. His wallet and cell phone were missing."

"Like someone assaulted him on the street? That doesn't sound like Etonville."

"Even small towns like Etonville can be susceptible to crime. And when someone is intoxicated . . ."

"Intoxicated? I never saw Jerome drink more than one at a time," I said.

"His blood alcohol content was .08. Just at the legal limit."

"No way. I mean, I did smell alcohol on him when he arrived at the theater, but not so much that he couldn't audition."

Bill snapped his head up. "He was drinking before he got to the theater? You didn't mention that."

"I didn't? I guess it slipped my mind," I said.

"Anything else 'slip your mind'?" Bill asked.

After I said my good-byes, I paused outside his door to read a text from Lola, who was checking in. Suki brushed past, glancing quickly at me, the faintest hint of irritation on her normally Zen-like face. Could it be about her goose chase to Sadlers? She knocked and entered Bill's office, leaving the door slightly ajar. I overheard her say "the substance on his trousers . . . a resin of some kind . . . synthetic latex . . . still working on it."

There was no point in arguing with Bill over Jerome's blood alcohol level. Facts were facts, but I still had a tough time with it. Just didn't seem like Jerome. The courteous soul who loved to read thrillers, left the Windjammer after one double Scotch, and patiently waited on lines of ticket holders at the theater, even when they badgered him for better seats. The random robbery-and-murder theory didn't sit well with me. It was possible he'd met the murderer after auditions and had a few more drinks and then . . . what?

The rain had stopped by the time I stepped outside the Municipal Building. I walked briskly back to the Windjammer to help set up for the dinner rush. Gillian was on the phone taking reservations, Benny was behind the bar, and Carmen was fast at work helping Enrico make chicken stock and prepping the rosemary potatoes.

I collapsed into my booth with the cast list and the rehearsal schedule, as well as the restaurant's wine order and staff calendar. As long as I didn't get the Windjammer staff measured for costumes or the *R and J* cast bussing tables, I'd be fine. It was like juggling two jobs.

My ring tone chimed, and I checked the number and clicked AN-SWER. "Hi, Carol."

"Uh, no, it's me. Pauli." Then he added, as if he needed to explain using Carol's cell, "I'm at Snippets."

"Hi, Pauli. What's up?"

"Did you want to work tonight?" he asked carefully.

"On the website? I think we can wait 'til the weekend. I had a few more ideas about the pictures on the home page, and maybe we can add a bit of history. You know, like the Windjammer was owned by a sea captain who—"

"I meant that other thing."

"Oh. Right." I looked around the dining room. Things would begin to heat up in the restaurant in another hour, and I needed to stay through dinner. But afterward I planned to head to the theater to speak with Lola and meet with Chrystal about costume fittings. I had no idea what Pauli's rules of engagement were on school nights. "Could you stop by the theater instead of the restaurant later? I'll be over there working. Around eight-thirty? Check with your mom."

"Okay."

I could hear muffled voices in the background.

"Hi, Dodie. I can bring Pauli to the theater later," Carol said.

"You're sure it's okay? I'm not interfering with his homework or something?"

"Not a problem. He does homework off and on all day, as far as I can figure. Most of the time his face is buried in the computer."

"He's really talented," I said.

"Thanks. Anyway, I need to speak with Chrystal about hair issues so I'll catch her when I drop Pauli off."

"Okay, and I'll bring Pauli home."

"No need. His friends will pick him up. They're working on a project, he said."

Pauli had more than one project going.

The cast was on a break and a production conference was in progress when I opened the door of the Etonville Little Theatre. Sitting on stage, Walter was debating the pros and cons of balcony construction with the set crew head—JC—while out in the house, Penny and Chrystal fussed over costume business, and Lola fingered satin and velvet fabric swatches.

"The balcony needs to be three feet higher and reinforced," Walter said, jabbing his forefinger at a blueprint of the set. "There's going to be a lot of action up there."

JC stared at Walter's finger. "That's going to take more time and money."

"We'll rehearse with a ladder until it's ready. We've got a ten-foot one in the shop."

A ladder? I was glad I didn't have to scramble up and down—

"Dodie, what do you think of this material?" Lola stared at the samples in her hands.

"Penny, we need these measurement sheets filled out this week," Chrystal said firmly. Then she turned to me. "At least we don't need sizes for the codpieces." She snickered.

"Here's a draft of a measurement schedule," I said, handing her a sheet of paper. "It's based on who's called what nights this week."

Chrystal's eyes opened wide. "Uh . . . thanks! This is great."

Penny looked sullen. "I would have done it if Walter had asked."

"Of course you would," Chrystal said.

"I think I like this blue." Lola held the swatch at arm's length.

"That's good because Walter wants the Capulets in blue and the Montagues in red."

Definitely the Jets and the Sharks, I thought.

Actors had just begun to trickle back in, some alone, some in twos, when a sudden whoop erupted from the lobby, followed by some yelling and hooting. I looked at Chrystal, and Penny darted up the aisle and wrenched open the door. Romeo and Tybalt were chuckling and jabbing each other in the ribs like little boys on a playground.

Abby flounced past Penny and paraded herself down the right aisle of the theater. Everyone froze.

Under her breath, Chrystal muttered, "Oh my Lord. I asked the ladies to bring in a rehearsal skirt from home."

Abby was dressed in a flaming-red Elizabethan gown complete with starched ruff and a bodice cut way too low, with a score of colored feathers jammed every which way in her hair.

Juliet and another young Lady-in-Waiting ran into the theater just as Abby halted, one Elizabethan-clad foot in front of the other, as if she were walking a tightrope. Juliet playfully nudged the other girl, who lost her balance and tumbled into Abby. Caught off-guard, she yelped, wobbled sideways, and landed on her back with a cloud of billowing red satin held aloft by a petticoat made of wire and muslin.

The two girls dissolved into a fit of giggles. Abby flailed her arms and legs and screamed at the top of her lungs. "Get me up!"

There was a mad dash to her side, Chrystal pulling while I pushed, grabbing a handful of wire and satin and inhaling feathers.

"Penny, what is going on?" Walter demanded.

Lola and the rest of the cast stood wide-eyed, mouths agape, while Penny threw up her hands in dismay and then made notations on her clipboard.

"Rehearsal skirt, I said, not full costume. That's not even your character," Chrystal said to a tearful Abby, who was by now upright.

"I could have played Juliet," Abby whimpered to no one in particular.

Abby's dramatic entrance had thrown the rehearsal schedule askew. By the time we had her and the cast under control, we'd lost at least twenty minutes. Walter didn't help move things along, either. He was still using present-day British vernacular like "you lot" and "bugger off" and the cast either laughed or exchanged expressions of "huh?" And sometimes Walter communicated via theatrical directions that were a little old-fashioned and just a bit pompous. "Hence" he would say, and "dress the stage."

I hadn't been able to pull Lola aside and talk with her about turning Jerome's ledger over to the police. Though Walter "borrowing" from the box office had nothing to do with Jerome's murder, I wanted Bill to see the notation that indicated Jerome had had a meeting planned with an MR for the day after he died. Which may have been as innocent as a haircut or a doctor's appointment. Still, I was feeling some guilt at holding back this information and remembered my great aunt Maureen's favorite saying, that she had crocheted on a wall hanging: *In life's wardrobe of emotions, guilt is the itchy wool turtleneck that's three sizes too small.* I'd been scratching for several days now.

Carol and Pauli walked in the door. Carol made a beeline for Chrystal to consult on hair and wigs, and I set Pauli up in the box office. I told a few folks he was doing his homework.

"I'm working on some new software that can help identify passwords. What it does is—" Pauli said.

"Some kind of forensic program?" I asked.

"Sort of. Do you want me to explain it to you?"

"No, that's okay. Just go ahead." I watched him sort through all of the information we had collected on Jerome, his forehead furrowed.

"I'm leaving," Carol called into the box-office window.

Pauli looked up and nodded and then went back to work.

"He's really into your website, isn't he?" Carol asked.

"Yeah. Did you get the hair straightened out?"

"There are a few wigs in storage that I'll pull out. Mostly everyone'll wear their own hair and I'll fool around with styling. Pauli, home by eleven, okay?"

He nodded again.

"Bye, Dodie."

"Bye."

"You got anything to write on in here?" Pauli asked.

"Let me take a look." I opened the top drawer under the ticket counter; it had been cleaned out, presumably by Lola. I checked the second drawer and found only rolls of circus tickets. I rummaged around in the bottom drawer and lifted up a handful of old programs and some ticket reconciliation sheets. A pale, rose-tinted envelope slipped out of the pile and fluttered to the floor. I picked it up, and my heart skipped a beat. Someone had written *MR* on the front of it.

Chapter 13

A half hour later, two clones appeared in the lobby. They were exact duplicates of Pauli: shaggy hair in their earnest faces, a smattering of acne across their foreheads, hoodies, sneakers, and baggy jeans. They approached the box-office window.

Pauli brightened immediately. "Hey," he said.

"Hey," one said.

"Hey," the other responded.

"I'm going, okay?" he said to me.

"Fine. I'll call you tomorrow about the website," I said, and he smiled slyly as he packed up his laptop.

I watched the kids exit the theater and then withdrew the envelope from my bag, where I'd stashed it while finding Pauli some scratch paper. The stationery had a subtle floral pattern and a vaguely rose-like scent. I lifted it to my nose and inhaled. The envelope was empty, but the initials on the front, along with the last page of the ledger, suggested that Jerome's mystery lady and MR might be one and the same. I made up my mind. I took the ledger from my bag and carefully detached the back page. I could give Bill both the page and the envelope and not even mention Walter. I could just say I'd found the loose page in one of the drawers when I was searching for—

My cell rang. I punched ANSWER. "Hi, Carol. Pauli left ten minutes ago with his friends."

"Dodie!"

"What?"

"I just got a call from Rita, my shampoo girl, who got a call from her cousin Monica. The one you—"

"—talked to. Right."

"Well, she said the police are all over her street." Carol was breathless.

"Ellison? Jerome's street."

"Yes. And they're going into his house. What do you think is going on?"

"I don't know. Thanks, Carol." I grabbed my bag.

The lobby door banged open, and Penny stuck her head in the box office. "Walter wants you to see him after rehearsal," she said gruffly.

"Sorry. Tell Lola and Walter I'll check in with them later. I have to run." I headed for the exit.

"But Walter's redoing the circle of light tonight because the trust has been broken and—"

Walter would have to regain the trust without me.

I ran to my Metro, hopped in, and cranked the engine, shooting up Main and over Fairfield. I drove down Ellison and came to an abrupt stop two doors from 1428. I recognized the white car in the driveway from my previous visit. Red and blue flashing lights atop the police cruiser had begun to draw attention. Front porch lights snapped on, and neighbors ventured out and gathered in small knots of murmuring humanity. I cut through a neighbor's yard just as Officer Ralph Ostrowski raced his police vehicle down the street and slammed it into the curb. He jumped out and waved his arms at the handful of people who lined the sidewalk.

"Okay. Nothing to see here. Let's break it up."

I darted to the porch, wracking my brain for an excuse to get into the house, when the front door opened.

"Hello! It's Dodie, yes?" Charles Waters stood there bobbing his head and smiling merrily. He ran one hand through his tufts of white hair and eased back on his bedroom slippers.

"Hi, Charles. May I come in?"

Charles opened the door wider and I slipped through, Ralph close on my heels. Over Charles's shoulder, I could see and hear Bill and a woman, probably Betty Everly, in the living room—he was nodding patiently as she flapped her arms around, talking rapidly.

". . . so I went upstairs to check on the plumbing in room three because the tenant was complaining about the trap in her shower and there it was. The door to room two was partly open and everything was ransacked." She was still in her work apron, her hair a feather duster of flyaway tendrils.

Ralph tapped me on the arm. "This is a crime scene. No civilians permitted. You'll have to stay outside."

"It's okay, Ralph. I'm a friend of Charles. Mrs. Everly's father?" I gestured to the older man, who grinned his agreement.

Ralph hitched up his pants and jammed his nightstick into his belt. "It doesn't matter who you're friends with. You can't come in here and trample on evidence."

"Why don't you check with the chief?" I said politely.

Bill appeared in the hallway, Mrs. Everly two steps behind him.

"Chief, she says she's a friend of—"

"—Charles. He let me in."

Bill looked quizzically from Ralph to me to Charles. "Uh-huh." He paused. "Ralph, take care of crowd control," he said quietly, and jerked his head in the direction of the street, where the tiny knots of people had morphed into one big neighborhood bunch.

"Are you sure?" Ralph was clearly disappointed, but Bill only nodded and opened the door for him to exit.

"This is Ms. O'Dell. She's . . . helping with the investigation," Bill said firmly to Mrs. Everly.

She drew her sweater around her midsection and glanced at me skeptically. Then her eyes fell on poor Charles. "Dad, take off those slippers and put on your shoes. You're going to trip and fall," she barked.

His body sagged and he shuffled off to the back of the house. Betty Everly was never going to be his checkers partner.

Mrs. Everly led the way to the second floor and stood aside as Bill entered Jerome's room, careful to leave everything untouched. I peered over his shoulder and gasped. The bedroom was in complete disarray: the mattress had been yanked off the bed, the covers thrown about. Someone had inserted a knife into pillow seams and polyester fiberfill had burst out, layering the floor with white balls. The lamps were tipped over, shades askew. Even the paintings had been slashed. Someone had done a thorough job of rummaging around.

"Who's going to pay for all of this?" Mrs. Everly wailed.

I walked to the closet and peered in. "What happened to his clothes?"

"I gave them away to Goodwill," she said defensively.

Her words landed with a thud. As if discarding Jerome's clothing was a second burial of Jerome himself.

I hung back and leaned against the archway leading into the living room, chock-full of tchotchkes and furniture. Every surface was covered with china figurines and coasters of various materials and shapes; moving around end tables and easy chairs required the agility of a tap dancer. Bill sat with Mrs. Everly on the sofa.

"What time did you return home?"

"Nine-thirty. Same as every night," she replied. "I work at Lacey's Market. Frozen foods."

"Did you leave the door unlocked?" he asked. "There don't appear to be signs of forced entry."

"Sure. Someone's always ringing my bell because they forgot a key. I just got tired of waiting on them."

"Was there anyone in the house earlier in the evening?"

"Well, one of my renters has been out of town all week and the other works a night shift."

"What about Charles?" I asked.

Bill and Mrs. Everly swung their heads in my direction in unison: he with curiosity, she with thinly veiled suspicion. "I don't like Dad to answer the door. Once it's open, he's been known to wander off."

Bill coughed and frowned, warning me to back off a little. "Have you noticed anything unusual in the neighborhood lately?"

"Like what?" she asked, her mouth turned down at the corners.

"Like anyone hanging around? Someone you didn't recognize?"

Mrs. Everly pondered the question for a moment. "Not really. Of course, there are the Banger sisters."

"Who?" he asked.

"Two old ladies on the next block up who are always causing trouble. Busybodies. Always have their noses in everyone's business."

Sounded like most of Etonville to me. I knew the two chatterboxes from their frequent dinners at the Windjammer.

"The night Jerome died, they knocked on my door after the police left and wanted to know if they could borrow a cup of sugar. Do you believe that?"

She looked from Bill to me and back to Bill again. We shook our heads in unison.

"Anything to get into my house and have a look around."

"So no one or nothing out of the ordinary. Besides the Banger sisters," Bill prompted her.

Mrs. Everly nodded. "What do you think they wanted? Why tear the bedroom apart? There's nothing much of value up there. I'm going to have an awful time cleaning up."

"We'll need to dust for fingerprints in the room. We'll let you know when we're finished."

"I hope it doesn't take too long. I need to rent that room," she said curtly. "It's my main source of income."

Bill nodded. "I understand."

I wondered if he regretted trading Philadelphia's urban police force for Etonville law enforcement. He stood up and tiptoed around the coffee table, careful to avoid bumping ceramic Doberman Pinschers guarding the entranceway to the living room.

"Mrs. Everly, did Jerome ever have any visitors?" I asked quickly. Bill paused.

"What kind of visitors?"

"Oh, you know . . . friends."

Mrs. Everly rose. "I don't interfere in the business of my renters."

"I didn't mean to imply that you did. It might be helpful to know is all."

"I run a respectable establishment here."

I nodded and turned to leave and found my face squarely in Ralph's chest.

"Chief," he said, stepping aside to talk to Bill, "I got the Banger sisters out here, and they claim they saw something."

"What did they see?" Bill asked.

"A dark car cruising down the street. First up then down. More than once," he said significantly.

"What time?"

"They were watching *Jeopardy*. So that would be . . ." Ralph paused to calculate the time.

"Okay, I'll have a word with them. Why don't you dust for fingerprints. Thanks for your help, Mrs. Everly." Bill nodded brusquely and headed for the door.

I followed him out.

Ralph had done a decent job of dispersing the crowd, but there were still a number of folks hanging out on their porches in fear of missing something. Standing on the sidewalk next to Bill's squad car were the Banger sisters.

Bill tipped his cap courteously. "Ladies, I understand you saw a vehicle cruising up and down the street tonight?"

The sisters giggled, their heads bouncing, thrilled to be, momentarily, the center of attention. "Oh my, yes," said one. "We were watching—"

"*Jeopardy*," said the other. "And Alex Trebek had just read the Final Jeopardy question."

"So that would be almost seven-thirty?" I asked.

"Oh, Dodie, is that you?" said the first sister.

"Can you remember the make of the car? Or its color?" Bill gently steered them back on track.

"Well, let's see. . . . It was definitely dark. . . . Maybe black."

"Like one of those cars the FBI uses on television. You know, the big bulky ones."

"SUVs?" he said.

"That's right." The sisters turned to each other and smiled.

I had a sudden thought. "Do either of you remember seeing anyone visit Jerome here?"

They frowned. "Jerome usually came and went alone," one sister said. "Other than that one time."

My pulse quickened. "That one time?"

"We were walking around the block and saw a car stop just about here. . . ." She pointed to the street where Bill's cruiser was now parked. "But we weren't close enough to see who she was."

"A she?"

"Oh my, yes. She had on a skirt and her hair was—"

"Up in a French twist," I said, a tad triumphantly.

Bill just stared at me.

"That's the third sighting of the SUV," I said and shifted sideways to face Bill. We were leaning against his squad car.

"That's assuming it was the same SUV you saw the other two nights."

"Trust me. It was. How many big black SUVs are in Etonville? For once, the Banger sisters might have gotten it right."

"Yeah."

"Much to Mrs. Everly's annoyance."

"I just wish we had the license plate number."

"Right."

"There are a lot of loose ends here," he said.

I reached into my purse. "And here are a couple more." I withdrew the envelope and ledger sheet and handed them to him.

"What're these?" His brow puckered.

"I found them in the box office."

He took both pieces of paper and studied them.

"MR on both of them," I said.

"Four-sixteen. The day he died."

"Might have been a doctor's appointment. Or something more important . . ." I let the thought dangle.

"Like a meeting with this mystery woman?" he said.

"Possibly."

He hesitated. "Where did you say you found these?"

"In a drawer in the box office."

He examined the ledger page carefully. "Looks like this might have been torn out of something."

"Really?" I said innocently.

He cut his eyes in my direction. "I'll log them into evidence." Bill shook his head. "I just wish I knew what was really going on here. What was the intruder looking for?"

"Maybe it was a random robbery."

"Like the night Jerome was murdered?" he asked pointedly.

"Yeah, I know. Hard to swallow. A single, older man in a rented room. Not exactly a great mark for a robbery. Especially a high-end robbery. The SUV was an Escalade."

"The Banger sisters only described it as a big, bulky—"

"I knew it was an Escalade I saw the first time I drove by the house."

We stood in silence as a night breeze ruffled my bangs.

"Guess I'll head back to the station," he said.

"Guess I'll head back to rehearsal." I slung my bag over my shoulder.

Bill nodded. "Between the restaurant and the theater, you're a glutton for punishment."

"Yeah."

"With a good nose for detection."

I felt some heat rise in my face. "Is that a compliment?"

"I suppose so," he said abruptly. "Don't let it go to your head."

Chapter 14

It was after ten-thirty and rehearsal was probably over, but I figured I could touch base with Chrystal and share my box-office find with Lola. Not to mention the break-in at Jerome's place.

"What's going on?" I said to Penny, who was standing at the back of the theater, so flustered she'd fogged up her glasses and misplaced her clipboard. Unlike most nights, when the cast disbursed quickly to homes or the Windjammer, where the bar would be open for another hour, actors were milling about, agitated. The rumbling level, as well as the tension level, was rising.

"Walter tried to get them into the circle of light and they refused. I've never seen that before." Penny jiggled her head for effect. "It's like a . . . a . . ."

"Rebellion?"

Lola took a look out into the house and spotted me. She ran up the aisle. "Oh, Dodie, thank God you're here." With a nod to Penny. "Sorry, Penny, but I think Dodie needs to handle this."

"Walter said I was the production stage manager. That means stage managing the production." She stomped off.

"Above her pay grade, huh?" I said.

"Where have you been? It's pandemonium around here."

"Didn't you hear? Jerome's room was ransacked."

"Jerome's—?"

"Someone broke into the house on Ellison. Although it looks like the door was unlocked so technically there was no break-in. But whoever it was did a number in his bedroom."

"Whatever for?"

"He or she was looking for something. And remember that black SUV I told you about? The Banger sisters saw it on the street the hour before."

"The Banger sisters? They're nutty old coots."

"Maybe not this time."

Walter was looking around. "Lola?" he whined plaintively.

"So what happened here? Besides the non-circle of light?"

"Walter is shuffling around some of the servants and Ladies-in-Waiting and didn't even get to Act II tonight so he changed the re-hearsal schedule, and now he's calling the cast in on Sunday. Everyone."

"But the ELT never rehearses on Sunday. That's the day off. I had everything arranged to maximize efficiency and minimize wast-ing everybody's time."

"He's getting nervous about the text," she whispered.

"Lola!" Walter called out.

"You're being summoned," I said as she groaned and moved off.

"I thought your schedule worked perfectly."

I whipped my head around. "Hi, Elliot. I thought so, too, but ap-parently Walter didn't."

"He's just a little anxious. He needs to let the cast settle in. They'll be a lot fresher if they have Sunday off, but, well . . ." He shrugged.

"I hear you have a lot of experience. Maybe you should be di-recting *Romeo and Juliet*. It all seems to be sending Walter into a state of . . ." I searched for the right phrase.

"Panic?"

"I was thinking manic depression."

"I don't have the patience." He laughed warmly and ran a hand through his hair.

"And Walter does?"

Elliot peered at a small crowd that was growing more vociferous. "Say, I'm going to try to quiet a few people down before they leave. But after that, would you like to have a drink with me at the Wind-jammer? Unless that feels like a busman's holiday?"

"Sure. I need to stop in and check on things anyway. Just come by when you're finished pacifying ruffled feathers."

Walter waved me over, but I pretended to be so busy in conver-sation that I didn't notice. It might be good for him to stew in his own juices. Maybe he should do his own rehearsal schedule in the future.

"I don't have the energy to tackle Walter tonight. He'll have to wait until tomorrow."

"I know what you mean." Elliot touched my arm lightly and sauntered away.

The ELT could use a few more like Elliot Schenk.

Abby flounced up the aisle and pushed her face into mine. "Walter said I should understudy the Nurse instead of Juliet."

Now that made sense.

"Instead, he gave it to her." She pointed to Edna, who was beaming, one of the few actors apparently not discontented.

"I don't even have any lines. All we do is stand around waiting."

Last time I checked, that's what the Ladies-in-Waiting did. "Sorry, Abby."

"Huh," she said and hiked up her red velvet gown.

"You didn't miss much. It was a quiet night. Here, that is," Benny said and wiped down the bar.

"The rumor mill is working overtime?"

"Oh yeah. One of Jerome's neighbors came in. He supposedly talked to the Banger sisters, who supposedly talked with Jerome's landlady, and I heard it all. Jerome's room, the SUV, gunfire—"

"There was no gunfire. Where do they get this stuff?"

Benny shrugged. "Maybe a car backfired?"

"Word travels fast."

Benny started to count on his fingers. "Sure does. Between the Banger sisters, Edna, Snippets, and Ralph . . . of course he was at the crime scene. . . ."

"It must drive the chief nuts."

"No secrets in Etonville," he said and laughed.

"Except who murdered Jerome," I said thoughtfully.

"Good point." He nodded to a customer who approached the bar. "What can I get you, Elliot?"

We sat in my back booth, Elliot sipping Johnnie Walker while I relaxed into the faux leather black seat and blew on a cup of coffee to cool it off. "You and Jerome liked your whiskey neat," I said.

"That we did," Elliot replied and cupped his glass with both hands. "Being at the theater feels like a way to stay connected to him."

"I know what you mean."

"We were two lonely bachelors who spent many a night here after rehearsals and shows . . . of course, that was before your time."

"And before you left. According to Lola, the stories about your exit from Etonville were apparently very colorful."

"Oh?"

"They involved financial shenanigans, rehab, and an abandoned child."

His eyes twinkled. "I'm afraid my leaving was much more mundane and far less exciting."

I waited for him to continue.

"I had a job offer in Pittsburgh. An investment banking opportunity."

"It didn't work out?"

"I grew bored so I returned to Wall Street. Life in the Midwest is not the same as life in the big city." He studied me over the lip of his glass. "So you see, the reports of my demise have been greatly exaggerated."

"Mark Twain."

"He's one of my favorites," Elliot said.

"Jerome and I loved mysteries. Cindy Collins was our favorite."

"That was an interest we didn't share. I lean more toward American classics. Twain, of course, Hemingway, F. Scott Fitzgerald, Steinbeck. Jerome was enamored of crimes, detectives, and general mayhem. A retired English teacher!"

"We were always in competition to figure out whodunit," I said.

"Who won?"

I leaned across the table. "Between you and me, I was much better at it than Jerome."

Benny flashed the lights to indicate last call for the half dozen occupants of the restaurant.

"I assume things have cooled off at the theater?" I asked.

Elliot took out his wallet. "Somewhat."

"I think you're good with people." I brushed away his offer to pay.

"It's just my natural charm," he said breezily and closed his wallet. "Thanks. I hear we missed out on some excitement this evening."

"Right. A break-in at Jerome's former residence."

"That's what Edna said." Elliot's brow wrinkled. "I hope the police are on top of this. Jerome's murder might require more resources than small town law enforcement can provide."

"Chief Thompson certainly has his hands full. By the way, did Jerome ever mention a . . . special friend?"

Elliot cocked his head. "Special friend?"

I smiled. "A woman."

"Jerome? I don't think so. Of course we'd been out of touch for much of the last couple of years." His eyes twinkled. "I wasn't privy to his love life."

"Right."

"He was much smarter than I when it came to marriage," Elliot said ruefully.

I wondered about that.

Elliot said good-night and, once again, reminded me that the ELT remained in desperate need of my management skills. I promised to speak with Walter tomorrow.

Benny sidled over to my booth, broom in hand. "Henry was a little upset tonight. His Thai fish curry kind of bombed, and Enrico burned the grilled eggplant."

"I think he's getting a trifle too experimental for Etonville's tastes."

"And he was asking about the theme food for *Romeo and Juliet.* Got any ideas there?"

"I'm drawing a blank. I've given up on Italian and romance. . . . What's left?"

Benny thought. "Murder?"

"Good one."

Benny resumed his work and my cell binged, telling me a text was waiting. It was my old boss inviting me back to his new restaurant for Memorial Day weekend. I closed my eyes and got a shore rush: warm sand and cool sea breezes, the screeching of sea gulls and the pungent smell of suntan lotion. I opened my eyes to reality: the faint odor of stale grease and a dirty coffee cup. I loved my job at the Windjammer and all of my Etonville friends, but how long could I stay here? Maybe I did belong below the Driscoll Bridge.

* * *

Georgette's pastry shop, to pick up some desserts for the Wind-jammer, was the first thing on my list this morning. Afterward, I swung by Snippets to see Carol. It was a madhouse. Besides the normal wear and tear on one's hearing there was the break-in chatter.

"Thanks for the call last night." I appraised the salon. "I guess that's all everyone can talk about today. Jerome's room."

"I hear they had to break down the door."

"No, they didn't. All they had to do was walk in. Even the front door was unlocked. Have the Banger sisters been in already?"

"Rita talked with her cousin."

"Right. Monica Jenkins. I didn't see her in the crowd last night."

"Apparently she was in bed with the flu but through her bedroom window had a bird's-eye view of the street. Being sick didn't keep her off the telephone."

"Or hinder her imagination," I said.

I watched Carol's hands swirl around the stainless-steel sink as she rinsed stray hairs and a skim of shampoo down the drain. "Monica gave me a pretty good description of the woman who visited Jerome. And the Banger sisters confirmed it was a gray-haired female. But Mrs. Everly, Jerome's landlady, said she never saw anyone drop by the house to see Jerome. Of course, she was a little cranky last night."

Carol brushed a curl out of her eyes. "I've done a couple of perms for her. I know what you mean." She dried her hands. "How's Pauli doing with the website?"

"Great." That reminded me I needed to check on his password progress. . . .

Bill beat the lunch rush at the Windjammer—the place was still empty—and slid onto a stool at the bar. I poured him a cup of coffee. He looked tired and agitated.

"The town's in an uproar," I said.

Bill frowned. "Yeah." He unfolded a copy of the *Etonville Standard* and passed it over to me. The headline read BREAK-IN AT VICTIM'S FORMER HOME. "They stopped the presses and delayed printing to get this story in. Called me at six this morning," he grumbled.

I scanned the story. "Who told them there was gunfire?"

"The same person who said we had to break down his door." He spread his arms as a question mark. His walkie-talkie squawked and Bill pressed a red button. "What is it, Edna?"

"We got a 480."

"Hit and run? Who called it in?"

"Mrs. Parker. Her car got banged up on Belvidere over by the library."

"Okay. Did she get a plate number?"

"Nope. Just a description. A black SUV."

Bill's eyes met mine, sending my heartbeat racing. It was either the SUV or his royal-blue orbs that absorbed my life force and took my breath away.

He grabbed his cap and bounded to his feet. "Edna, find Ralph and tell him to meet me at the scene."

"10-4, Chief."

I wanted to follow Bill to the hit-and-run site, but I needed to stay in the restaurant.

Enrico stuck his head out the kitchen door, his face a mesh of worry lines. "Dodie, we have a problem," he said quickly.

I downed the last of my seltzer and hurried into the kitchen. The icemaker had experienced an electrical problem, and everything inside had melted. The water had begun to leak out and overflow a floor drain designed to keep the tiles dry.

"I'll call the plumber and an electrician. Enrico, can you handle the floor?"

Enrico grabbed a mop and I punched numbers into my cell phone. Henry kept cooking his homemade tomato soup.

I got the kitchen sorted out and helped Gillian to prep for the lunch rush. Folks scurried in the minute the doors opened, and everyone wanted to talk to me about the latest turn of events.

"Dodie, wasn't that just the most attractive picture of Jerome in the paper? It was from the Etonville High School yearbook." One of the Banger sisters. "We're friends with Mrs. Everly. We know what goes on."

"I witnessed the hit-and-run on Belvidere, you know," said Mildred from the library. I was shocked to catch her in the Windjammer for lunch.

I perked up. "You actually saw the vehicle hit Mrs. Parker?"

"Well, I was on my break and I stopped in the ladies' room and then looked out the front window to see if it was still raining, and just a few minutes later Mrs. Parker had the collision with the SUV."

"But you saw the SUV hit her?" I prompted.

"Well, almost." She smiled graciously.

"But not really."

"No, but I can swear to Mrs. Parker's character, if the chief needs me to."

"Right." I planted myself next to the cash register and vowed not to move for the next hour.

"Hey, Dodie, my take-out order ready?" Edna frequently picked up lunch for the police department.

"Is B—uh, the chief back yet?" I asked casually.

"After the 480, actually it was only a 481 misdemeanor because there was no real damage and we didn't have to call an 11-85, that's a tow truck—he had a 1091A and an 11-86."

I stared at her blankly.

"That's a stray animal and a defective signal, for you civvies."

You had to hand it to Edna; she loved her work. "I'll check on your order."

"Hey, tell Henry he can throw in some of that Thai curry if there's any leftover. Suki goes nuts for that food."

"Will do."

"Dodie, you're coming back to rehearsal aren't you? Walter feels bad about screwing up your schedule, and I know if you just talk with him. . . ."

I glanced at Edna. "I'll be there."

By two-thirty, things had settled down in the restaurant. No news from the police station; though I was dying to call in, I restrained myself. I'd stand a better chance of getting information from Bill later if I didn't bug him now.

Lola trudged in the door, damp from the steady rain that had been falling since late morning. She removed her stylish, deep purple rain jacket from REI and plopped into a seat opposite me. "I couldn't sleep all night."

"The show?" I asked.

"The show, Walter, the budget, learning lines . . . maybe this was a huge blunder. Doing Shakespeare at the ELT."

"You've got lots of time yet. Four more weeks to get it together."

"I think the Nurse may quit because her granddaughter is giving birth any day now in North Dakota and she wants to visit, and Romeo's having a fit over his costume and Chrystal can't get some of the men to try on their codpieces." She pursed her lips. "They don't see why they need them."

We locked eyes and she giggled. *As if.*

"You will be there tonight, won't you?"

"Walter's going to have to use my rehearsal schedule."

"He will," she said firmly. "He knows he needs you, and I guarantee he'll be as good as gold after last night's eruption."

"Okay. After all, I've got some skin in the game now."

Benny poured Lola a cup of coffee, and she smiled gratefully.

I lowered my voice. "I didn't get a chance to tell you last night . . . I gave Bill the back page of the ledger you found in the box office."

"You did?" Lola said anxiously.

"Don't worry. I ripped it out of the book. Bill will never know where it came from. Walter's financial . . . issues don't have any bearing on the murder. But I did feel like Bill needed to see the initials and date. MR 4/16."

"I understand," Lola said.

"Especially since I went digging through the box office drawers last night and found an envelope with the letters MR on the front."

Lola's mouth dropped open. "No!"

"Yes!"

"What kind of envelope?" she asked.

"Pinkish, kind of a floral design. Scent of roses."

"The kind that would hold a love letter?"

"Exactly, but the envelope was empty." My cell phone rang. I checked the caller ID. "Hi, Carol."

"Uh, Dodie, it's me."

"Oh, hi, Pauli. I was just thinking about calling you."

"We're in," he said ambiguously.

I glanced at the wall clock; it was time for Gillian's break, which meant I had to cover the last table in her section. "In what?" I asked.

The line went quiet. "*In,*" he said with emphasis. "The dead guy's email," he whispered.

Oh my God, I thought.

"Pauli, that's . . . amazing,"

Lola looked up and searched my face. I nodded. "Yes, we can work on the website. Can you come down here in the next hour or so?"

Pauli snorted. "The website. Sweet." I heard a rustling on the line. "Hey, Mom, I'm going to the Windjammer, okay? To work on the . . . *website.*" I could hear the quotation marks and imminent laugh gurgling up from his throat.

"See you soon." I clicked off, my heart pounding, my palms sweaty.

"It's wonderful to see Pauli engaged in these computer projects. He is such a smart guy," Lola said.

She had no idea.

Chapter 15

Pauli entered the Windjammer at four o'clock and slipped into the booth next to me. Benny brought him a Coke.

"How did you do it?" I asked sotto voce. "How did you find his password?"

Pauli looked like the proverbial cat that had munched on the canary, and I didn't blame him.

"I just tried to think like he did."

"What a good idea." I paused. "What does that mean?"

"Well, like, remember when you said he read thrillers and then like he spent all of his time at the theater? And then like I said I was working on this program to take like different clues from people's lives, you know, and search through lots of combinations?"

"Digital forensics, right?" I said and ruffled the hair on the top of his head. He blushed.

"Yeah. Anyway, I took the names of those books you gave me like Cindy Collins, and she writes these murder mysteries. . . ." He paused as though to absorb the irony of Jerome's reading habits juxtaposed with his death. "And then I asked at the theater what plays he was in."

"You did? What a cool idea."

"He was the detective in *The Mousetrap*."

"Right."

"We did that at school three years ago. It's like kind of boring," he said.

"I know what you mean. I've seen better plots in a cemetery."

Pauli guffawed. "Yeah, and anyway you said he just got the email address like in the last few months so I figured he probably used something recent since we didn't get a hit on like his birth date or the usual stuff or whatever."

"Wow, I'm impressed."

"Yeah, and I worked them through the algorithm . . . and finally I got it."

"The password. So don't keep me in suspense. What is it?"

Pauli picked up a napkin off the table and wrote it out: *JAdetective*.

How elegant: his initials and his alter ego.

"Pauli, you are really something."

He shrugged and proceeded to punch in the password.

I could feel the little hairs standing at attention on the back of my neck as we sat in my booth and watched Jerome's email materialize on the screen. Still, it was too soon to take a victory lap.

Since Jerome hadn't logged on for over a couple of weeks there was a lot of junk mail. Pauli began to scroll methodically through the inbox from the last few days. We worked our way back to the day he died and then started to search in earnest bypassing advertisements and offers. Jerome apparently didn't believe in cleaning out his inbox.

Then I started to see a pattern.

"Pauli, I'm going to need to study these." I carefully folded the napkin with Jerome's password on it and stuffed it in my pocket. I didn't want to take the time to read separate emails in front of Pauli; I wasn't sure what I would find out. But I was equally unsure what to say to him now. "Pauli, about all of this . . ."

He held up his hand. "The first rule of digital forensics is confidentiality," he said gravely.

"Right. So mum's the word until I can sort it out?"

"Sweet." He shut down his laptop.

"What's the second rule?"

"Like, never give up or whatever," Pauli said, grinning.

After the dinner hour at the Windjammer, my plan had been to sort things out at the theater and then hurry home to read through Jerome's email. I prepared myself to do battle with Walter over the rehearsal schedule, but I needn't have bothered. There was already a battle going on. Walter and Romeo stood toe-to-toe on the stage while

Lola sat in the first row, nervously twisting a lock of blond hair, and Juliet, perched atop a ten-foot ladder, texted nonchalantly.

Penny approached me, jerking her head in the direction of the stage.

"What's going on?"

"Walter is about to strangle Romeo."

Walter gesticulated broadly, then climbed up and down the ladder to demonstrate how easily one could master the steps. Romeo was having none of it. His every gesture said, "No way."

"Angoraphobia," said Penny confidently.

"Fear of rabbits?" I asked innocently.

"Heights."

"But traditionally it's Juliet who's on the balcony. Not Romeo," I said.

"This production is not traditional." Penny took off her glasses and cleaned them on her sweater. "Walter has this vision that he wants the scene to look like *West Side Story*. You know, in the movie where Richard Beymer tries to reach Natalie Wood on the fire escape and he hangs on to the railing, and their fingertips just about touch."

"And bad-boy Romeo won't climb a ladder," I said.

"Yeah. Plus Walter's saving money by doing the balcony scene on the cheap."

"On the ladder? You mean it's not just for rehearsal? I thought JC was building the balcony?"

"He was until Walter found out what it would cost," Penny said.

"Good thing Juliet isn't afraid of heights."

"Penny! Where is my prompt book?" Walter was now beside himself.

Penny ran onstage and thrust the binder at Walter. "Maybe we can just do the balcony scene the . . . traditional way?" She turned and looked at me.

Walter looked like he could chew nails and still come back for a helping of chain link fence. "Penny, my production is not traditional! I have a vision. They fall in love. On a balcony. He climbs up to meet her, they kiss. It's the most important scene in the play!"

"Why can't we just meet in a garden like in *Downton Abbey*?" Romeo asked. "I mean who meets on a balcony? How real is that?"

The possibility for stupid was growing by the second. Walter looked out at Lola and exhaled audibly. The man was aging before my eyes.

"Walter," Lola said softly, "why don't we rehearse it for now with Juliet up there and Romeo . . . here." She pointed to the place where Romeo had defiantly plunked his body, the bottom rung of the ladder. *The way the scene was usually played*, I thought.

Walter nodded and Romeo began his *What light through yonder window breaks?* bit.

The ladder teetered slightly and Juliet gasped. Penny placed herself—Atlas-like—under the ladder, one arm on each leg. Romeo droned on, indifferent to the meter, Juliet's beauty, or his predicament as a Montague in a Capulet compound. Walter had to remind Romeo to look at Juliet.

So much for Walter's vision.

"This isn't going to work," Walter fumed. "I want you to be able to touch." He scrutinized the petulant Romeo and decided not to push the issue. "I'll stand in for Romeo."

Romeo was suddenly alert. "What do I do?"

Walter smiled sarcastically. "You speak and I will play the lover on the balcony. A little like Cyrano," he said.

"Like who?" Romeo asked.

"Never mind." Walter scrambled up the ladder, pretty nimbly for someone his age, until he was face-to-face with the youthful Juliet.

Romeo threw down his script. "How am I supposed to act with you up there?"

"I want you to be the one on the ladder, but since you are afraid of—"

"I'm not afraid of heights. I just don't think Romeo has to be on a ladder."

"A balcony," said Penny.

"Whatever. I'm not rehearsing." He crossed his arms insolently.

Lola crept onto the stage and called up to Walter. "Why don't we take a break and let's just read the scene on the ground and pretend that it's a balcony. That way, Romeo and Juliet—"

"You want to take five?" Penny asked Walter.

"No. I don't want to take five." Walter was furious. "I want to rehearse the scene."

In frustration, he slammed the prompt book on the top rung of the ladder, startling Juliet, who reached for the cell phone that had popped out of her jacket pocket. Her foot slipped, and she started to slide down the ladder's top steps. Lola jumped up, I ran to the stage, and Penny came out from under the A-frame of the ladder just as Juliet bounced down the next few rungs, her foot connecting with an unprepared Romeo.

It was ten o'clock by the time Walter had decided to stay off the ladder for the rest of the evening. I informed him firmly, but respectfully, that either he worked with my schedule or I was off the theater "payroll." Lola backed me up.

I guided my Metro out of its parking space and flipped on the wipers. A mist covered the windshield, colored by the orangeish glow of streetlamps. It was an eerie sensation, driving through Etonville during a spring rain that had scooted folks off the streets. It felt like a ghost town.

At home, I made a cup of strong coffee to accompany a slightly stale jelly donut I had in the fridge and huddled with my laptop at the kitchen table to run through Jerome's emails. I went methodically through his inbox, beginning with the day before he died, April 15, and worked my way back several months. What had caught my eye earlier, and what I had not mentioned to Pauli, was a series of four emails from a business called Forensic Document Services stretching from late February up through the beginning of April. Who or what was Forensic Document Services?

I opened each email, all from a Marshall Wendover. The first one was obviously in response to Jerome's query about some "valuable, historical" item, never actually described, that he needed authenticated. The language in each email was cryptic, as though neither Jerome nor Marshall wanted to say too much over the Internet. Both appeared to be covering their tracks. The "item" was just referred to as the "document," and Wendover, after apparently determining that Jerome had something that he thought was worth the company's time, stated that the retainer for their services was approximately a thousand dollars.

I Googled Forensic Document Services and Marshall Wendover to find a website, an address, a phone number. But there was no link to a company by that exact name headed by a Marshall Wendover. I found a Forensic Services, a Document Services, even a Forensic Documents Service. After half an hour, I gave up searching for Jerome's correspondent and checked out the other websites. There were a number of companies around the country that offered a range of forensic applications, including photographic and microscopic analyses of a document's paper, ink, handwriting, erasures, and impressions. Ostensibly, this information would answer questions regarding the originality, authorship, and provenance of the item. Some heavy-duty investigation. There was no listing of fee structures for this work.

I spent another hour searching for other questionable emails, but aside from advertisements and promotions, and announcements from the ELT, there was little else of interest. Nothing from an MR. I yawned and stretched.

I closed the lid of my laptop and trundled off to bed. I didn't need Cindy Collins tonight; I had my own mystery to solve.

I dreamed I was living inside the old Chutes and Ladders game I had played with my brother on rainy shore days, falling down ladders, bumping off of one A-frame after another, and having to begin the climb back to the top again. I woke in a cold sweat. I closed my eyes and tried to re-enter sleep, but it was impossible. The only solution was coffee and the paper. Yesterday's leaden gloom had been blown away by overnight gusts. The sky was a cloudless, deep blue and the sun warm on my shoulders as I opened the front door, got a lungful of clean, crisp air, and retrieved my *New York Times*.

My cell clanged. The caller ID wasn't familiar. "Hello?" I said cautiously.

"I hope this isn't too early?"

So this was what Bill sounded like in the morning, slightly hoarse, slightly sexy. I glanced at the wall clock above the sink: eight-thirty.

"No, I've been awake for hours." Sad but true.

He cleared his throat. "I thought you might want an update on the SUV incident."

You bet, I thought. "Would you like me to stop by the station?"

"How about Coffee Heaven in an hour? I have to go by the Unitarian church first to deliver their May Festival permit."

"Right. The May Festival. Henry's doing the catering." I paused. "Are you sure you can talk in public?"

"We'll sit in a back booth. Anyway, whatever I have to say is probably already around town. See you in a few."

He clicked off and I stared at my phone. What was I doing entertaining thoughts about Bill? Sure, he was a terrific-looking guy with a body to die for. And he seemed on top of things. He was unattached, as per the Snippets crowd, and he apparently was able to get my engine revved. Still, what did I know about him, other than the Philly connection and NFL experience? Maybe I needed to do a little investigation of Etonville's chief of police.

I was into the Arts section of the *NYT* and my second caramel macchiato, this one a decaf, when Bill slid his compact frame onto the bench across from me.

"Sorry I'm late."

"Problems with the May Festival?"

"Reverend Taylor wants to close Amber Street in front of the church all day, and the permit is only for four hours. He is being difficult."

I nodded. "Small-town life."

He smiled. "Don't get me wrong. I love it here. I just need to get used to the place." Jocelyn set his coffee on the table and he took a swallow from the steaming cup.

"So the hit-and-run?"

"More like a bump and run. Mrs. Parker thought she had put the car in drive but really put it in reverse. She banged into the SUV, not the other way around."

"Still, the SUV took off, right? Didn't wait until you arrived."

"True."

"I assume no license plate number?"

"Nope. Only Mrs. Parker's description. 'A big black sport utility vehicle.'"

I waited for him to go on.

"I'm feeling like it's some kind of phantom automobile. I never see it," he said.

"Counting the Banger sisters, there are four people who have seen it," I said.

"Yeah, and three of them are certifiable." He downed the last dregs of his cup.

"I certainly hope I'm number four."

His walkie-talkie squawked. "Yes, Edna."

"Chief, Officer Shung is looking for you. State police dropped off an analysis of Jerome's—"

Bill pressed the volume button. "I'll be right there."

"10-4," Edna said.

"Sorry, gotta go. If you see the SUV, let me know."

I nodded. "Will do."

And that was that.

Chapter 16

It was all hands on deck for chopping at the Windjammer. Henry had two kinds of salad, soup, and homemade marinara sauce, for vegetable lasagna, on the menu, and that meant a ton of veggies, not to mention the fruit for his dessert medley. Henry, Enrico, and Carmen had each staked out a corner of the kitchen.

I grabbed a bundle of table napkins the laundry service had delivered an hour ago and set myself up at the bar. Ever since I was a kid, kitchen tasks—folding napkins, setting the table, chopping vegetables—have always been restful activities for me. My hands did their thing while my mind wandered or, as necessary, focused. I'd spin imaginative stories with fanciful characters while helping my mother to prepare dinner; it was our special time together and the only time I was allowed to play with knives.

Right now, folding napkins provided the opportunity for me to hunker down mentally. Where the devil was this SUV? Bill was spot-on about one thing: the vehicle *was* a kind of phantom, appearing suddenly in various parts of town, and then disappearing just as quickly. Despite the fact that there were more pieces to the Jerome puzzle available now, the picture still was not taking shape. What was Jerome's connection to Forensic Document Services, and who was MR?

"Dodie." Enrico had sidled up to my elbow without my noticing. He was whispering.

"Hey, Enrico." I escorted myself back into the present moment.

"I am worried about Henry. He is afraid of La Famiglia."

"Afraid?"

Enrico nodded. "That is why he is creating vegetable lasagna," he said confidentially.

"It's just another restaurant," I said.

"But Henry has his pride. He was the first and best in Etonville for a long time," he said seriously.

"There are enough customers to go around."

"It's hard to surrender your position."

I patted Enrico on the back and sent him back to work. It was difficult to believe that Henry felt threatened by a small Italian bistro. Couldn't two restaurants live in harmony in the same town? Maybe seeing *Romeo and Juliet* rehearse was affecting my perspective, but the competition between the Windjammer and La Famiglia was feeling more and more like the Capulets and Montagues, without the sword fights and the poison.

I looked up as Benny walked in the front entrance. "The beer and soda delivery should be here any minute."

"Good morning to you, too," Benny said teasingly.

"I put on the coffee."

"Thanks."

"And would you remind me to tell Henry that he needs to call Reverend Taylor about the May Festival at the Unitarian Church?"

"Got it, chief." Benny saluted. "Anything else?"

"Probably, but I can't think of it yet." I smiled.

Lola banged through the door. "There you are. I went by your house and didn't see your car so I figured . . . oh, hi, Benny." Back to me. "We need to talk."

Benny raised his eyebrows.

"Come on, Lola, let's go to my 'office.' "

She followed me to my back booth.

"Coffee?"

She nodded, and I signaled Benny.

"Whew. I need a vacation. Maybe I'll get out of town for a few hours later," I said.

Lola stared at me uneasily. "Dodie, are you okay? Is the Jerome business getting to you?"

"Yes and yes. What's up at the theater?"

Lola filled me in. The balcony crisis wasn't going away since the budget couldn't afford the lumber and hardware. Chrystal was insisting on velvet and satin for the costumes, and Walter was pushing for cheaper muslin. Romeo claimed he had a sprained ankle this morning, the Nurse finally quit, and Lola didn't think Edna had the role in her.

I shook my head. "Everyone is on edge."

"Tell me about it. Walter and I don't know what to do to hold it together. If Elliot wasn't in the cast, we'd be in even more trouble."

"All of this happened this morning?" I asked.

"Most of it through email." She paused. "Some days I hate the Internet."

"Speaking of the Internet . . . I have news about Jerome."

Lola's eyes got bigger. "What?"

"You can't talk about this to anyone. Not Walter, not Carol, especially not Carol, at least right now."

"Tell me," she demanded.

"I need to tell the chief, but I'm not sure I should yet."

"I'm going to burst if you don't—"

"Did Jerome ever mention an historic document to you? Something of value?" I asked.

"Never."

"Well, you know how we said if we could find out who Jerome was seeing, we might learn something about his death?"

"Yes."

"And how the best way was through his email?"

"Okay."

"Well, you know how clever Pauli is with a computer. . . ."

Lola's eyes opened even wider as I related my hacking story, concluding with the discovery that Jerome had been in correspondence with Forensic Document Services.

"So where might he get his hands on something like that? And why was he keeping it a secret?" I asked.

"Jerome had a lot of secrets," Lola said thoughtfully.

"I've got a little more digging to do."

"If I can help, let me know." She stood up. "See you tonight?"

"Wouldn't miss it."

Lola promised to keep the email story to herself, while I promised to show up at the theater.

The jury was out on Henry's vegetable lasagna. Mildred's husband, who had progressed from soup and salad to entrees, wondered why he couldn't use meat like in "regular lasagna," and the Banger sisters said it tasted "too mushroomy." I defended Henry: he was just trying to broaden the palate of Etonville. Abby's Jim said his palate was doing just fine, thank you.

I was relieved to turn over the helm to Benny after dinner and headed next door to the theater. I relaxed into a soft seat cushion in the theater's last row, house left. I'd brought my laptop to do a little more surfing on the Internet in case I got bored. Walter was avoiding me and focusing on the night's work: swordplay. God help us.

He had a limping Romeo, an impatient Mercutio, and a silly Tybalt all flexing foils and horsing around, slapping one another on the butt.

"Hey, you guys. Knock it off. Those things aren't toys and they cost money," Penny yelled. "This is where the gang stuff starts," she said to me. "Jets and Sharks." Then turned her attention back to the cast. "Two minutes until end of break."

I watched Walter take the men through their paces, counting beats and choreographing steps until somebody invariably ended up on his backside. At which point, the whole process began all over again. I wanted to touch base with Chrystal, but she wasn't due in for another hour and I was getting restless witnessing the men's antics with swords, so I opened my computer.

It wasn't a stretch to believe that Jerome might have had an historical item of great value—I read recently about a baseball card collection worth over a million dollars. People found treasures in their attics and garages. But Jerome had neither, so I had no idea where he might have found his. I Googled rare letters and diaries and learned that they could fetch hundreds of thousands of dollars. But it was all theoretical without knowing what I was dealing with.

Just for fun, I typed in *William Thompson law enforcement* and, no surprise, there were dozens of links. I restricted my search to *Deputy Chief William Thompson + Philadelphia* and there he was. The first link was a story from the *Etonville Standard* quoting Bill on Jerome's murder. The second link was a reference to the anniversary of Bull Bennett's death and mentioned Bill's NFL career in Buffalo and Cleveland. The third link dated from a year ago, and there it was: a story about some scandal in the police department in Philadelphia. This might have been why he took the job in Etonville.

"Hello, Dodie. Having fun?"

I blushed and snapped the lid of my laptop shut as if I had been caught by the teacher viewing unsavory websites. "Hi, Elliot. Just keeping an eye on things. You're not due in tonight," I said.

"Just keeping an eye on things, too." He smiled and jerked his head in the direction of the stage. "I don't know who's getting the worst deal. Walter or the actors."

I stifled a grin. "Maybe the swords?"

We both cackled, and Penny shot us a stern look, her finger plastered vertically on her lips.

I lowered my voice and made a quick decision. "Elliot, did Jerome ever mention a valuable document in his possession?" I fervently hoped I would not regret opening this can of worms, but someone had to know something and Elliot was Jerome's friend.

Elliot frowned and shook his head. "What kind of document?"

"Maybe something historical?"

"Not that I recall. Why?"

"I'm not sure. It's just something that has come up," I said.

"Oh." Elliot waited.

"I thought that since you were friends, he might have said something about it."

Elliot shrugged. "I'm sorry, but if he had a document like that it's news to me." He hesitated. "Sometimes Jerome could be . . . reticent about his personal life."

"I'm beginning to see that," I agreed.

By the final hour of rehearsal, Mercutio, Tybalt, and Romeo had nearly poked each other's eyes out brandishing the swords as Walter tried to choreograph the big fight scene. When Tybalt whirled right instead of left and whacked Walter on the rear end with the flat edge of his sword, Walter decided to call it a night even though it was only ten o'clock. I'd already buttonholed Chrystal about the dress rehearsal schedule and had listened to her lament on the budget. She'd managed to find a compromise on the principles' costumes and had agreed to settle for cheaper, and slightly less authentic, undergarments. Who would know anyway?

It had been a long day and I was exhausted. Even my skin was tired. I offered to drop Lola off at home since her Lexus was in the shop again—I thanked the stars for my sturdy Metro—and things seemed to be cooling a tad with Walter. Lola stopped to speak to Elliot, and, as she turned to go, he gave her a brief hug. Hmmm . . .

Chapter 17

L ola slammed my car door shut. "Could we drive to Belvidere on the way to my house? I have a book I'd like to put in the overnight library drop. It's due tomorrow."

Since budget cutbacks had started last year, the library now closed at eight on weeknights.

"Sure. But do they really check that kind of stuff?"

"I had a five-dollar fine last year."

I remembered Jerome's overdue copy of Sherlock Holmes. I wondered if Mrs. Everly had bothered to return it.

We rode down Amber a few blocks, and I turned right onto Belvidere. The street, like most of the others in Etonville at this time of the night, was dark, lit only by a handful of streetlights and a haze of ambient light from the moon.

I drove past the entrance to the Etonville Public Library, where the windows were transparent in the dark, and coasted through the parking lot to the far corner of the building, where the book depository was located. Security lights illuminated this side of the lot, where an asphalt paver and a backhoe had spent the day blacktopping.

Lola grabbed the door handle. "I'll just be a second." She hopped from the car and stepped ten feet to the library wall.

Idly tapping the steering wheel as I waited, I glanced out the car window, past where Lola was standing, and detected a sliver of light that leaked out from a lower-level window. Odd, I thought, when everything else was dark. Then the light disappeared. *Maybe it was my imagination.*

"Done. I can check that off my list," Lola said as she slid onto the seat.

"Did you see that light?"

"What light?"

I pointed into the inky night. "There. Just beyond where you were standing."

Lola stared through the windshield. "I didn't see anything."

I put the car in drive, turned the corner of the building, and slowly proceeded to follow the wall of the library. We passed a bank of lower-level windows, all of them dark. "I could have sworn I saw a light."

"The library's been closed for hours. Who would be working there this late?"

I reached the end of the north wall and was about to turn left when I saw a broken window.

"Look. The glass is shattered," I said.

"Probably some kid with a rock."

I jammed the car into park and peered into the first floor. I debated getting out and investigating. All that was left of the window was a series of jagged splinters outlining the metal frame. I flicked on my cell phone flashlight. The circulation desk was visible. I knew the layout: to the right of the desk was a conference room, to the left, a reading room. Behind it a hallway with smaller meeting rooms and the computer area where I talked with Mildred. All was quiet.

"Maybe somebody broke in," I said and clicked off my flashlight.

"Another robbery?" Lola asked.

I turned off the engine. "I'll call Bill." But before I could access recent calls a door creaked open, then shut at the back of the building.

"What was that?" Lola whispered.

"Shh."

There was a moment of silence; then a figure emerged from the shadows along the library wall. We bent down to avoid detection. My heart stopped in my mouth and Lola closed her eyes. All was still for a moment. Then the soft tread of shoes hitting pavement reached our ears.

"Maybe I should follow him." I started to move, but Lola grabbed the back of my jacket. "Dodie, no! Wait for the police."

From down the block, a car engine hummed to life.

I called Bill's cell number.

"Chief Thompson," a voice said wearily.

"Bill? It's Dodie. Lola and I are at the library, and there's been a break-in—"

His voice grew alert. "Where are you exactly?"

"In the car."

"Stay put. I'm on my way."

Bill arrived first, in his personal automobile—a late-model BMW, who knew?—and walked over to my Metro. "Are you two okay?"

"We're fine," I said.

"Tell me what you saw."

I described the broken window and the fleeing figure and the car motor.

"Stay here while I take a look around." He switched on his flashlight and started for the building.

"I'm coming with you," I called out and opened the door.

Bill stopped. "I'll signal you when the place is secure."

"But—"

He took off.

Suddenly, Mildred pulled up behind us in a modest compact car. "What's going on? The police department called Luther, and Luther called me."

"Someone broke into the library," I said.

"We heard him run away," Lola added.

"Bill . . . Chief Thompson is investigating right now."

Luther Adams arrived in an ancient Cadillac. He was a little man with beady eyes and pursed lips. I'd only crossed his path once before at an ELT opening night reception. Benny had spilled fruit punch on his white bucks. He had not been pleased. We filled Luther in and waited around for what seemed like forever until Bill returned.

"Chief, I'm Luther Adams, the director of the library."

"Mr. Adams, it looks like someone broke into the lower level."

"This is horrible. Just horrible," Mildred said, holding back tears.

"Could you follow me to turn on the lights?"

"Of course."

Mildred and I went along, and Lola stayed in the car.

Luther unlocked the front door and turned on the lights. The first floor was untouched, and the upstairs stacks were not disturbed. The lower level was another matter. The shelves of the media room were empty as though someone had run his arm down every aisle and swept all of the contents onto the floor, but the special collections area had been hit the hardest. Rare and oversized books were scattered about the room; some were opened with spines bent and broken. A locked case had been shattered, shards of glass everywhere, and the most valuable of the library's holdings flung with total disregard into a pile that formed a mini-volcano. A handful of brown boxes had been stomped on.

"Who could have done this?" Mildred said, then bent down to turn a chair right side up.

"Please don't touch anything until we've had a chance to dust for fingerprints in the morning," Bill said.

Mildred straightened up quickly. "Sorry."

Bill called Ralph to come to the library and cordon off the crime scene.

"What can we do?" Luther asked. "Nothing like this has ever happened before."

"My team will secure the area. In the morning, after we've investigated the scene, we'll need a complete inventory of anything that is missing. Right now, there's nothing you can do. I suggest you return to your homes."

That included Lola and me, I guess.

Mildred and Luther thanked Bill, but decided to hang around until they could lock up.

Meanwhile, Bill took my official statement. "What were you doing here so late at night?"

"Like I said, Lola had to return a book in the night depository. Then I noticed a light in the lower level and saw the broken window. I heard the perpetrator—"

Bill cocked his head.

"A back door opened and closed. I saw a figure and then heard him running away."

"Can you describe the figure?"

"Sorry. It was dark. It looked like a male, though."

"Was he carrying anything?"

I shrugged. "Not that I could see."

"And then?"

"We heard the engine of a car down the block."

"Is that everything?"

"Yes, that's everything," I said simply.

"Okay. Good."

"Whoever it was could have taken some of those first editions and sold them for a lot of money," I said.

Bill nodded.

"So maybe it wasn't books they were after."

Ralph's squad car arrived, lights flashing, houses on all sides of the library lit up. But it was late and only a few people briefly viewed the proceedings from their porches. I could visualize what the town would do with tonight's events.

"Oh, Chief," Mildred said, blotting her eyes, "Who would want to harm these precious books?"

Mildred was childless so the prized volumes in special collections were like offspring, to be cherished and well cared for. I knew how she felt. I had a thing for old-fashioned paper and binding. I couldn't get into Nooks and Kindles.

"I don't know, Mrs. Tower, but we're going to do our best to find out," Bill said and gave her a brief, sympathetic smile.

"Mildred, did you see anybody strange wandering around the library recently?" I asked.

I could feel the heat from Bill's eyes even before I turned to see his frown. I might be overstepping my bounds, I knew, but someone had to plunge in here.

"I can't say I have. But there are so many people coming and going in the library. You know, even with the budget cuts and closing early and eliminating programs and staff, there's still more happening than we can handle. I warned Luther."

"About—?"

"About what?" Bill said simultaneously. He whipped around to face me. "Do you mind if I do my job?"

I stepped back. "No problem."

"Now, Mrs. Tower," Bill said with a trace of irritation, "what do you mean?"

"Well, we've had new donations from estate sales and some William Carlos Williams items for our New Jersey authors' shelf, and well . . . we can't keep up with everything. I'm not sure exactly what the holdings are in the special collections."

"Isn't anyone in charge of curating the collection?"

Mildred's voice dropped. "Not since Mary left. I told Luther that letting her go would be a disaster." She teared up again. "And I was right.

How are we going to take an inventory of what's missing? There are boxes of books that have not been catalogued."

I couldn't help myself. "Who is Mary?" The little hairs were dancing.

"Mary Robinson. The special collections librarian."

Bill was either oblivious or doing his best to ignore my rising excitement. "And where did she go?" I asked.

Mildred turned up her nose in disgust. "Luther downsized her. Said he had to let some staff go. Budget decreases. She was devastated, poor dear." She crossed her arms. "But he kept his personal secretary. If you ask me—"

"Mary. Robinson. MR. The mystery lady." I could barely contain myself. "I don't think we ever met. Could you describe her?"

"Mary? She was seventyish." Mildred smiled. "But a young seventy. Gray hair . . ."

"Which she often wore in a French twist?" I asked.

"Yes, as a matter of fact. Why do you ask?"

I turned to Bill. "She fits the description of the woman with Jerome."

"Jerome Angleton? Who was murdered?" Mildred asked, eyes round.

"Mildred, did Jerome ever visit Mary here? Were they friends?"

"I couldn't say. Remember, I told you that Jerome came here to use the computer."

"Right."

"Sometimes he stopped down in the special collections."

"To see Mary?"

"Not exactly to see Mary, I wouldn't think. More like the classic first editions down here. He was a retired English teacher, you know. Mary was very knowledgeable about the collection."

"Would you know whether they socialized outside of work?"

Mildred's laugh was a gentle tinkle. "Oh, goodness no. Mary didn't date, as she told me many times. She had her two cats, her nieces and nephews in New York somewhere, three of them, and the special collections. She tended to keep to herself."

"Where is she now?" I asked.

"I don't know. I think she left town. The last time I saw her was the day Luther informed her that she was let go."

* * *

We sat in my Metro in front of Lola's house. It was twelve-fifteen, already the next day. "I feel sorry for both of them. Jerome and Mary Robinson."

Lola stifled a yawn. "It's been quite a night. And my feet are killing me." She removed one espadrille and massaged her toes. "Poor Jerome. He had it bad for a woman who was only into cats and books and relatives."

"We don't know the whole story. Maybe Mildred was wrong. Maybe he and Mary *were* dating. Jerome was very discreet. Mary sounds like she was, too. He spent a lot of money on jewelry. That has to mean something."

"He was a thoughtful guy," Lola said.

"I wonder what happened to the gold bracelet he bought at Sadlers in Creston," I mused.

"I'll bet Mary Robinson's got it. I'll bet she turned over a new leaf, started to see Jerome, fell in love. . . ." Lola said helpfully.

"I'd like to think so, for both their sakes," I said. "I don't know, it just doesn't add up. There's something missing."

Lola squeezed my arm. "I have to go in and collapse. Big night tomorrow. We run Act I. I am spending the whole day with the script."

I gave her a hug. "Thanks for being around tonight."

I stayed put until Lola was in the house, the door locked and the upstairs lights switched on. Then I drove carefully home, one eye out for the sinister SUV, and wracked my tired brain about how all this was connected to Jerome's murder—if at all.

Chapter 18

I overslept, unusual for me, and awoke groggy, one eye slit open sufficiently to read my alarm: eight-thirty. My sinuses felt stuffed and my throat scratchy. I burrowed back under the covers and refused to face the day. I was feeling emotionally hungover after the library break-in—thrilled to discover MR, but disheartened about the missing pieces in the whole investigation. I couldn't shake the idea that Mary Robinson held the key to it all. I sneezed.

On days like this, I tended to force my way upright with the promise of a caramel macchiato, or maybe fresh pastries from Georgette's Bakery. But neither was enticing me to hit the shower this morning. I stared at the ceiling and noticed the thread of a crack that ran diagonally from one corner of the room to another. *I need to contact my landlord*, I thought and—

The audible vibration of my cell phone, still plugged into its charger on the bureau, got me up and I grabbed it.

"Hello?" I rasped.

"Dodie, are you all right?" Carol, at least, was hard at work, given the racket in the background.

"I might be getting a cold."

"From last night? We heard about the library break-in. You must have been terrified."

"Well, Lola and I weren't really in danger—"

"You saw his face, right?"

"I—what? No, I—"

"Annie Walsh said he was over six feet tall—"

"She what?"

"—and had a bushy beard—"

"Carol, stop!"

"What's wrong?"

I closed my eyes. I could not face Etonville today. Not Snippets, not the Windjammer, and certainly not the Etonville Little Theatre where *Romeo and Juliet* was being thrashed into life.

"Nothing. It's all rumors. It was too dark to see anything. No one knows anything at this point."

"I should have known. Annie does have a tendency to exaggerate."

"I'm just going to take it easy today. Maybe I'll call in sick," I said.

"That sounds like a good idea. Drink some orange juice and pop a few echinacea tabs. Do you need some?"

"No, thanks."

"I'll let you go then."

"Okay. Thanks for calling." I was grouchy but also grateful. I had good friends who checked in on me. "By the way, did you know Mary Robinson? She used to work at the library."

"Sure. Quiet, reserved, a bit old-fashioned. I remember cutting her hair on occasion. Always the same cut. No color. But the last time she came in she said she wanted a new look. Something younger. She never came back. I hope she finds another good salon in Poughkeepsie."

My dancing hairs started to tingle. "Poughkeepsie?"

"That's where her nephew lived."

"How do you know?"

"One of my customers played bridge with her. But that was a while ago. In recent years, I think she mostly kept to herself."

I was coming to life, blood rushing through my veins, the top of my head quivering, back in business.

"I'd like to find Mary and ask about Jerome. I understand they were friends."

"You can find anyone on the Internet," Carol said.

"True," I said. "Gotta' go."

I hummed as I showered and planned my strategy for the day. First, a call to Henry to tell him I wouldn't be in today. Then, a call to Lola to see how she was doing and let her down easy: I would not be wrangling Penny, actors, or Walter tonight. They were on their own. Then, I'd visit Bill.

Best laid plans.

Benny was out with a sick kid but would be in for the dinner rush. I sucked it up and told Henry I'd cover the bar and register during lunch, fuming at fate that interrupted my well-conceived schemes.

Lola panicked when I called and begged me to see a part of rehearsal. At least Cheney Brothers' delivery showed up on time and complete; they'd been good as gold since my gentle reprimand.

I had an hour to hit the Etonville Police Department before I had to be at the Windjammer. I walked past the lobby display in the Municipal Building and turned down the hallway to Bill's office. I hurried past Edna's dispatch window, thinking I might escape detection. No such luck.

"Dodie, that was real brave of you last night," Edna said efficiently.

"It was really just an accident that Lola and I were even at the library."

"Still, you called it in. A 459."

"I'll bet that's a break-in."

"Yep. Burglary. Don't know if it's a 10-29F or 10-29M. Felony or misdemeanor. Depends on the damages."

"Is the chief in?"

"Yes." Edna's line buzzed and she waved good-bye. I continued down the hallway and paused by Suki Shung's cubicle. "Is the chief busy?" I asked.

"I'll see." Suki looked up from her console and studied me coolly, her expression solemn as always.

"Thanks."

She pressed a button. "Chief, Dodie's here."

"Okay. Send her in."

I walked into his office. Bill looked like he needed sleep, too; he had dark rings under his eyes, the lids heavy.

"So far no usable prints from the special collections room," he said before I even asked.

"The perp probably used gloves," I said.

He cocked an eyebrow at my vocabulary. "Probably."

"So I've got new information," I said.

Bill's mouth curved up a little and he inclined his head. "Is this going to take a while?"

"Well, I have to be at work . . ." I glanced at my watch. "In half an hour."

He rapped a pencil against the top of his desk. "How about we talk later?"

"When later? I'm at the Windjammer 'til three and then I have some things to do at home. . . . And then at rehearsal for part of the night."

Bill nodded and leaned back in his chair, hands atop his head. His shirt tightened, considerably highlighting his pecs. "Let me take you out to dinner. Kind of a thank-you. We could talk then."

Was this what I thought it was? "Well, I . . ."

"I have to work late. How's eight-thirty? That give you time to get all of Shakespeare's ducks in a row?"

"Make it nine. Just to be sure."

"Done. What about La Famiglia? Ever eat there?"

Uh-oh. I'd be eating with the enemy.

"I like Italian. What about you?" he asked.

I'd only done take-out once from La Famiglia. "Fine."

"Good. Meet you there at nine."

I settled in at my kitchen table to find Robinsons in Poughkeepsie, New York. I was banking on one of her nieces or nephews having the same last name. I started with the White Pages and then progressed to a few social media websites.

As I worked, my mind was on dinner. I took a break, stretched, then crossed to the front door and stared out at my lush, green lawn, the result of a rainy spring. What was I going to wear tonight? This would be the first time Bill and I had even attempted anything re-motely resembling a social activity. It wasn't *really* a date. Still, I wanted to look my best. Maybe my white dress with the kitten heels?

I went back to work and focused on Mary. I got a couple of names in Poughkeepsie itself. But also a bunch in other towns, too, like New Paltz, Red Hook, and Garrison. I spent the next hour calling every Robinson I could find in a twenty-mile radius of Poughkeep-sie. No one answered at ten of the residences, so I left messages, seven or eight had never heard of a Mary Robinson, and one lonely soul tried to keep me on the line and convince me to buy Girl Scout cookies.

There had to be some way to find her, but it was not going to hap-pen today. I had to get ready for my "meeting" with Bill after the the-ater, anyway.

* * *

I took a sip of my wine—an expensive bottle of an Italian cabernet that Bill chose from an extensive wine list. "You seem to know your way around reds," I said.

"I'm an Italian foodie and I read the *Wine Spectator*."

It was hard to concentrate on the menu once I laid eyes on Bill. He had replaced his uniform with a black shirt, open at the throat, gray slacks, and a pale gray mohair blazer. The aftershave was a scent I didn't recognize, something woodsy and minty at the same time. His face had a fresh-scrubbed shine, the brush cut of his straw-colored hair neatly combed.

"You look nice," he said, assessing my appearance.

"Thanks." My auburn hair hung loosely to my shoulders, and I wore my white, sleeveless knit sheath, cut respectably low in front, that fell softly from waist to hem. I'd bought it for a wedding last year that I'd never attended because the engagement was called off, and I had been dying to take it for a spin.

From our corner table, I looked around the candlelit dining room of La Famiglia, a dozen tables, most full, occupied with folks I didn't recognize. This was not the Windjammer crowd; maybe out-of-town patrons. Still, a good gathering for a Wednesday night. The atmosphere was warm, inviting, and altogether cozy.

I felt the urge to slip out of my Jimmy Choo knock-offs.

"So how is everything in *Romeo and Juliet* land?" he asked, his lip curve in action.

"Well, let's see. Walter is in a frenzy because the ELT can't afford a full-blown second-story balcony, and when he tried to substitute a ten-foot ladder, Romeo threw a hissy fit because he's angoraphobic—"

"Don't you mean—?"

"Acrophobic. Sorry. It's a Penny-ism. If Walter's in turmoil, so is Lola, and Penny just stands around with her clipboard. Oh, and the Nurse quit because her granddaughter had a baby so Edna is stepping in."

"Yeah, she informed me," he said. "The department won't be the same until this show is over." He speared a piece of radicchio in his green salad.

"At least she's sane and happy. She and Elliot and a few others. It's the grumblers who are driving Walter crazy." I poured buttermilk dressing on my own leafy greens.

The waiter arrived with our entrees—Bill went with a traditional eggplant parmigiana and I chose sautéed scallops with a butternut squash caponata. They melted in my mouth; Henry would die to have this on our menu. I wondered who supplied their seafood.

"There's something in here that's just . . . wonderful," I said.

"I'll bet it's the rosemary, raisins, caper combination. Mixture of the sweet and tart," Bill said.

"I'm impressed."

"I've had it here before," he said.

"You're a loyal customer?"

"Hey, a guy can eat in two restaurants, you know?" His eyes crinkled as he dunked a bit of Italian bread in herb-infused olive oil. "So. How did you get from business management to the Windjammer?"

"By way of a lovely beach restaurant whose owner was a laid-back old surfer bum. We specialized in ocean breezes and barefoot dining. It was rated a top pick on the Jersey Shore."

"Sounds like a great job."

"The days and nights were grueling during the summer season, but the patrons were fun and you couldn't beat the location."

"How long were you there?" he asked.

"The shore? All my life. Bigelow's . . . five years."

"Until . . . ?"

"A fifteen-foot elm landed on the roof of my house. Hurricane Sandy," I said.

"Sorry to hear that. No family?" he asked.

"My parents live in Florida and my younger brother Andy's in California. I miss them."

"I know what you mean." Bill smiled regretfully.

I wondered who he was missing.

"You traded fundamentals of accounting . . ."

"And finance and blah blah blah for a career managing restaurants from burger joints to seafood shops to Bigelow's. After my internship at a restaurant in Philadelphia. Of course I'd spent my summers waitressing down the shore so I was already food-friendly."

"And now Etonville," he said.

"It beats being a desk jockey with my nose to a computer screen surrounded by Excel spreadsheets."

Bill frowned. "That sounds like my job some days."

"But not every day, right? I mean, look, it's exciting about Mary Robinson, yes?"

"Well . . ."

"Now that it's confirmed she and Jerome were friends, or at least acquaintances, it makes sense they might have had a meeting planned for four-sixteen."

"Confirmed? Makes sense?" Bill set his fork down and took a sip of his wine.

"There's the sheet of paper and the envelope I found in the box office, both with the initials MR. It appears as if Jerome had a get-together of some kind on the calendar for the day after he died."

"So you think they were involved."

"He bought a diamond ring and a gold bracelet. I'd say that's pretty serious." The wine was going to my head. It made me courageous. "Did you find anything interesting in Jerome's checking account?"

The vino must have had the same effect on Bill because he answered without a beat. "Nothing much in his checking account, a couple thousand in savings."

"Oh."

"But his credit card was another matter. He'd racked up about three thousand in bills over the last two months. A pattern that was significantly different than the previous twelve months."

I let loose a low whistle. "So something was going on. What else was he buying?"

"Women's accessories. Jewelry. Sadlers and elsewhere."

"Aha!" I said.

"We can't jump to conclusions," he warned me. "But . . . it does look as though something in his life changed."

"You heard Mildred. Jerome spent time in the special collections. I think he was interested in more than the books."

Bill shrugged. "Possibly."

"Jerome read popular mysteries and thrillers. We liked the same authors. Not the kind of books you find in the special collections."

"Even if it were true, what's the connection with the murder?"

"That's what I haven't figured out yet," I said, breaking off a piece of crusty Italian bread. "I did find out that Mary's nephew lived in Poughkeepsie."

Bill opened his mouth, then closed it. "How did you—?"

"Snippets." I grinned. "Don't underestimate the power of the hair salon. Gossip central."

"Well, I'll be. . . ."

"I've been searching for Robinsons in the Poughkeepsie area. Nothing yet, but—"

He shook his head and laughed. "Great work, but keep me—"

"Posted. I know."

We chewed over the rest of the case along with the last of our meals. I hated to see my scallops disappear.

"By the way, the lab guys identified some stuff on Jerome's pants. It was a synthetic substance, a type of polymer."

The synthetic latex I'd overheard Suki mention outside Bill's office. "Really?"

"Yeah. An acrylic casting resin used to create rubber objects. Like tires. "

"That sounds like a factory material. Maybe the resin had been on his pants for a while."

Bill shook his head. "They said it was fresh. Hardened, but fresh. Recent."

"All of this evidence is like having nothing but consonants in a Scrabble game," I said.

"Meaning?"

"Each of the tiles is valuable, but—"

Bill cut me off. "Taken together, they don't add up if there are no—"

"Vowels," I finished.

Bill insisted on ordering dessert: tiramisu for him and peach gelato for me. We emptied our coffee cups in companionable silence; I was feeling really relaxed, stuffed, but definitely wound down. Before I could think too much about the advisability of potentially ruining a lovely evening, I decided to tiptoe into deeper waters. "I've been meaning to tell you something all night."

His body shifted slowly from tranquil to tense, shoulders hunching forward, hands interlaced in front of his jaw to form an inverted V. After all, I could be introducing any one of a number of matters: personal, theatrical, criminal.

"And what's that?" he asked.

Suddenly I wasn't as confident of the reception I might receive when Bill knew about Jerome's email. But it was too late. The wine had loosened my tongue, and my body felt rubbery and vulnerable.

"Remember when I said it would be a good idea to see who Jerome might be communicating with because if it was an MR, or somebody else, then maybe we could find out what led to his murder?"

"Go on."

"So I got Jerome's email address from his audition sheet—"

"The audition sheets. Yes. Penny delivered them to me."

"Right, well, I was able to get into his account and discovered something interesting. It looks like—"

The waiter set the bill on the table discreetly and we both fell silent. Bill inserted a credit card into the pocket of the folder, barely glancing at the total, and handed it back to the young man. He lowered his voice.

"How did you get access to his email?"

"I had the address and then got the password—"

The waiter returned the sales slip and credit card, and Bill scratched out a tip and total. "You mean you hacked his private account?"

"I guess you could say that. After all, he's not around to complain about his privacy."

"That's not the point."

"But isn't it more important to know what I found? Jerome was corresponding with a company called Forensic Document Services. They deal in rare documents. It's got to have something to do with—"

"Hacking into someone's email is a serious offense."

"I know. But it won't interfere with the investigation. It's just a lead."

Bill scoffed. "You have absolutely no respect for my office, do you?"

"I have respect for you. But I don't get it. You're not curious about what I found?"

"I can't use evidence obtained illegally, Dodie," he said firmly.

"It's not evidence. It's just some information. Do you want to solve Jerome's murder or don't you? Simple as that."

"Nothing's simple where you're concerned," he said.

We sat in a tense silence for a moment.

"Look, I'm sorry." He rubbed his hand across the top of his head, placing the spikes of his brush cut at various angles to his scalp. "But it's frustrating. Trying to play by the book when someone is thwarting your every move."

"I'm thwarting your every move?"

"I didn't mean it that way," he said.

"I'm just trying to help solve a murder." I could feel my mouth clamped shut, tight across my face.

"And I get that, but there is protocol that needs to be followed." His voice softened. "I've been through this before. I left a department that was full of corruption and had never heard the words 'by the book.' I don't want any part of that."

So what I'd surmised from the Internet article was right. A scandal in Philadelphia law enforcement had sent Bill running straight to Etonville.

"I understand protocol. But I want to find out who murdered Jerome." I took a pen and a scrap of paper out of my purse, and wrote, *Forensic Document Services. fdsnj@gmail.* "Jerome was corresponding with a Marshall Wendover." I pushed it across the table. Bill pushed it back.

He stood up peremptorily. "Let's go."

The mood had changed drastically, and I was mentally kicking myself for launching into Jerome's email.

He walked me to my Metro, which was parked next to his BMW, his mouth a straight line with no hint of the playful curve. I got in the car, started the engine, then opened the window. "Thanks for dinner."

"Be careful, Dodie. You're on thin ice."

I put the Metro in gear and pulled out of the lot.

Geez, I thought, *that didn't end well.* The evening was a shambles. Now, Bill felt he couldn't trust me. There was nothing to do but limp home, lick my wounds, and climb into bed with a good book.

I drove the half mile back into Etonville center. When the light at the corner of Islip and Gates turned yellow, I stepped on the gas, calculating how long it would take me to make it through the intersection. I sped through and the light turned red. I glanced in the rearview mirror. I was surprised to see that the vehicle behind me had sped through the light, too. When Islip dead-ended at Anderson Road, I paused at the stop sign and slowly turned left. It was the black SUV. I sat up straighter in my seat and began to pay attention.

My chest thumped. I could see the intersection of Anderson and Main up ahead where the light changed from red to green. I knew I'd be safe if I could beat the SUV through the light and speed down Main to the Etonville Police Department on Amber.

I checked my rearview mirror again. Only the two of us on the street at this hour. I stepped on the gas, and my Metro jerked forward obediently as if it knew I needed help; the SUV kept pace. I tapped on the brakes, slowing down a bit, and the black hulk followed suit. I leaned into the steering wheel, tightening my grasp on the rim, and took deep breaths. My heart and stomach were a trampoline act.

I ignored the traffic light. I pressed the gas pedal and began to turn the wheel hard to the left so I could tear down Main. The angry growl of the SUV's engine erupted into the night. It swerved around me, barely missing my front bumper. We were like two graceful athletes, two vehicles making a synchronized turn in tandem. I was on the right, avoiding parked cars and negotiating the correct side of the white line in the middle of the road. The SUV was on the left—in the lane of oncoming traffic. We straddled the center line for two blocks. I had no choice but to keep going, fast. We passed the Windjammer and the theater, and I could see the dimmed lights of Coffee Heaven ahead.

The SUV roared again. It shot past me and veered abruptly into my lane, directly in my path. I jammed on the brakes, and I could feel the car going into a skid that brought me a few feet from the passenger door of the SUV. *This is it*, I thought. It would all end here. I held my breath, half expecting an armed assailant to emerge and make short work of me. The silence lasted seconds but seemed like hours.

Out of nowhere a pickup truck—minus a muffler—rattled down Main behind me. By the time it was within ten yards, the SUV had backed up, then swung around in a wide arc and headed the other way down Main Street. The truck passed me, oblivious.

I forced myself to breathe through my mouth until the blood moved back into my clenched hands. I was shaking and my mind raced. Images, thoughts, what-ifs tumbled helter-skelter, bouncing off each other. What if my Metro had not stopped in time? What if the driver in the other vehicle had jumped out and taken a baseball bat to my windshield? What if he/she had a gun? What if the pickup had not appeared when it had?

I wound down the window and stuck my head out into the night. The temperature had dropped, and an evening breeze blew wisps of damp hair off my neck. This time, the stillness was peaceful, non-threatening.

I leaned back into the headrest, realizing I had been too rattled to get a license number, again. But I also grasped another fact: someone wanted to scare me off the investigation. And they were doing a damn good job, too. I started the engine and drove slowly back home. I could not go to Bill about the SUV again without a license plate number.

I parked on Ames Street near a streetlight instead of in my dark driveway. I checked the neighborhood before I alighted and hurried up the sidewalk to the front door. I tested all door and window locks—dead bolts and chains—and drew the curtains. I lay down on top of the bed just to rest my eyes. In two minutes, I was fast asleep.

Chapter 19

I'd come in early to the Windjammer to work last night out of my system. If I focused firmly on taking inventory and ordering supplies, I might be able to ignore my regret over the spoiled dinner and my terror at being stalked by the SUV.

A half hour after I arrived, Henry trudged in, glanced at me silently, and tied an apron around his middle. I noticed he'd been adding a few extra pounds these last months. Was he eating out of frustration?

"What?" I said.

"Did you enjoy yourself last night?" he asked glumly.

Uh-oh. I decided to bite the bullet. "Yes, as a matter of fact, I did." Which was only partly true.

Henry grumbled and started to unload vegetables from the refrigerator.

"Look, Henry, La Famiglia is just another restaurant. Okay, so they have a . . . different kind of menu. But the Windjammer has its own special character."

Henry wasn't buying it. "Their food was better?"

I could still taste last night's caponata. Henry's specials were tasty and sometimes a trifle experimental, but for pure culinary sophistication, one couldn't beat La Famiglia. And that was bad news for the Windjammer.

"Of course not. This is silly." I remembered Bill's defense. "People can dine in two restaurants. You have regulars who I'll bet have never eaten at La Famiglia."

"What did you have?"

"Uh, just . . . a scallop dish. With squash."

Henry stopped slicing eggplant and looked up with interest. "Scallops and squash?"

"Butternut squash." I said carefully, and filled in a requisition. "I've got shrimp on the order. Didn't you talk about some Asian fusion dish . . . ?"

"With spicy fruit salsa."

"Let's put it on the menu for the weekend."

He nodded, not completely over my treason, but at least he had a battle plan that included a new experiment with seafood.

Gillian had the dining room under control so I planted myself by the cash register to handle take-out orders. At noon, Edna bounded in, a frown replacing her usual cheerful demeanor.

"Hi, Edna, let me get your order."

"Dodie, I wish you had stayed for the entire rehearsal last night," she said without preamble.

"How did it go?" I said.

"Okay for the first hour. But then all hell broke loose."

I stopped in my tracks. "What?"

"Walter kept stopping the run through and giving notes which frustrated just about everyone, especially Lola, and Elliot just up and confronted Walter."

"Polite Elliot?" After Jerome, he seemed the next most gracious member of the ELT.

"Yep. The two of them got into it." She gave me the eyeball.

"What about?"

"Elliot said Walter left something to be desired as a director of Shakespeare—"

"Oh no."

"And then Walter said Elliot only came back because he had no place else to go and was a bust in Pittsburgh and if it hadn't been for Jerome, Elliot would never have been a member of the ELT."

"What does that mean?"

Edna dropped her voice. "Walter never liked Elliot. I think he was a little, you know . . ."

"Competitive?"

"Uh-huh. And word was, Jerome persuaded Walter to cast Elliot time after time."

"Jerome persuaded . . . ?" I thought it would have been Lola who had pushed to have Walter include Elliot.

"And then people wanted Elliot to direct and Walter got his ego bent out of shape and then suddenly Elliot up and left," she whispered. "He says he had a business opportunity two years ago, but I think it was Walter who drove him away."

"Wow. I'm surprised he agreed to do *Romeo and Juliet* after all that."

"Well, I guess it was a tribute to Jerome," she said.

"I suppose."

I'd have to call Lola and get more details. I could only guess what would happen tonight. I rang up Edna's order and made change; she said good-bye and left.

Benny dunked glasses in soapy water. "I heard Henry's beside himself."

"Someone must have seen me in La Famiglia last night with Chief Thompson," I said.

"No private life in this town." Benny gestured for me to come closer. "How was it? The food, I mean."

"I had sautéed scallops with butternut squash caponata." I closed my eyes. "It was to die for."

"Awesome." Benny sighed. "The specialty here was pot roast. Good pot roast but still . . ."

"I know what you mean." My cell phone rang and I hit ANSWER.

"Dodie?"

"Hi, Lola."

"Did you hear?" she asked.

"From Edna, yeah. Whatever possessed the two of them to slug it out in the middle of rehearsal?"

"I don't know. Walter *was* over the top with notes this early on. Romeo said he was treating the cast like puppets and everybody was getting frustrated."

"But Elliot? He seems so easygoing. Above the fray."

"I thought so, too. I guess Walter just pushed one too many buttons with him." She paused. "To tell you the truth, Elliot only said what others were thinking. But Walter is under a ton of stress and calling out the director of a show like that, well, it's just not done. Not at the ELT. Not anywhere."

"Then Walter fired back, right?"

"Oh, I think he really hurt Elliot's feelings. You should have seen his face. Like all of the air went out of a balloon."

"So where does that leave the show?" I had images of Walter and Elliot dueling it out with the *R and J* swords.

"Walter cancelled rehearsal for tonight but we're supposed to start staging Act III tomorrow."

"I'll drop in."

At three, I was ready for my break and some heavy thinking. I opted for fresh air instead of Henry's homemade soup. I took my jacket off the hook by the door and walked briskly down the street. After fifteen minutes, I passed Betty's Boutique, Coffee Heaven—avoiding the temptation to settle into a booth with a caramel macchiato—and the Unitarian church. I went another couple of blocks before I stopped to lean on a picket fence that outlined the property of one of Etonville's quaint, eighteenth-century houses. Early spring rituals were under way as landscapers cut grass and trimmed bushes despite the rumble of thunder off somewhere north of Etonville. Normally, the pungent smell of fresh-cut grass made me feel happy. Summer was definitely on its way. But today I was distracted and needed to focus my mind.

I sat down on the curb. Bill was right. He was the police chief; I had no business one-upping him as he tried to do his job. But I felt I owed something to Jerome, regardless of how illogical that seemed. One thing was clear: I could not call his office until I had something tangible to bring to him. Like information on Forensic Document Services. It was a cinch Bill would not pursue this angle if he thought information was obtained illegally. But I had so such qualms.

I turned out the lights and locked up. The Windjammer had been fairly empty the last couple of hours; a few ELT regulars showed up, tight-lipped and weary-looking. At home, I changed into comfortable sweats and fuzzy slippers, poured myself a glass of chardonnay, and hunkered down with my laptop. There had to be a way to locate Forensic Document Services. I began with the assumption that it was a New Jersey business, and if it had a New Jersey business license it had to be registered with the State Department of the Treasury.

I scanned state websites for information on registering a corporation.

After twenty minutes, I found the "New Jersey corporation and business entity database." I could do a name search! I followed the steps outlined and entered Forensic Document Services on the line indicated. Seconds later I had my answer: a business registered in that name had a filing date of September 2010 and a location in Piscataway, New Jersey. I stared at the screen. I couldn't believe it. I called information and received a phone number. Tomorrow, I planned on calling it and requesting a meeting with Marshall Wendover.

I felt giddy. The little hairs danced and my heart pounded. Needless to say, I was awake for hours.

Just when I thought things had calmed down with Henry, I had to hold his hand, figuratively, in the kitchen. He was peeved at a review for La Famiglia in the *Etonville Standard*. The food and service had received four stars, and the chef's specialties—roasted red bell pepper pasta and, my favorite, scallops with butternut squash caponata—were described as "superb." I had to agree.

To make matters worse, La Famiglia had taken out a half-page ad touting its stars and quoting the review. Last year, the Windjammer earned three stars. The rivalry was taking a toll on Henry's mood.

"I don't care what ratings La Famiglia earned, no one can beat your homemade soups," I said encouragingly.

"I never get four stars," he griped.

"It's the *Etonville Standard*, for Pete's sake. Who cares what they think?" I didn't have to wait for an answer. Henry cared. "Look, let's get that Asian fusion dish on the menu, and what about the gourmet stew you were thinking about?"

Henry shrugged. "Maybe I need to throw out the entire menu and start over," he said dramatically.

Geez.

I still had half an hour until the lunch crowd would appear. I slipped outside and sat in my Metro to get a little privacy as I tapped out the number for Forensic Document Services. The phone rang five times before a gravelly voice spoke.

"Hello?"

"Is this Forensic Document Services?" I asked.

"Who's calling?"

"Mr. Wendover . . . ?"

"That's me."

"My name is Dodie O'Dell, and I'm calling because my uncle, Jerome Angleton, passed away recently and I'm trying to tie up some of his . . . business affairs." I waited for some response.

"Okay," he said.

"I understand he was in touch with you about a document that he wanted authenticated?"

"I'd, uh, have to check my records," he said.

"Would I be able to meet with you? I have a few questions—" I said.

Another phone rang in the background. "I'm not sure what I could tell you," he said reluctantly.

"I'd appreciate just a few minutes of your time," I said as vulnerably as I could.

"Well, I got a busy schedule. . . ."

"How is the day after tomorrow? In the morning?"

If he refused to see me, what was plan B?

"Okay. Eleven."

Marshall Wendover gave me his address and made it clear that he could squeeze me in for only a few minutes.

Back in the Windjammer, I confirmed the week's menus, checked the meat locker, took an accounting of fresh vegetables, and inventoried the bar. Lunch was well under way so I retreated to my back booth and studied the spreadsheet with staff schedules while I scooped up a spoonful of Henry's crab bisque.

"What do you recommend?"

I looked up into Elliot's tanned, handsome face. "Sloppy Joes with parmesan-cheese chips are the special. I hear they're going fast. And of course the crab bisque," I said, smiling.

"May I join you?" he asked, glancing at the array of paper in front of me.

"Sure." I folded the printout and set it aside.

"I hope I'm not interrupting important work."

"Staff schedules. I spend my life arranging other people's time. Here, next door . . ."

"Ah yes. Well, the theater needs your organizational skills."

I cocked my head as though weighing my judgment of his appearance. "You don't look half bad for someone who barely escaped a fistfight."

Elliot's sense of humor was still intact. "I could have taken Walter in two rounds."

"Lola said what you did just 'isn't done.' Criticizing the director in front of the cast," I said.

Elliot shrugged. "Someone needed to say it."

"What's going to happen now? The show must go on, right?"

"We'll all traipse in tonight, pick up our scripts, hit our marks, and pretend the other night never happened."

Gillian came over and took Elliot's order. He settled on the bisque.

"How is the murder investigation proceeding? I hear the town gossip at rehearsal, and it sounds like you've been busy."

"You know the rumor mill."

"Yes, but the burglary at the library was real."

Gillian brought Elliot's lunch and a table setting wrapped in a black cloth napkin. "Here you go. Enjoy."

I thought about Mary Robinson and Forensic Document Services. "I think there should be a break in the case soon," I said, with more confidence than I felt.

"Really?" Elliot paused, his soup spoon half way to his mouth.

"There are some leads."

"Oh? So the chief is on top of things?" Elliot continued to eat.

"Yes, I think so."

"Well, that is good news," Elliot said. "You asked about Jerome's love life the other day . . . ?" He smiled mischievously.

"Did you remember something?"

"It's not much, but I think that Jerome might have been seeing someone."

"How do you know? Did he mention anyone?"

"Not directly. You know Jerome . . . little cagey about himself. But he referred to a 'friend' the last time we spoke. I got the feeling he wasn't talking about a guy he shared a beer with. If you know what I mean." He laughed.

I certainly did. "When was this?"

Elliot put his soup spoon on the dish and thought. "Possibly February."

"Just a couple of months ago." I paused. "Maybe I'm mistaken, but I thought you said you hadn't spoken with Jerome in quite a while."

"Did I? I don't remember that." He smiled again and finished his lunch.

Was there anything else Elliot had neglected to mention about Jerome?

I finished the restaurant schedules and looked over tonight's rehearsal plan. My cell clanged.

"Hi, Carol," I said.

"Dodie, Pauli just texted me. He said he would be a few minutes late."

"No problem. I'll be here. Can you ask him to bring his camera?" I wanted to add a picture from the herb garden out back. Henry had an extensive array of herb pots—rosemary, basil, thyme, chives, parsley, cilantro—on a patch of ground behind the restaurant. It had a kind of English garden, idyllic vibe and would give the Windjammer a country feel.

"Of course."

"Will you be at rehearsal tonight? Lola mentioned something about hair and wigs," I said.

"I have to work 'til seven but I could stop by afterward and pick up Pauli, too," Carol said.

"Great. I'll feed him dinner."

It was four o'clock by the time Pauli got out of school and picked up his digital camera. "Do you want to see your website," Pauli asked eagerly, sucking back a Coke and barbecue potato chips.

"Sure. But let me get Henry." Henry could use a pick-me-up, and the website might be just the medicine he needed.

We stood over his shoulder as Pauli unveiled the site like it was a gourmet meal. He was busting his buttons with delight. And he had every right. The Windjammer had never looked so good! The dining room appeared welcoming, the menus mouthwatering, and the pictures from the street made the place look almost stylish. *Eat your heart out, La Famiglia*, I thought. "This is wonderful, Pauli. Right Henry?"

"Yeah." Henry looked pleased and scanned the pages as Pauli pointed out a few required bits of editing here and there.

Pauli's eyes glittered. "We really crushed it."

He'd done a beautiful job with the website, and the Windjammer came off looking appetizing and classy.

"Let me know what I owe you, Pauli," Henry said, patting the kid on the back before he headed off to the kitchen.

Pauli and I stood on the back stoop of the Windjammer. Next door was the ELT. Its loading dock was still framed in yellow crime scene tape. On either side of the dock was an extra-large garbage can with the debris of the scene shop: pieces of lumber, some old plaster board, paint buckets. Midway between the two cans were the faded remains of the white chalk outline where Jerome's body had lain.

I averted my eyes and forced myself to study the patch of ground that Henry used as his garden. The entire area was about six square yards, with a brick walkway surrounding a plot of land now overgrown with an assortment of weeds. The perimeter was outlined with a wire fence to discourage grazing critters. Henry had only recently moved his herb pots from the kitchen to outdoors; it would be a few weeks before he planted the herbs in the ground.

"Looks like Henry needs to do some work here," I said and pulled a tall stalk of common pigweed that was threatening to take over. In the corners of the yard, dandelions poked their heads through cracks in the brick pathway. Altogether, the herb garden was not the most photogenic site.

Pauli gazed through the viewfinder as he meandered around the yard and checked out angles.

"Do you see any possibilities here?" I asked doubtfully.

"Uh-huh." Pauli snapped photos, standing, lying down, facing the restaurant, and facing the alley behind the restaurant that served as a back entrance to a row of houses and businesses.

I walked around, trying to find different points of view. Following Pauli's lead, I sat on the ground looking up at a forty-five degree angle through the spiny stems of the rosemary plants. "Pauli, come look here. Maybe you can sharpen the rosemary in the foreground, and blur the back wall of the theater."

Pauli duly marched over and plopped himself down beside me. He clicked off picture after picture, then scooted on his butt a few feet right and left to capture the lacy sprigs of the parsley and the rich green plumpness of the basil leaves.

"Awesome," he said.

I leaned back on my arms and closed my eyes while he worked and absorbed the warmth of the late afternoon sun. My mind wandered to this morning's phone call with Marshall Wendover. What did he know that he wasn't saying?

"Uh, Dodie?"

I squinted. "Yeah?"

"I think I have enough."

I brushed off my hands and shifted my weight forward to stand up. I looked up and over the garden to the ELT as I got to my feet. "I didn't notice that before," I said.

"What?" Pauli was busy scrutinizing his handiwork.

"That window," I said.

Pauli glanced up. "It's broken," he said.

A second-floor window at the back of the theater had been punched out. All that remained was the serrated outline of a large hole. Reminded me of the library.

"I'll bet no one even knows about it. We've had some heavy rains lately. I hope nothing important got wet," I said.

Pauli nodded to be polite and tucked his camera into its case.

"Thanks for your work on the website, Pauli."

He shrugged. "Okay."

"And thanks for your work on that other . . . project."

Pauli grinned. "Piece of cake."

Chapter 20

The atmosphere in the theater was much as Elliot had predicted: businesslike and professional, with one additional element. Uneasiness had permeated the rehearsal, and I could sense folks waiting for the other shoe to fall. Elliot was his charming, jovial self, Lola's smile flickered like a flashlight with a failing battery, and Walter was grim-faced. Nevertheless, the show had to go on.

Pauli, sprawled in the last row of the house with his laptop, edited the Windjammer web page while I doodled thoughts on theme food. When Lola took a break, I intended to ask her about the rooms upstairs and check out the broken window.

"Hi, Dodie," Carol said, panting as she sank into a seat beside me. "Long day?"

"I had four perms, five colors, and seven cuts. I was there by myself for four hours. Two of my girls are still out sick. I think something is going around," she said as Pauli sneezed.

She raised her voice. "Pauli!"

He removed his iPod earbuds.

"Take the echinacea when you get home."

He grunted an assent.

Walter called the cast to the stage, delivered some general notes about professionalism and learning lines, and continued to stage Act III, pushing actors around the set and having them mimic his line readings. Romeo was right about one thing. Walter was making the cast look like puppets.

Lola crept up the aisle and whispered, "Let's go to the dressing room. I have the makeup sheets and hair notes there."

Carol pulled herself upright. "Pauli, stay here. We'll go home in a few minutes."

He nodded.

We followed Lola down the aisle and onto the far right side of the stage, trying to create as little disturbance as possible. We needn't have worried. Walter was lying on the floor prostrate with grief as he demonstrated Juliet receiving the news that Romeo had killed Tybalt. The Nurse—the bearer of the bad tidings—wrung her hands and wailed. Edna was having a ball overacting and Lola grimaced. "Oh, brother."

Carol opened a door at the back of the stage that led to a green room and two decent-sized dressing rooms, one for men and one for women. Lola unlocked the women's and flicked on the lights, a series of bulbs outlining mirrors mounted above a counter that could accommodate half a dozen actors. Across the room was a corresponding set-up.

Lola and Carol bent their heads over sketches of hairdos and makeup.

"What's upstairs?" I asked Lola. "I'd like to check out the rooms. Are they locked?"

"Why?"

"Today when Pauli and I were out in the herb garden behind the Windjammer I noticed that there's a broken window on the second floor. Somebody should check out any damage."

"All right, there's not much up there. A prop shop, some storage, nothing else. I wonder how a window got broken." Lola pulled out a key. "Here's the master," she said. "It will lock or unlock all of the doors in the theater."

"Thanks."

"The light is at the top of the stairs," Lola said.

"Got it."

Lola and Carol resumed their conversation as I stepped into the hallway and faced a flight of stairs that led to the second floor. Though I'd been under the stage in the costume shop, I'd never been above the stage. The propped-open dressing room door sent a shaft of light onto the first few steps. At the top of the steps, a short hallway was flanked by doors at either end. I flipped on a wall switch and nothing happened. I tried a few more times for good luck, but again, nada. I pulled my cell phone out of my pocket and hit the flashlight app.

I stood still to get my bearings. The door to my left was marked

STORAGE, and when I unlocked the door and peeked in, I saw racks of costumes and dozens of boxes stacked floor to ceiling, but no broken window. The Windjammer would be to my right, I reasoned. I unlocked the door at the other end of the hall. It was unmarked but had to be the prop shop.

Inside the dusky interior, the room was spooky. An odd collection of objects used in previous ELT productions filled shelves: kitchen utensils, bottles of every shape and size, shelves of books, several dolls with scary, painted features, bouquets of fake flowers in dirty glass vases, and three cowboy hats. The room gave off the odor of mold, and the floor was grimy. It needed a good cleaning. A large center table, marked up and gouged, was obviously the construction area. On it were a hot glue gun, a stapler, and containers of fluids.

I directed my flashlight at the far wall and lit a small bank of windows; the middle one had a large hole in the center of the pane. I moved to the wall and was about to reach for the window frame when my foot crunched shards of glass. I had been thinking kids had thrown a baseball or a rock. But if someone had thrown an object at the glass from the outside, a substantial number of broken pieces should have been on the floor. But they weren't; there were only a few fragments. *Maybe the window was broken from the inside*, I thought.

I waved my light around the walls and floor more carefully to see what I might have missed on first entering. I bent down. There were lighter, cleaner square patches on the floor, the same size as the table legs. The table had been moved. Something was wrong here. The air was stifling and oppressive, and I felt like I couldn't get my breath. The room began to whirl and I dropped my cell. I put out a hand to steady myself, grabbing a shelf of books, and volumes tumbled down, clattering to the floor and creating a pile at my feet. I stooped to retrieve my flashlight. Burrowing my hand in the heap of books, I pulled a paperback from where it was hidden partway under the bottom shelf of the bookcase. I felt the hairs on my neck rise.

"Dodie, are you okay?" Lola said from the doorway.

She and Carol had heard the noise and came up to see me sitting on a mound of books, speechless. I held up the paperback: it was Cindy Collins's latest mystery, *Murder One and a Half.* Jerome had been reading it the night of auditions.

"What is it?" Carol chimed in.

I tried to fan the pages open, but they stuck together, held in place by a thick, hardened, dark splotch of something. My hands shook.

"Dodie, talk to me." Lola entered the room and stood above me.

"I think I know where Jerome died."

Theatrical scoop lights saturated the prop shop with a harsh brilliance to help the crime scene investigation unit do its work. Ralph was standing guard at the bottom of the stairs leading to the upper hallway, and Suki was assisting the CSI team.

I sat on the top step with a container of caramel macchiato that Carol insisted on buying for me. Downstairs, it was chaos, according to Lola. Once I had called Bill, Lola had stopped rehearsal, much to Walter's irritation, and informed everyone that the police would soon be at the theater—again. The actors had taken the occasion to cut out, and Penny was flapping her arms and nudging her glasses, trying to maintain order. Fat chance.

"You doing okay?" Bill asked me quietly.

I nodded and sipped my drink. "I think so."

"That was some skillful detection out in the herb garden."

"Just an accident," I said.

He frowned. "Could have taken us months to discover this place."

I had the feeling he was speaking about himself, maybe kicking himself for not having the entire theater thoroughly searched.

"Do you think there's other evidence in the room besides the book?" Unaccountably, I had begun to shiver despite the fact that the upstairs was warm. Bill gave me his jacket.

"Even though the murderer obviously cleaned up well, there are always microscopic traces of blood they miss. But the book is a major find."

"What was the dark stuff on it?" I asked, even though I was pretty sure I knew the answer.

"We'll take it to the lab to check it out."

"Chief?" Suki poked her head out the prop shop door.

Bill followed Suki into the prop room. From below, I could see Lola moving up the steps.

"Oh, it's all too much," she said and sat down beside me.

I put an arm around her shoulders. "At least I didn't have to watch rehearsal." I tried to lighten the mood.

"Dodie, that's not even funny. Things are going haywire. With the police here and Walter freaking out and actors insecure, I'm think-ing we should cancel the show."

"You can't do that, can you?"

"The ELT has never done it, that's for certain." She shook her head. "It could mean the end for Walter. That and the missing money."

The missing money made me think about a thousand dollars, which made me think about the documents service. I whispered, "You know how I told you about Pauli and me in Jerome's email?"

"Yes. And the document company."

"I made an appointment to go there."

Lola grabbed my arm. "You did? When?"

"Tomorrow. Don't say anything about this to anyone. I haven't even told Bill."

"Why not?"

"When I mentioned Jerome's email over dinner, Bill went a little crazy because of the hacking. Illegal, etc."

"Oh. But maybe he'll think differently now that you've found out where Jerome was murdered."

"Maybe. But I want to have something definite to give to him."

"Mum's the word," Lola said.

Bill walked into the hallway holding one of the containers that had been on the table, now in a plastic evidence bag. "Looks like a nail in the coffin. So to speak." He held it up. "Liquid polyurethane."

"Jerome used that to make props. You create a mold and then pour it in. It's like rubber," Lola said. "He'd made firearms and stat-ues and all kinds of things."

"When the lab guys examine this, I have a feeling it's going to match resin that was on Jerome's trousers."

"So he was definitely murdered here?" I asked.

"Looks like it," Bill said.

"And the broken window?"

"It's preliminary but the fracture pattern is consistent with gun-shots. A weapon was probably fired in there. We'll check out the ground outside beneath the window."

Carol took Pauli home and Lola and I hung around for another hour, waiting to see what other secrets the prop room revealed. But aside from numerous evidence bags with wood splinters from the floor and bookcase, and samples of dirt from various surfaces, there was little else to report.

I said good-night to Bill, and we trudged down the stairs. Walter was in his office, his head in his hands, bent over the prompt book. For once, Penny was not at his heels, waiting to do his bidding.

"Walter, I'm going," Lola said simply.

Walter looked up, dark rings under his puffy eyes, his face slack and ashen. *Romeo and Juliet*—and possibly Jerome's murder investigation—had taken a substantial toll on him. "Walter, are you all right?" I asked.

He looked at me as if I were crazy. "Of course not," he said and began the litany of rehearsal crises. Walter did have a lot on his mind, but much of it was his own doing. Not that I thought he was capable of seeing the truth.

"Are they finished upstairs?" he asked.

"Still at it," I said. "Do you want me to hang around and lock up? I'm pretty wired and doubt I'll get to sleep anytime soon. Besides, tomorrow is my day off."

Lola shot me a look of pure gratitude. "That would be thoughtful, wouldn't it, Walter?"

He nodded numbly.

"Come on, Walter, let's go home. Thanks, Dodie." She smiled and held Walter's jacket for him. I watched the two of them walk out, Lola's arm around his shoulders.

I had two options. I could lounge inside the theater or sit in Walter's office, the holy of holies. He must have been really disconcerted about the evening's events to let me stay here alone. I gazed at the interior of the office. In addition to the props and costume pieces piled on each of the two desks, there were now a handful of foils leaning into one corner, a lady's hoop skirt in another, and three two-by-fours stacked up against the drawers of a filing cabinet. All of this *Romeo and Juliet* paraphernalia was more evidence that Walter was juggling too much, trying to negotiate rehearsal and scenery and costumes.

I sat at his desk and pulled some blank sheets of paper from a wire mesh basket marked SCRAP. Maybe I could analyze his budget and find money somewhere for a real balcony and Elizabethan underwear. I knew Walter was a little sloppy when it came to bookkeeping, but I'd seen him stash a file in the top drawer of the desk when he thought no one was watching.

I assumed the desk was locked, but no harm in giving it a try. To my amazement, the drawer opened, revealing a compartment filled to the brim with papers, old programs, pencil stubs, ball point pens that didn't write, and assorted rubber bands and paper clips stuck in place by a sticky brown gunk which I recognized as spilled coffee. On top of the debris, a manila folder was jammed into a thin slice of space. I withdrew the file and shut the drawer. It closed halfway, then refused to budge. *Geez.* A half-open drawer would be a dead give-away that I had been snooping. I yanked and pushed and jiggled for a few minutes, then decided to start from scratch. I pulled the drawer out and off its tracks. When I'd removed the file initially, I must have inadvertently shoved something that slipped down behind the drawer.

I reached into the open space. My fingertips just barely touched an object, but it was too far back for me to grasp it. I got down on my knees and angled my body so that my arm extended another inch or two into the drawer space. Now I came in contact with the offending item. It was hard and smooth. Glass, I imagined. I cautiously traced its outline.

"What are you doing down there?"

"Arghhh!" I yelled and turned my head to see Bill at the entrance to Walter's office. "Don't creep up on me like that."

"Sorry," he said. "Why is your arm inside the desk?"

"There's something blocking the drawer," I said between gritted teeth.

I extended my fingers and shifted the object just enough to be able to grasp its sides. "It's a bottle." I withdrew an empty pint of alcohol and studied the label. "Chivas Regal."

"Walter was drinking on the job?" asked Bill.

"Walter doesn't drink. But this was the only liquor Jerome drank."

Bill's eyes constricted. "Where's Walter?"

"He left with Lola a few minutes ago. I sent him home to sleep and said I'd lock up."

He reached for the bottle. "I'd better take it. Have CSI guys check it out at the lab. I'll give Walter a call in the morning."

"I can't believe that Walter would have had anything to do with . . ." I stopped myself from finishing the thought.

"We're done upstairs. Do you need a ride home?" he asked kindly.

I shook my head. "I'm good."

"How about I follow you home? You've had a . . . busy night."

"Thanks, but I'm okay. Really." I forced a smile, my face muscles worn out.

Bill stared at me. "Come on. I'll be right behind you."

I was too tired to argue.

He hesitated. "About the other night . . ."

"I get it. No problem."

I locked up, Bill trailing behind me as I tested the door handles to make sure all was secure. I waved good-bye, climbed into my Metro, and pulled out of my parking spot. Bill's cruiser kept pace until I turned into my driveway; then he waited until I was in the house before he drove off.

Chapter 21

If I thought Etonville was abuzz over the break-ins, it was nothing compared to the hullabaloo that erupted the next morning. I was awake half the night, and when I finally nodded off, I dreamed of a large black hole, like a swimming pool, that I dove into, completely unaware of what I would hit when I landed. Exactly how I felt upon awakening and remembering the events of the previous evening. Jerome dying at the theater and the future of the ELT in question. The only comforting thought was that I had the day off. Benny would take over as assistant manager and handle the bar. Gillian and Carmen would take care of the dining room.

The appointment at Forensic Document Services was at eleven so I had a couple of hours to relax yet. My head was still firmly planted on my pillow when my cell phone vibrated. I closed my eyes and toyed with the notion of pretending to be asleep. But curiosity got the better of me and I rolled out of bed. "Hello?"

"Hi, this is Maggie Hemplemeyer from the *Etonville Standard*."

"Who?"

"I'm writing about the Jerome Angleton murder at the ELT."

I blinked my eyes and tried to clear my head.

"I understand that you discovered where Jerome was murdered."

"Not really. I mean, it's still—"

"Look, we know about how you found the broken window and the book in the attic and the liquor bottle."

"I think you should talk with the police department before you—"

"The *Standard* already published a story on the ELT being the location of the murder. Just hit the stands. I'm talking about a follow-up article. Kind of a human interest thing. You know, local gal thwarts crime spree."

Huh? "Maggie, I'll get back to you."

"But—?"

I clicked off for one second and it buzzed again. I answered without looking at the screen. "Look, I told you . . ."

"Dodie, it's Carol. I'm looking at the paper. What's going on?"

"What's the headline?"

"Windjammer Manager Locates the Scene of the Crime."

"Okay."

"The subheading is 'Artistic Director's Involvement Questioned.' It says you found a Scotch bottle in Walter's desk drawer that belonged to Jerome?"

"I found the bottle, but I'm not sure what it says about Walter's involvement."

"Just a minute, Dodie." I could hear a tumble of voices in the background; Snippets must be beside itself. "Okay, okay, I'll ask her." Then a rustling on the receiver. "The shampoo girls are wondering if they will arrest Walter?"

"Carol, I have to go."

"Okay. I'll check in later."

I was about to jump in the shower when my phone dinged with a text. "Are you up? Call if you are." It was Lola. I punched in her number.

"The town's going berserk. You wouldn't believe what people are saying," she said. "What happened after we left?" She sounded scared and upset.

"I found an empty pint bottle of Chivas Regal in Walter's desk."

"Walter didn't drink," she said.

"But Jerome did and that was his brand, and he was almost legally drunk the night he died."

"What was it doing there?" she asked.

"I don't know. I was getting the show budget out of the desk drawer and—"

"You were what?"

"Whatever. The drawer stuck, and when I took it out to see what the problem was, I found the liquor bottle shoved in the back," I said.

There was silence while Lola processed everything.

"This is a nightmare. One problem after another."

"Lola, Bill took the bottle to be checked out by the CSI unit. But it probably means nothing."

She hesitated. "I've been troubled by Walter lately. His financial issues, the way he's been treating the cast, his fighting with Elliot. But I would never think he'd . . . have anything to do with Jerome's death."

"There's no point in jumping to conclusions," I said hastily. "There has to be a logical explanation. Bill is going to speak with him this morning."

"This seems so trivial, but I guess we should think about the show," she said.

"Maybe Walter needs an assistant."

"He knew Shakespeare was going to be a challenge, but he wanted to put the Etonville Little Theatre on the map," Lola said.

It was on the map all right.

I let the hot water ping on my face and cascade down my body. How had things gotten this out of control? I forced myself to step out of the shower, towel off, and dress. It was 10 AM when I backed my Metro out of my yard and onto Ames Street. Across the way, my neighbor Mrs. Dugan waved and smiled her approval. She'd obviously seen the paper. I was a reluctant local celebrity, starting to feel as if the citizens of Etonville needed to get a life.

I craved the anonymity I'd enjoyed down the shore. Too many people and too much happening there for anyone to care what I did with my time. Of course, I hadn't been smack in the middle of a murder investigation. After my appointment this morning, I had to make a decision. To tell Bill what I'd learned or not. My great aunt Maureen called indecision the graveyard of good intentions. I didn't want to end up with my name on a tombstone.

Piscataway, New Jersey was a forty-five-minute ride from Etonville by way of the Garden State Parkway, U.S. 1, and 287 North. It was a large township by New Jersey standards, fifty thousand people and a mix of ethnicities, with a full range of suburban neighborhoods, corporate parks, strip mall businesses, and light industry. I'd had a couple of occasions to visit Piscataway when I was in college and dating a guy from Rutgers University whose family lived there. I spent an agonizing Thanksgiving around a formal dining room table listening to conservative political ranting. We split up by Christmas.

Even with traffic on Route 1 and 287, I arrived on time at ten-fifty-five. Forensic Document Services was located on a busy street a mile outside downtown Piscataway. Set back a hundred feet from the road, the office was a single-story, yellow-sided building, modest in appearance, with a row of parking spaces adjacent to the front entrance. I pulled into an empty space and shut down the engine.

I entered a reception area—really just a row of red molded plastic chairs and a matching coffee table covered with *People*, *Time*, and *Car Mechanics*. There was a reception desk, but it was unoccupied.

I wasn't sure what I had expected, maybe something a little more refined, academic, or artsy. After all, the business was probably dealing with historical documents, books, and other printed materials. From the look of things, this could be the generic DIY office of an accountant, credit counselor, or small-time lawyer. Maybe even a private investigator. I could hear a voice rising and falling from somewhere further inside the building.

"Hello. Anybody here?" I called out.

There was a scuffling from a hallway behind the desk. A bald, overweight guy in the middle of a cell phone call rolled himself out of a room in an office chair and waved for me to come on back. I followed the man in the chair to an office on the left.

"Jay, Marshall here. Woody had a stroke last night. Yeah. Too bad. Right. Anyway, you need to send Harry to Plainfield to cover for him, and tell Marge to get out of Edison and go to New Brunswick. When she gets there, she can send Al to Jersey City. What?" He glanced at me and waved to two chairs, one of which was buried in files and papers. I sat down on the other one.

I saw a series of business cards slotted in a holder on his desk: besides Forensic Document Services, there was ABC Trucking and Sam's Auto Body Repair.

"Listen to me," he yelled into his cell. "We can't afford to wait and see if Woody survives this. I mean, we all want him to, of course, but meantime, chop chop. Get on the horn and get this stuff in motion." Marshall clicked off. "Sorry. Busy morning. Can I get you something?" He stuck his head out the door. "Angela?"

"She's not here yet," I said.

168 • *Suzanne Trauth*

"Hard to get good help. Even if it is your sister-in-law." He giggled in the high-pitched titter of a young girl. "So?"

"As I mentioned on the phone, I'm Dodie O'Dell. My uncle was Jerome Angleton." I waited to see any flicker of recognition. Nada. Marshall pursed his lips and crossed his arms on his ample chest. "Maybe you heard about his death? He was murdered in Etonville two weeks ago."

"Murdered? I don't know nothing about any murder."

"Well, I'm following up on his business affairs . . . after his untimely passing."

"Uh-huh."

"And I noticed that he was in email communication with you about a document."

Marshall blinked. "What kind of document?"

"I'm not sure," I said. "There were four emails from February 20 through April 12."

"Uh-huh."

"I reviewed the correspondence. It looks like he was interested in hiring your company to do an authentication."

"Maybe." Marshall tilted his head, then stared up at the ceiling. Thinking. "I might remember the guy. Seemed to me he was asking about prices and how authentic our authentication service was, and how long it would take."

"There wasn't any specific information about the process or the cost—"

"Look, we never say too much in an email. I don't trust the Internet and some of the stuff we work on is very valuable, if you know what I mean." He giggled again.

"You didn't meet with him?" I asked.

"Nope. Only contact was through email."

"So you never found out what the document was?" I asked.

He shrugged. "Never thought he was serious. Every once in a while we get a joker who cleans out an attic and thinks we're *Antiques Roadshow*. Just wants free information." He leaned in. "I'm not in the business of handing out freebies."

I nodded at the business cards. "You're in a lot of businesses," I said and smiled.

Marshall studied me. "You could say that."

I looked around. "So is this where the authentication process happens? Testing paper and dating the ink?"

Marshall barked a short laugh, this one from his gut. "Nah, that's done in Woodland Park. My brother runs the lab."

"Interesting mix of companies. A document service and a car repair."

Marshall squinted at me. "And trucking. And a few others." His cell rang and he examined the caller ID. "Anything else? I need to take this," he said in a hurry.

"Could I get the name and address of the lab? Maybe your brother's contact information?"

"Hang on, Jay." Marshall grabbed a business card stamped with FORENSIC DOCUMENT SERVICES and scribbled a phone number on the back. "That's Morty's office number. But he won't be able to tell you anything. Like I said, we never made personal contact with the guy."

I took the card. "Thanks."

He waved good-bye. As I moved down the hallway, I could hear Marshall shriek into the phone, "Jay, Jay, I don't care what Woody's wife wants. Business is business."

Charming guy, I thought as I exited the building. I wondered if he was on the level. If he was telling the truth about not meeting with Jerome. Or if his brother knew anything.

I took my time driving back to Etonville. The temperature was rising so I wound down the window to let the gusts of warm air circulate through my Metro. I felt elated that I'd made an actual connection between Jerome and the document service but disappointed that I'd gotten so little information. Nothing, really, that I hadn't known before. Other than the fact that Marshall's brother was responsible for the actual authentication in another location.

My stomach growled, reminding me that I had bypassed breakfast and almost missed the lunch hour. A stop at Coffee Heaven was in order. I left my Metro in a parking space and walked the half block to the corner of Amber and Main. I pushed on the glass door with the OPEN sign displayed prominently and was greeted by a wall of noise. The place was full—which meant that I would probably have to sit at the counter.

Jocelyn looked up from pouring coffee for a customer and gave me a big grin. "Dodie!"

Her voice was loud and it reverberated around the diner. Within seconds, the room went still as people twisted in their seats and looked to the door, where I stood like a deer in the headlights. Then, one by one, they started to applaud. One thing you had to say about Etonville: it was a grateful town.

I nodded self-consciously, slipped onto a stool, and picked up a menu as the clapping died down.

"Coffee's on the house," Jocelyn said. "You're a regular hero, investigating that prop place and finding that liquor bottle." She leaned in close. "Tell me, did Walter have anything to do with it? I always thought he had shifty eyes."

"I think the chief's still investigating," I said softly. "And I'll take two eggs over easy."

"Gotcha," she said.

As I waited for my food I texted Lola to see how she was doing. I was feeling bad for Walter. I couldn't imagine he'd had anything to do with Jerome's murder, even if he was nipping at the box office till.

Ten minutes later, Lola called my cell.

"Where are you?" she asked.

"Coffee Heaven, having a late breakfast."

"Can you talk?"

A large woman on my right was borrowing half of the stool next to me, in addition to her own, and the man on my left had tilted his upper body forty-five degrees so that his armpit was dangerously close to my whole wheat toast. "Let me call you back in a few."

"I'm calling an emergency meeting at the ELT," she said dramatically. "Me, Elliot, Penny, you, I hope, and Walter, of course. Elliot said he could make it by four o'clock."

"I'll be there. And calm down, okay?"

"Oh, how did your meeting go? Did you find out anything about Jerome?" she asked.

I switched my phone to the other ear and leaned down over my eggs. "Nothing much."

I clicked off as Jocelyn sidled up. "More coffee, hon?"

I smiled my thanks. I thought about all the problems at the ELT. Then Jerome's murder. In my mind, I was an official unofficial part of the investigation. Maybe something would develop from my meeting with Forensic Document Services. And then there was Bill. . . .

I picked up my check—minus the cost of the coffee—and slipped a tip under my plate. I was headed for the cash register when my cell rang again. It was Bill.

"Hi," I said cautiously.

"Dodie, can you stop by the station this afternoon?" He sounded weary.

"Did you get any sleep?"

"Not much."

"Sure. I'm leaving Coffee Heaven now."

"Thanks."

The Municipal Building was hopping. Two crime scene techs I recognized from last night passed me on the way to Edna's dispatch window.

"Dodie, you're the toast of the town today," Edna said as she answered a 911 call and held up her hand for me to wait.

"Mrs. Parker, you're going to have to get that husband of yours to find Missy. Did you check up in the tree? We're just too busy today. We have more important things to do. Good luck." She cut Mrs. Parker off. "Dodie, I'm worried about the play. If Walter is . . . incapacitated, who's going to direct us?" she asked plaintively.

"I don't know, Edna," I said honestly.

"It's my first real role. I've been tweeting my relatives from Pennsylvania about rehearsals."

"You're on Twitter?"

"I'd hate to have to uninvite them."

She looked sad and I felt sad for her. Closing down *Romeo and Juliet* would be a shame. "Let's just see what happens, okay?"

Edna nodded as her switchboard lit up again. "Go right in," she said and went back to her calls.

I knocked on Bill's door, and when I heard "Enter," I did.

He was on his walkie-talkie. "Suki?" He waited. "Come in. This is base to squad one." He waited some more.

"Chief, Suki here."

"Did you find Ralph?"

"Eating lunch."

"Get him on the road. They're filling potholes over on Anderson and he's on traffic duty."

"Copy that."

"He can take his lunch with him," Bill said.

"10-4."

I sat down then. "Have you seen the paper?"

Bill nodded and exhaled heavily. "Sorry you were targeted. I don't know where they get their information. I spoke with someone early this morning, but all I gave them were the absolute facts. No theories."

"If you're not talking and neither is Suki . . ."

Bill shook his head.

"That leaves the crime scene unit—"

"They're on loan from the state police and don't have a dog in this hunt."

"And Ralph?" I asked.

Bill looked surprised, then stern, and finally resigned. "I'll have a word with him."

"So what are the facts?"

Bill leaned back in his chair. "Traces of blood on the floor and table in the prop room matched Jerome's type, and the resin on his trousers was similar to what we found in there."

"So it gives us the location of the murder. Isn't that good news?"

"Yes, but finding that bottle of booze complicates matters. I spoke with Walter this morning."

"What did he tell you?" I asked, almost afraid to hear Bill continue.

"Apparently shortly after Lola left the night Jerome died, Walter went into the lobby to turn out the lights and he heard a noise in the box office. When he knocked on the door, Jerome opened it."

"Jerome—? So he hadn't left the theater?"

"He was drinking from the bottle, somewhat inebriated and clearly agitated, according to Walter. When Walter questioned him about being in the box office at that hour, Jerome said he had a meeting in the theater and that Walter should mind his own business. That's when things got testy."

"Oh no."

"Oh, yeah. Jerome confronted Walter about the missing money and threatened to go to the board. Walter came clean with me about his borrowing from the till."

Uh-oh.

"I think there was a little shoving and pushing, and Walter took the liquor as evidence of Jerome's irresponsibility. Maybe get him kicked out of the ELT."

"It's true there was no love lost between them these last months. But why didn't Walter come forward?"

Bill shrugged his shoulders. "He doesn't know why. Didn't have any reason."

"And the bottle?"

"He *says* he forgot about it the first time we questioned him."

That's hard to believe.

I sat in stunned silence. "At least we know Jerome was planning on meeting someone in the theater. What does this mean for Walter?"

"Technically, he's now a person of interest."

"Meaning?"

"He's not a suspect, but he had information that might impact the investigation," Bill said.

My mind played through a catalogue of investigative themes gleaned from my mystery novel fixation. Opportunity and motivation were at the top of the list. Walter certainly had the former. "What was his motivation?"

"Money? He admitted he was deeply in the red because of his alimony. Jerome was the only one who suspected him of embezzling from the theater."

"And his alibi?"

"Questionable. He said he watched Jerome leave the theater and then he stashed the bottle in his desk. But he can't prove he left the theater when he said he did. There are no witnesses. When I thought the murder took place elsewhere, that wasn't an issue. But now that we know it occurred in the prop room. . . ." He drummed his fingers on the desk.

"So now what? Do you arrest him?" I asked tentatively.

"No, but we'll be bringing him back for more questioning. I want to interview the cast and anyone else who was at the theater the night Jerome died. It's possible someone saw or heard something at the auditions."

"Guess those sheets Penny gave you will turn out to be helpful after all." I slouched in my chair. It was depressing news for Walter and Lola and the ELT. I wanted to climb back into bed and pull a blanket over my head. "Thanks for the update."

"Thanks for the interest you've taken in the case." He hesitated. "Let's keep each other posted on any developments."

"Will do." I turned to leave. "And thanks for trusting me."

"No problem . . . partner."

Chapter 22

Bill called me his "partner." I was feeling guilt as well as indecision. Still, I could not tell him about my meeting this morning without raising the issue of my hacking Jerome's email. Would he continue to think of me as a partner if he found out I was investigating on my own?

I forced my attention back to Lola.

"Cancelling the show is not on the table," Lola said firmly, her posture diva-like and imperious. "I've thought it through and discussed it with the board. We agreed that it just is not in the best interests of the theater."

We'd sat ourselves on stage around a large banquet table, hemming and hawing for twenty minutes, ignoring the elephant in the room—Walter—and throwing out thoughts about *Romeo and Juliet's* progress.

"We've only got three weeks," Elliot said carefully.

"You've done it before, right, Walter? Remember *Dames at Sea* and the kid who broke his leg and had to dance with a crutch?" Penny punched Walter lightly on the upper arm, but he didn't respond.

Since we'd arrived, Walter had sat glumly, silently, picking at his beard and propping up his head with a closed fist. If it was possible, he looked even worse than last night. The usually meticulous artistic director wore wrinkled clothes and sported tousled hair.

"Why ask me anything? Just go ahead and make all of my decisions for me!" he groused.

"Walter, we all sympathize with your . . . situation, but we have to think of the company. We're all in this together." Lola's color heightened, and two red splotches formed on her cheeks.

The tension felt like a shroud that enveloped all of us. Penny pushed her glasses up her nose and tapped a pencil on her clipboard.

Elliot concentrated on a crease in his trousers, and Lola studied her nails. I had been silent so far. Partly because I was distracted by last night's events and partly because Walter knew who had discovered the liquor bottle in his desk drawer. He'd been staring daggers at me. I cleared my throat. "We need a plan of action."

"Yes, Dodie, good thinking," Lola nodded. "What did you have in mind?"

"Well, you've basically staged everything, right, Walter?" I said. Walter nodded forlornly.

"What needs the most work?" I asked.

"Tonight we're working with Romeo, Juliet, and the Nurse," Penny said. "But everybody needs help with lines."

"Since most of the cast will be available, maybe we can put some of them to work catching up with the set and costumes. Chrystal needs help in the shop so, Lola, why don't you gather a few folks and get them to work there tonight?"

"That is an excellent idea, Dodie," Lola said with relief.

"Walter, if you can rehearse someplace else part of the night . . ."

"You can run lines in the dressing room," Lola said.

"Penny, you might want to get a crew in here to paint the Verona backdrop. JC was complaining about having time on the stage last week," I added.

Penny bobbed her head.

"I'll text other actors and see if I can get them to come in and run lines for a few hours. When they're not working with me, they can help with costumes or painting," Elliot said.

"Thank you, Elliot," Lola murmured. "Walter?"

"Fine," he said grudgingly.

The meeting ended with Penny going into high gear on her set assignment, and Lola and Elliot working on rehearsal details with their heads together. Walter watched, offering a suggestion periodically. I signaled my exit and left. Since I was next door to the Windjammer, I elected to stick my head in, though it was still my day off. The dinner service was in full swing, the dining room loud, Gillian bouncing from customer to customer, and Carmen bussing tables.

Benny, frazzled, bounded past me, five plates balanced on his tray. "Great day to be off," he muttered and practically dove onto a table.

Copies of the *Etonville Standard* were on many tables, and a few people saw me and poked dinner companions. I rushed to the kitchen and hid behind the swinging door. Henry looked up and shook his head.

"Don't say it," I said.

Benny crashed into the door. "Those Banger sisters are bonkers. Know what they said?" He grabbed three burgers and fries and two bowls of chicken soup.

"I'm afraid to hear."

"They heard Jerome was dating Walter's ex-wife. That's why he shot him."

"Now that at least would make sense," I said.

By six-thirty, the cast and crews were sorted out: Walter had the use of the stage for two hours, after which JC and a few actors would be painting; Lola and Chrystal had gathered a costume crew and were noses to the grindstone with seam rippers and sewing machines. I much preferred to pretend to use a needle sitting down, than paint a backdrop of Verona on my hands and knees. So I offered to join them for a while.

After several hours, we had altered a stack of rented bodices, nipped and tucked to fit the ELT cast, and worked our way through the Ladies' skirts, hemming each with a hot glue gun—more efficient said Chrystal. Though most of the crew had gone by ten-thirty, Lola struggled with pleated strips of starched muslin, trying to create the folds of a fan, for the Elizabethan ruff Walter insisted on wearing. Carol dug through the theater's stock of boots to see if there was anything of use. I had pricked my finger for the fifth time.

"Has anyone seen my bag?" I asked. I was sure I had brought it with me from the house to the basement shop.

Carol pulled her head out of a cardboard box and wiped dust off her hands. "I don't think anyone has been in these shoes since *Little Mary Sunshine*."

"Two years ago? Really?" Lola looked under her bolt of muslin. "I don't see it, Dodie."

"Guess I left it upstairs." I slipped off a stool, stretched my back, and headed for the door.

"While you're up there, would you ask Walter for some petty cash? Chrystal needs about fifty dollars," Lola said.

I stopped. "Are you sure we should disturb him?"

"Of course. Chrystal needs to do some thrift shopping tomorrow." Lola was taking no prisoners this evening.

I climbed the stairs that led from the underground costume shop to the backstage. I opened the fire door expecting a bustle of activity, but I was met with silence. The house lights were off and the only illumination was provided by the security light stage right. Apparently the scene crew had decided to call it a night. I bent over to check out a half-painted pastoral vista of Verona, spread out across the upstage floor. Good work, I thought.

I stepped carefully around the backdrop and into the house, found my bag in Row D where I had left it, and, relieved, walked up the aisle. In the lobby my eyes adjusted to the darkness broken only by the light that outlined the edges of Walter's office door. I knocked gently.

"Walter?" I heard a creak and a slam.

"Who is it?" he asked abruptly.

"Dodie."

After a moment's hesitation, Walter's shoes clomped as he moved to the door and unlocked it.

"Yes?" he said through a two-inch crack.

"Chrystal needs some petty cash. Fifty dollars."

He stared balefully at me and, for the first time, I actually felt sorry for him.

"I'll get the money. Wait here." He shut the door in my face.

I put my ear to the wood and could hear nothing. Then the whoosh of the door and his hand inserted into the opening, clutching a fistful of dollars. "Remind Chrystal I need receipts."

"Will do. Walter—?"

The door shut once more.

Clearly there would be no communicating with him tonight. I walked back through the dimly lit theater and my foot hit the edge of the first seat in row A, house right.

"Damn," I said aloud and massaged my ankle.

I climbed onto the stage just as a silhouette moved off to my left behind the security light. Fear surged up my throat and into my mouth. I choked, then called out.

"Lola? Carol?"

The silence was earsplitting. I could go back to find Walter or run to the stairs leading to the costume shop. In that instant, the security light went black. A crash echoed through the empty space, followed by running thumps as someone closed the distance between us. Instinctively, I shoved my arm into the void in front of my face and backed up. I heard heavy breathing, a soft grunt, and then I was roughly thrown aside. As the footsteps retreated, I tried to see who it was, but it was too dark.

I crawled to the stairs leading into the house. I sprinted up the aisle, rebounding off rows of seats, and burst into the lobby. "Walter!" I screamed.

All was quiet. Walter's office was dark and there was no sign of an intruder.

The door into the lobby flew open. I scrambled to assume a fighter's stance. "Arggh!" I shrieked.

The lobby was flooded with light. "Dodie, are you okay? We got worried when you didn't return to the shop. Who turned out the security light?"

"I'm fine." I told them about what happened. "He appeared so quickly."

"What do you think he was after?" Lola asked.

"He was snooping around backstage," I said.

"Where's Walter?" Lola asked.

"He must have left."

Walter's office was secure and the painted backdrop was untouched. Break-ins were becoming too frequent: first Jerome's, then the library, and now the theater. Whoever was prowling around wasn't looking for box-office receipts. He had bigger fish to fry.

"The theater is getting to be a dangerous place," said Lola.

Carol and I nodded.

"Should we call the chief?" Carol asked.

I had my cell phone out. "I'm already on it."

The following morning, I ducked into the theater and saw Bill on stage. He stepped gingerly around the edges of Verona, spread out before him on the stage floor. "Not bad," he said.

"Yes, they do a good job here. But what do I know? I have trouble with paint-by-numbers."

He laughed, then got serious. "So show me where you were," he said.

I walked Bill through my attack, from the shadow on stage smashing the emergency light to pushing me to the ground.

"There doesn't appear to be a forced entry. Someone might have had a key."

"He could have slipped into the theater through the loading dock door after the crew left and Walter was still in his office."

Bill nodded thoughtfully. "They're checking back here, upstairs in the storage and prop rooms again, and downstairs in the scene and costume shops. I doubt the guys will find any prints. The costume shop was ransacked."

"After Lola and Carol came looking for me. It'll take Chrystal a day to straighten up. I wonder where he's going to strike next," I said. "Each place has had a connection to Jerome."

"And since Jerome died in the theater, this seems like the most significant venue," Bill said.

"That's good because I think we've run out of places."

"Yeah," he said. "Come on. We need to write this up and I'll need your statement."

"Did you interview the cast and crew yet?"

"Oh, yeah. I've seen about half the cast so far," he said.

"Anybody notice anything important?"

"If you don't count Benvolio in a snit because Romeo read twice while he only got to read once, and a Lady-in-Waiting angry because Walter precast the show before auditions—"

"That would be Abby."

"No, nothing significant," he said.

I finished giving my statement and waved good-bye to Edna as I left the Municipal Building. I hoped for her sake, for all of the ELT actors, that the show would, indeed, go on. Lola called to say she'd met with board members and they wanted to support Walter and have him continue as director, but only if he agreed to have Elliot as assistant director, in case of an "emergency." Like if he had to give notes from a jail cell.

I managed to get through lunch at the Windjammer without having to tell my attack story; I had no desire to be front-page news in the *Etonville Standard* again or to fend off Maggie Hemplemeyer's attempt at a human-interest article.

I settled into my booth with coffee and yesterday's chicken pot pie, a copy of Henry's menus for the weekend in hand. I ran down the bill of fare. "Uh-oh."

Benny leaned on the back of my booth. "I'd like to switch some hours with Gillian next week, okay?"

I nodded, distracted.

"What?" he asked.

"I think we're in trouble. Here's what Henry has planned for Friday: caramelized fennel salad and roasted mackerel with dill and lemon. And Saturday is spaghetti with anchovies and hot peppers."

"You don't think he's reacting to . . . ?"

"La Famiglia? Yes, that's exactly what I think. A little bit of innovation is fine, but this is the Windjammer."

Benny raised an eyebrow. "Game on."

I slumped against the seat. I felt like taking a nap.

Henry burst out of the kitchen sputtering, cell phone in hand, ranting. I heard "website," "sabotage," and "revenge."

"Slow down, Henry," I said and glanced at Benny. "What's this about the website and a La Famiglia link?"

"They called 'to thank me for putting a link to their place on our website.' People are visiting our site and calling them for a reservation!" His face was fire engine red, his forehead damp.

Oh no. "I don't understand. Let me call Pauli and see how this happened," I said as soothingly as I could.

Henry trounced off. "I knew that website stuff was going to be a problem."

I'd finally gotten Pauli on the line and discovered that, in his eagerness to impress Henry, he'd added a page on Places to Visit in Etonville—with links to websites for businesses all over town, including La Famiglia.

Geez.

I stayed late to close up and let Benny go early. I snapped off the overhead lights, and slipped the key in the front door lock. I pulled my jacket around my middle and tucked my bag into my belly. You'd never know it was late April; tonight the air was chilled, the inky sky crystal clear. Constellations resembled a connect-the-dots drawing. I would have thought it was early March.

I climbed into my Metro, glancing up and down an empty Main Street. I couldn't be too careful these days. But since last week, there had been no sign of the errant SUV. I turned down Fairchild and onto Ames. As I approached my house, I saw a car in the driveway. By the streetlight I could see a dark vehicle with the shadow of someone in the driver's seat. I pulled to the curb several doors away from my own and switched off the engine. Who would be visiting this time of night?

I opened my car door and slipped out, shutting it again carefully. I could play it safe and try to sneak into my house, or screw up the courage to approach the car and confront the driver. I crept stealthily around the front end of my Metro and moved from tree to tree until I was a mere ten feet away. I walked straight to the driver's side door. The window was open. "Can I help you?" I said loudly and firmly.

The woman inside turned her head. "Oh! I've been waiting here for hours."

"Who are you?"

"My name is Mary Robinson. Jerome's friend."

I was flabbergasted. Her look was Marian-the-librarian—seventy-ish, unfussy gray hair in a French twist, glasses dangling from a cord around her neck. Just the way Monica had described her. But her voice was pure Kathleen Turner—resonant and throaty. All remnants of my exhaustion vanished.

"We need to talk," she said.

"Let's go inside."

Despite the late hour, the disconcerting confrontation, the extreme circumstances that had brought her to my house, Mary Robinson was composed and alert. Dressed in black slacks and a matching sweater, she could have been having afternoon tea with an old friend.

"Would you like something? Coffee? Tea?" I asked after we had settled ourselves in my living room.

"No thank you."

We sat on my sofa. "How did you find me?" I asked.

"I was a reference librarian for twenty years before I assumed responsibility for the special collections. I know how to find things. With and without a computer. Besides, you called me."

Mary's nephew had been among the Robinsons in Poughkeepsie I'd contacted. The message I'd left had included my landline, which would have been Mary's connection to my address.

"I'm sorry you had to sit in my driveway for so long. Why didn't you just call me?"

"I wanted to see you in person. I like to see the faces of the people I confide in," Mary said.

Confide? This should be interesting. "So you're staying with family upstate?"

"Temporarily. I love my nephew and I appreciate his taking me in, but with his four children, his wife, and all of the animals, I have no privacy. I'm used to living alone."

"Where does he think you are tonight? Should you call him?" I asked.

Mary silenced me with a gesture. "He knows I'm staying overnight. At the Eton Bed and Breakfast."

"You can't stay at your home?"

"I sublet my apartment when I left town to a kind young woman who offered to take care of my cats."

"Mary, do you know why I was looking for you?"

"I think so," she said sadly. "We, Jerome and I, never intended for things to get so . . ."

"Out of control?"

She glanced up at me, helpless. "Yes."

"Maybe you'd better start from the beginning."

Chapter 23

We talked for two hours. Mary had met Jerome when he came to the library to use the computer lab and accidentally ended up in the special collections. Their friendship had blossomed, she claimed, over shared interests in rare books and classic first editions. It was a side of him I hadn't known about.

"Someone had left a box of old volumes at the library, and Luther told me to bring it down to special collections. It was part of an estate sale. We receive a number of those donations." She paused. "I was cataloging a book on bird-watching."

"When you . . . ?"

"Came across the item in question," she said. "Very neatly folded at the beginning of Chapter Three. I was intrigued. It was over one hundred years old."

"A hundred years? Wow. What kind of document is it?"

She hesitated. "A letter . . . from a father to his son during the Civil War. A very famous father. I did a preliminary check on several websites. Similar documents from that time were sold for a great deal of money to collectors."

"Why is it so valuable?"

She shook her head and looked me straight in the eye. "I'd rather not say any more until I turn it over to the authorities."

"You told Jerome about it?"

"Yes. By that time we had grown . . . quite close."

"I see."

"He wanted to have it authenticated. He thought we could get four to five hundred thousand dollars if the document was authentic. We were making plans for the future."

I nearly fell off the sofa. "Mary," I said gently, "why did you decide to take the document out of the library? Wasn't that stealing?"

She sat up straighter. "The Etonville Public Library," she said bitterly, "was firing me after forty years. They called it downsizing, but I know they thought I was too old and useless." She stiffened. "Jerome was outraged when he heard. It was his idea to take the letter. No one was aware of the document. Besides, it served them right."

I nodded. "Go on."

"Jerome found a company named Forensic Document Services that could provide authentication."

Bingo. "Did you contact them?"

"Jerome did, but there was some issue about the initial fee of a thousand dollars. He felt it was excessive. I offered to pay it, but he refused. Then, I left for Poughkeepsie, and poor Jerome . . ."

She started to cry. I gave her a tissue.

"I know," I said. "We all miss him."

Mary sniffed. "I wish I had never found that letter."

"Where is it now?" I asked.

"I have it right here."

"With you?" I whispered.

She nodded and looked into her lap.

I noticed for the first time that she had been clutching a red and green quilted bag, large enough to accommodate file folders.

"I had it hidden for safekeeping in the library at the beginning, then gave it to Jerome when he emailed the document service. But when I was let go, I decided I should take it with me to Poughkeepsie until Jerome worked out the details. I thought it would be more secure."

And all this time, someone was ransacking Etonville for it.

"Maybe I should have left it with Jerome. Then maybe he wouldn't have been murdered."

She quietly wiped her eyes.

"We should call the police," I said anxiously.

She nodded. "In the morning we can go to the station." Mary hesitated. "I never wanted things to get this complicated."

"Someone wants that document badly enough to kill for it. They've broken into Jerome's apartment and the special collections—"

"The special collections?" Mary asked, immediately distraught.

"Yes and the Etonville Little Theatre." I said. "Someone tried to run me off the road the other night."

Mary covered her face with her hands. "I'm so sorry. I never thought . . ."

"Look, it's two a.m. Why don't you stay here tonight? It might be safer than staying in the B and B with the letter."

Mary stood up and pulled her sweater tightly around her shoulders. "No, I'm fine, dear," she said. "I'm accustomed to taking care of myself."

"Then maybe you should leave the letter with me," I said. "Just until we get to the police station."

Mary shook her head.

"At least let me follow you to the B and B."

"I'll be all right."

When it seemed pointless to try to persuade her any further, we walked out into the night air, and she slid into the driver's seat and started the engine.

"Ms. O'Dell, I don't know exactly why you became involved in Jerome's murder, but you have. That tells me you are a smart young woman with a heart." She paused. "I hope I can help clear up this horrible mess."

"I'll meet you at the Municipal Building at eight?"

She nodded and backed out of my driveway.

My body was beat, but my mind was spinning. I began to knit pieces of the story together. Mary and Jerome were in love. Too lonely seniors looking to get a second lease on life. I reviewed the facts. Mary had found the document and, rather than turn it over to the library administration, told Jerome about it. He'd contacted Forensic Document Services to get the document verified. But verification had never happened. Or had it? Where had the figure of half a million dollars come from? Was it a guestimate? But what had precipitated Jerome's death?

I awoke early and powered up my laptop. I wanted more specific information, such as what was considered truly valuable—what kind of nineteenth century document might fetch half a million dollars. I clicked on news reports of large auction sales of historical documents and books. True enough, it seemed that the figure of half a million or more for a rare item was not out of the question for rich collectors and well-funded museums.

* * *

Mary sat primly in a straight-backed chair opposite Bill.

"So Mary, let's talk about the document," he said.

She sat taller in her seat, both tough and fragile. "Of course."

"You said the document service was Jerome's idea?"

"Yes, but he had an introduction from an acquaintance."

"And he never mentioned this person's name?"

"No. But when he contacted them, there was a problem with the business arrangement."

"Such as?" he asked.

"They wanted a thousand dollars upfront just to see the document. That's before any real authentication."

"I see." Bill stopped to gather his thoughts.

"As I told Ms. O'Dell, Jerome thought it excessive."

I looked in his direction. "Do you, uh, mind if I . . . ?"

"Go ahead."

"Mary, when did you leave Etonville?" I asked.

"Let me think. I received my pink slip March first and was told I had thirty days. But I was not about to let them fire me so I turned in my letter of resignation March fifteenth," she said triumphantly.

"And moved to Poughkeepsie?"

"I left town April first and sublet my apartment. I only intended to be with my nephew for a few months. Until Jerome sold the document and we could settle down someplace." She leaned back in her chair. "All we wanted was enough money to keep us healthy and independent. We didn't want to have to rely on others to take care of us. The letter seemed to be a gift that fell right into our laps."

If you assumed that confiscating the property of the public library was a gift. I knew what they intended to do was illegal and obviously dangerous, but I sympathized with them.

"When was the last time you heard from Jerome?" I asked.

Mary considered. "We talked at the beginning of April. I think he might have been changing his mind about the document."

"Why do you think that?" Bill asked quickly.

"Because he was having some problems with the company. He asked me if I was certain I wanted to go ahead with selling the letter. I told him I was." She studied her hands in her lap. "That was selfish of me and might have gotten him killed."

"Was that the last time . . . ?"

"I called him April fourteenth. I remember because my nephew was filing his tax return that night," she said. "But no one answered. I waited a few days, and when I couldn't reach him, I called Mildred. I thought maybe someone at the library might have seen him." She touched a handkerchief to her nose. "It was too late. He was already dead and the funeral had taken place that morning."

"Mary, did you have a meeting planned with Jerome for April sixteenth?"

"A meeting? No. After I heard he'd died, I wanted to return to Etonville with the document, but I was frightened. I wasn't sure what to do. Then I received your call."

Mary paused and Bill looked at me. I shrugged.

"I thought I should just come to Etonville and straighten everything out." Mary looked up at me and made a face. "But it was a couple of days before my nephew remembered to give me your message. So here I am," she said simply.

"You have the document in your possession?" Bill asked Mary, a note of impatience creeping into his question.

"Of course."

"May we see it?" I asked quietly.

Mary folded her hands in her lap. "It was a single sheet of parchment, discolored and fragile, written by Abraham Lincoln to his son Robert and dated February 15, 1863."

Bill and I gawked as Mary withdrew a file from her purse that held a piece of paper encased in a plastic sleeve. She held it up for us to see. It was, as she had described it, yellowed and crinkly with age. *Executive Mansion* was centered and engraved at the top of the sheet, with *Washington* and the date underneath. It was a short missive, a brief two paragraphs, and at the bottom of the letter was *Father*, with *A. Lincoln* in parentheses below it.

We were hushed for a moment, taking in the significance of what we were viewing. Then Bill came to life. "I'll need to take control of the document and keep it safe. It could be evidence in a murder investigation. Ultimately, you know it will need to be returned to the library, Mary."

"I understand," she said wistfully and slipped the letter in the file.

"You should probably leave town as soon as you can. It's safer in Poughkeepsie for the time being. I'll contact you when I need to speak with you again," Bill said.

Who knew what the killer had found out about Jerome and Mary and the document? "Someone will stop at nothing to get this letter. Your life could be in danger," I added. "You know that, right?"

"I can see that now."

Mary and I walked out of the Municipal Building. I wanted to take her to breakfast, but it would be impossible to find privacy at Coffee Heaven. I thought a little trip to Creston would offer the anonymity I needed to broach a sensitive topic: the diamond ring. Mary deserved to know. I had said as much to Bill, during a minute alone while Mary was in the ladies' room, and he'd agreed.

We chatted about the special collections, library issues, and Mary's family in upstate New York as I coasted down State Route 53. In Creston, I found a parking space on the street just outside a café. I decided on *café au lait* and a bagel; Mary ordered coffee, black; one egg, scrambled; and rye toast, unbuttered. I had studied her while she was studying the menu. Mary was a woman who knew her own mind and wasn't afraid to share it.

"I'm astounded that you had such a valuable piece of property in your possession."

"We could have lived the rest of our lives on the sum we would have received," she said, then laughed. "Jerome was planning on a trip around the world and a house in the country. It would have been a dream come true."

"Do you see that jewelry store across the street?"

She turned in her seat and looked.

"Jerome did some shopping there."

"That's where he bought this?" She lifted the sleeve of her blouse away from her wrist to reveal the gold bracelet.

"Yes." I plunged in. "It is also where he bought a diamond ring."

"A diamond . . . ?" Her face transitioned from confusion to clarity to embarrassment.

"Right now it's in the evidence lock-up at the station. It's beautiful."

She shook her head. "Jerome was so romantic. So much more than I had been used to. Before I met him, I thought that I was too old for . . ."

"Love?" I said quietly.

"Yes." She looked down at her coffee cup.

I waited for her to continue.

"I began to believe it was possible, even at my age. Silly, I know."

"I think you made him very happy. The night before he died, he was as excited as a little kid. Now I know why."

Mary's face crumpled. "I'd give anything if Jerome could be here with me again."

We drove in silence back to Etonville and when we had reached the Eton Bed and Breakfast, I urged Mary to get on the road as soon as possible.

"I'd like to make one stop before I leave Etonville," she said.

"Where . . . ?"

"I'd like to visit Jerome."

"Yes. He'd like that. St. Andrew's Episcopal cemetery."

She touched my arm. "Thank you."

I hugged her warmly. She hugged me back.

Chapter 24

"Penny," Walter whined, "Move the blocks and tape deck over there." He pointed his finger in the direction of a handful of cast members, servant types, hanging out in a corner of the stage. They were lounging on the floor, texting, and chatting quietly. "And you lot, dress the stage." He waved his hand ceremoniously. The actors stared at him dumbly: they still were not down with his lingo. But at least he was back at work and the cast was on stage, slogging through text and staging. But I wasn't certain that it was enough to have *Romeo and Juliet* ready in three weeks.

Penny announced an extended break so that Chrystal could do some costume fitting. She handed out the male actors' basic wardrobe: tights, white flowing shirts—which had made their debuts at Jerome's funeral—and codpieces. Within minutes, Mercutio, Benvolio, and Tybalt were busy strutting with exaggerated emphasis on their groins. Chrystal was on her hands and knees yanking a pair of tights up the legs of an obese Lord Montague. She had gotten as far as his knees and had braced herself against Penny for leverage. Lola was all Elizabethan: red velvet and satin and exposed cleavage. A much more handsome version of Abby's costume. Elliot appeared from a dressing room, princely in purple and gold.

"It's difficult to see anyone else in Jerome's place," I said to Lola.

"On show nights, we did crossword puzzles together in the green room when I wasn't on stage."

"When he wasn't out with Elliot?" I said. "How is Walter getting along with Elliot?" I asked.

"Oh, you know Walter. He huffs and puffs. But frankly, I think he's glad Elliot is around. Someone to share the burden."

"And the glory, if all goes well."

Lola crossed her fingers.

Penny and Chrystal congratulated themselves on reaching Lord Montague's waist with the tights, and rehearsal resumed with Walter prancing around, demonstrating period dance to Mercutio and Benvolio.

I coordinated added costume fittings with Chrystal and handed off a rehearsal schedule for the next two weeks to Penny, who scowled.

"Walter will have to approve it," she said.

Approve this, I thought, and went next door to the Windjammer to check on things. I holed up in the back booth with my laptop to find some specific information. I was curious what a note from Lincoln to his son Robert, written shortly after he signed the Emancipation Proclamation, was worth. I wondered. *Would* the sale of a letter dated 1863 from one of America's most famous presidents bring half a million dollars or was it worth more than that at auction? Either way, it was worth enough to make someone murder for it.

I stayed on the Internet until closing time, digging into sites for information on rare documents and their financial value. I had a list of the most sought-after materials and sure enough, anything with a first-degree connection to Lincoln was near the top of the list. Previous letters by him had gone for amounts that ranged from a quarter to half a million dollars. And then I found the motherlode: in 2008, an 1864 letter from Lincoln responding to a petition asking him to free all of the slave children in the country fetched over three million dollars at Sotheby's auction house. I closed my laptop. If Mary's find had been authenticated and a buyer confirmed, she and Jerome would have raked in a fortune.

By eleven-thirty, Benny looked stressed out and Henry was actively pouting—a customer suggested he add a touch more paprika to his spicy chicken breasts. I surveyed the dining room as Benny wrapped up behind the bar and Henry switched off the lights. I would be glad when *Romeo and Juliet* opened and I could go back to devoting my time to managerial instead of theatrical concerns. Although, the truth was that I liked hanging out in the theater and, apparently, I was doing a bang-up job of keeping things somewhat organized.

I locked up and met Lola outside the restaurant. The rehearsal over and her meeting with Walter and Elliot concluded, I had agreed to drive her home and fill her in on the investigation. Lola and I hopped in my Metro.

"Whew. I am glad this night is over," Lola said as she clicked her seat belt. "We've stumbled through four acts and only one to go."

"Fingers crossed."

"If we make it to tech rehearsal, it will be a miracle."

I pulled out onto Main Street.

"So tell me what's going on," Lola said excitedly.

And I did. From Mary showing up in my driveway with the document to our conversation with Bill to my discussion about the diamond ring.

"She and Jerome would have gotten rich off that letter," she said.

"Maybe."

"No wonder he was murdered," she said soberly. "And we still don't know who killed him."

"True, but I'm beginning to have an idea."

I was about to launch into a theory when a black vehicle at the corner of Main and Anderson entered my peripheral vision. It pulled away from the curb, made a left turn onto Main and drove by the front of Georgette's Bakery. I counted to five and then swung my Metro in a wide arc through the intersection.

"Dodie, what are you doing?" Lola grabbed the dashboard. "U-turns are illegal, and I live in the other direction."

"Didn't you see that car?"

"What car?"

"The black SUV."

"*The* black SUV?"

"Hang on," I said.

"I'll call 911." Lola stuck one hand in her bag and pulled out her cell. "Nuts. It's dead! What about your cell?"

I pressed the accelerator to the floor. "Forget about calling. Get out a piece of paper."

"What for?"

"You're going to write down the license plate number."

Lola tore through her bag while I tore down Main, closing the gap between us and the SUV.

We passed the Windjammer and the ELT, and were crossing Amber when the black hulk did a quick turn through a yellow light and headed down a side street, picking up speed. I followed.

"That was a red light," Lola yelled as my sturdy little car began to tremble. It wasn't used to speeds above sixty-five.

"I have to stay with him."

I was closing in on the SUV, but I hadn't counted on the side street being a dead end. The SUV stopped our cat-and-mouse game, suddenly, in the middle of the *cul-de-sac* at the end of the block. He waited just long enough for me to commit myself to another U-turn before he accelerated, flying past us.

"Get the plate number," I screamed.

"I can't see it!" Lola rolled down her window and stuck her head out.

I edged closer to the SUV, and when it hit the brakes, I slowed down, too. When it sped up, so did I. We went on like this for half a mile before it was forced to halt at a red light ahead.

"The license plate is orange," Lola said.

"That's not New Jersey. It's out of state."

"I think it's three letters followed by four numbers."

"Hah! I think that's New York," I yelled.

The light changed, the SUV shot forward a few feet, then braked unexpectedly, leaving me in the middle of the intersection with a car barreling down on my right. The driver hit the brakes as I swerved to my left and straddled the white line in the middle of the road.

"Oh!" Lola squealed.

The SUV was toying with me. I was beginning to take it personally.

"Can you read it?"

"T...B...U..."

"Write it down."

Lola bent over to make a notation just as the SUV crossed the town limits and zoomed onto the entrance to the highway. It must have been going ninety because I couldn't keep up. In seconds it was out of sight. I steered my Metro to the side of the road and put it in park. My heart was banging erratically in my chest, and my hands were damp on the steering wheel.

"Dodie, I'm sorry I missed the last three numbers."

"We have the plate color, probable state, and three letters. Bill should be able to do something with a partial number."

Lola's eyes were shining. "I hope so."

After delivering Lola to her doorstep in one piece, I drove twenty miles an hour through town to my place. I collapsed on my bed, but my eyes were wide open. Sleep was going to be a challenge.

At seven AM, I dressed and headed for Coffee Heaven. I decided to drink caffeine until Bill got to the station. Probably closer to eight. I had the partial plate and a plan of action. What more could he want? I was getting an image of his dimple, laser blue eyes, and turned-up mouth as he listened to my report, grateful for a job well done. I scribbled on a scrap of paper: *Jerome, Mary, Lincoln.*

"Refill, Dodie?" Jocelyn asked, coffeepot in hand.

"Thanks."

"You're here early."

"Couldn't sleep."

"This murder keeping you up?"

"A little," I said and sipped from the fresh cup.

"It's all anybody talks about in here now." She paused, hand on hip. "I saw this TV show last week about criminals and their motivations. This detective from New York was saying that the obvious suspect in an investigation was most often the guilty party. Do you think that's true?"

"I have no idea." But it made sense. Who knew about the Lincoln letter? As far as I knew only Jerome and Mary, and now Bill, Lola, and me. But who had the most to gain from its theft? Jerome was dead; Mary had turned it over to Bill, who I assumed would keep the document safe. Lola and I certainly had no designs on it. . . .

I remembered a philosophy class in college where the professor had spent an entire session clarifying a principle he referred to as Occam's razor. Basically it stated that among competing hypotheses, the one with the fewest assumptions should be selected. Jocelyn might be right. And that meant just one thing.

I glanced at my watch. Bill should be at work by now. I dropped some bills on the table and waved good-bye to Jocelyn, who was now filling cups at the counter.

Edna was at dispatch with her nose buried in the *Romeo and Juliet* script. She looked up as I entered and struck a pose, one hand flying into the air to gesticulate, the other hanging on to the play for dear life.

" '*Romeo is banished; and all the world to nothing that he dares ne'er come back to challenge you; Or if he do, it needs must be by stealth. Then—'"*

"Edna!" Neither one of us saw Bill enter the hallway.

Edna, startled, dropped her script onto her container of coffee, which teetered before she could catch it and splashed liquid on her headset. "Chief?" she said as she swiped Kleenex over the microphone.

"Is that play all anybody can think about these days?" he asked grumpily. "Get Ralph and if he's at Coffee Heaven, tell him I said to get his tail over to the Shop N Go. One of the Banger sisters swears someone stole her purse and she's been calling my private line. How did she get my private line, anyhow?"

Edna shrugged. "10-4, Chief."

He turned toward me. "Dodie, you're up early."

"Do you have a minute?"

Ralph's voice shot out of the speaker, whose volume level was at ten. "Edna, don't tell the chief I called in, but I have to stop by the bakery and pick up a cake for Ricky's birthday."

Ricky was Ralph's five-year-old.

"Uh, Ralph . . ." Edna shifted her gaze upward to Bill's face, which was quickly becoming a light shade of crimson.

Ralph chuckled. "Oh yeah, and I found this toy fire truck with a fireman who looks just like the chief. You know, face all scrunchy and stuff."

"Ralph?" Bill said.

There was silence except for Ralph's audible gulp.

"Is that you, Chief?"

"Get over to Shop N Go. Edna will fill you in."

"Copy that," he said meekly.

"And Edna, lower the volume on that speaker," Bill said. "Dodie, we can talk in my office."

I followed him down the hall, practically running to keep up.

Bill crossed behind his desk, staring out his office window into an alleyway where a delivery truck was dropping off cartons for Betty's Boutique next door.

"Bad day?" I asked tentatively. It was much too early to have everything crumbling around you.

"The mayor's on my case about the murder. Says it being unsolved isn't good for business. If it drags out until summer, the tourist trade will be affected."

Mayor Bennett was Bull's brother, and anything Bill did was not going to measure up to his older bro. If the mayor had his way, Bull would be policing Etonville from the grave. And the tourist trade? Etonville was named after Thomas Eton, one of George Washington's army officers during the American Revolution. Sometime in the early nineteenth century, Eton's farm had become a village, then grown to a town. Mr. Eton's farmhouse was renovated into the Eton Bed and Breakfast in 1910—a white clapboard affair with black shutters surrounded by a white picket fence—and placed on the historical register. It remained Etonville's claim to fame, along with an ancient cemetery that dated from 1759. The mayor must have been referring to the odd couple or two who showed up at the Eton B-and-B after getting lost on State Route 53.

"I don't think I'd let Mayor Bennett worry you too much," I said.

"Well, he's right in one sense. The longer this investigation takes, the colder the trail."

"But now we have the letter."

"And no suspect."

"That's why I'm here," I said. I laid the slip of paper with the three license tag letters in front of him.

"What's this?" he asked suspiciously.

I proceeded to relate Lola's and my adventure last night, as we chased the SUV around town, concluding with our triumphant acquisition of a partial plate. I assumed he'd be ecstatic or, at a minimum, grateful.

"Only three letters? Where's the rest of it? What good is a partial plate number?"

I felt the air whoosh out of my internal balloon. "It's a New York plate. Can't you run black Escalades with the three letters through the computer and limit the search?"

"I guess so. But it's going to take time. There's probably a bunch of black SUVs with those first three letters."

I doubted that, but there would be no arguing with Bill in this mood.

"Well, you're welcome, anyway," I said, miffed.

He rubbed his hand over the top of his head. "Sorry. I'll put out an APB to surrounding towns. And notify New York. Thanks for the information. But I wish you had called me. I might have been able to catch up with him."

"Called you in the middle of the chase? We're lucky we survived intact," I said.

Bill exhaled. "Bad morning."

I felt sorry for Bill. He was right, things were stalled. "I have this idea."

"Dodie, I have to get—"

"But first, I think you'd better sit down."

He slowly let himself sink into his desk chair. "Okay."

I proceeded to tell him about Jerome's email contact with Forensic Document Services and my conversation with Marshall Wendover. His face registered the five stages of unlawful investigation: disbelief, skepticism, impatience, irritation, and astonishment.

"I can't believe you actually went through with—"

"Just hear me out. Of all the people connected to Jerome, and admittedly there aren't many, who would know the most about priceless documents? And who was in contact with Jerome?"

"Forensic Document Services?" he said cautiously.

"Yes!"

"But you said according to Jerome's email, Marshall Wendover wasn't even in touch with Jerome for two weeks before he died."

"True. But what about his brother?"

"What about him?"

"Marshall said Morty runs the document services. I think someone should talk with him." I pulled out the business card Marshall had given me.

Bill took the card and studied it. "Well . . . I guess I could give him a call."

"Not you. Me." I smiled confidently.

"Huh?"

"If you go, you are the police chief interrogating him about a murder. But remember, I'm Jerome's niece and can say I have the document but still need it to be authenticated."

"I think this theater stuff is going to your head," he said. "Not to mention the detective stuff."

"Look, Bill, you said it yourself. We need to solve the murder. Now that we know about the document, this could be the break we need."

He tapped a pencil against his blotter. "Okay. I'll run the plate number to see if there's any connection between the SUV and the company."

I picked up the business card off Bill's desk. "I'll call and make an appointment for tomorrow morning early so that I make it back to the Windjammer for lunch."

"Okay, but I want to be in the vicinity. Just in case."

"Your own car. No uniform?"

He nodded. "It's not smart that you meet this guy alone."

"I'll be fine," I said.

"Let me know when you've confirmed contact."

"10-4."

"Dodie?"

"Yeah?"

"Is my face really all scrunchy?"

Chapter 25

I invited Lola to join me for lunch at the Windjammer.

"Henry's shrimp salad is wonderful today," Lola said, wiping her mouth and taking a sip of water.

"I'll tell him," I said. "I made the appointment with the document place for eight-thirty a.m."

"So let me get this straight. You're going to act as though you are Jerome's relative—"

"Niece. That was my story with Marshall. I'm there to see what this Morty knows about the document."

"Won't he want to see it?"

"I'll say it's in a secure place. For the time being. But we need to know if it's the real deal. Kind of a probate matter."

"Sounds believable," she said. "Are you afraid to go alone?"

"Bill is riding backup in plainclothes. I'll be fine."

Lola scrutinized me. "I think you like playing detective. You need to audition for the next ELT production. If there is one," she said gloomily.

"So tonight is Act V, if I remember correctly."

"Walter rearranged things a little bit. He's running the wedding night scene. God help us, with the Ladies-in-Waiting doing a kind of dream sequence."

"He changed the rehearsal schedule?"

"The Ladies have been complaining, and Walter feels like he has to give them more to do."

"But Romeo and Juliet's wedding night?"

"Oh, you'll see. I think it's unnecessary, but Walter has a vision. Ever since Elliot became assistant director, Walter's been a little manic."

"Dodie, Henry needs you in the kitchen," Enrico said, appearing at my side.

"Tell him I'll be right there. Lola, see you tonight."

Despite the seriousness of the scene on stage, I had to struggle to prevent myself from bursting into guffaws.

"This way, ladies," Walter said and demonstrated an upper-body-flapping-in-the-wind kind of gesture. Lola and I exchanged dubious looks, and Penny bit off a chuckle with clamped lips. "Lift your arms. Sway. Let your heads roll."

Walter had the six Ladies-in-Waiting/Servants/scenery movers lined up across the back of the stage trying to imitate his movement. Probably not what Shakespeare had intended: a break in the action so the "chorus" could interpret the emotional transition from Tybalt's death to the Romeo/Juliet wedding night. The Ladies looked confused, slightly embarrassed, and painfully awkward—none more so than Abby, who swung her arms defiantly as if daring anyone to laugh. She'd been sending ocular death rays to Juliet for several nights now.

"They look like insane chickens with their heads cut off," Lola stage-whispered.

Her voice carried to the stage and made it seem as if we were making fun of the actors. Walter glowered, and Abby's eyes darted into the house, her face bitter.

"I don't think this whole thing works," muttered Penny.

Romeo and Juliet, both looking slightly bored with each other, re-hearsed their wedding night on a makeshift bed, two four-by-eight platforms on short legs. They lay side by side like two dead fish on ice.

Beads of sweat clung to Walter's forehead, and one or two had trickled down his face.

"The two of you are reclining in each other's arms," he said. Not a bit of warmth between them.

Walter instructed the Ladies to circle the bed, still flapping and swaying. They spun faster and faster, running really, around the marriage bed creating a dizzying effect. Walter moved downstage, turning his back for a split second, and Abby pivoted around a corner of the platform, driving her elbow into the Lady ahead of her, who unintentionally bumped Juliet, sending her squarely into Romeo's chest. Their faces smashed together and—ready or not—lips locked. Juliet rebounded off Romeo's face, checking to confirm that all her teeth were intact, Abby sneered, and the other Ladies collapsed in exhaustion.

At nine-thirty, Walter gave up for the night, probably because the gaggle of Ladies tromping around the stage like demented seagulls was becoming too much even for him.

I took my time dressing, wanting to appear as mature, and also mournful, as possible. I settled on a brown tweed suit I hadn't even tried on in a year. With a dark green sweater, I looked professional but approachable. I pulled my Metro in front of the Municipal building and rolled down my window. Bill was waiting next to his BMW. He looked fantastic in a blue blazer, white button-down shirt, and khaki slacks.

"Morning," he said, smiling. "You ready for this?"

"As I'll ever be," I said, smiling back. "Try to keep up."

We left Etonville via State Route 53 and entered the Garden State Parkway, traveling north to Exit 153B. It took only minutes to get on and off Route 46 West and find ourselves in the center of town. Such as it was. I'd never been in Woodland Park, but I had Googled the borough, population about twelve thousand, and discovered that it was home to a couple of business colleges, bounded on one end by Garret Mountain and the other by the Passaic River. I made a couple of left turns, as per my GPS, and arrived at an office park overlooking a reservoir and acres of undisturbed landscape.

The office complex where the lab was located was in stark contrast to the nondescript building with yellow siding that housed Forensic Document Services in Piscataway. Here, the landscaping was intricate and impressive. Magnolia and dogwood trees were scattered throughout the lawn fronting the building and the flagstone walkway leading to the entrance was lined with purple coneflowers.

I parked next to a handicapped area and watched Bill ease his BMW into a space a few yards away.

In the marble-walled lobby, a directory indicated that the Forensic Document Services Lab was on the third floor, in suite 302. The elevator door shut, and I glanced at a security camera in the upper corner.

I stepped into the third-floor hallway and found number 302 directly opposite the elevator. On the door was stenciled LABORATORY SERVICES.

"Here we go," I said to myself and clasped my bag tightly.

The office waiting area was also a contrast to Marshall's domain: leather furniture, indoor carpeting, potted plants, and Muzak. The feel was pleasantly comforting and reassuring.

I approached the receptionist, a young woman with short blond hair, deep red lipstick, and earrings that dangled well below her earlobes. "Hello. I'm Dodie O'Dell. I have an appointment with Morty Wendover. I'm a little early."

"Please have a seat. I'll ring Mortimer." She picked up a telephone.

I was doubtful "Mortimer" had anything to do with the car repair or trucking aspects of the family business.

"Ms. O'Dell, Mortimer will see you now. First door on your right." She pointed to a hallway on her left.

I followed her directions and walked into his office. Between Marshall and Morty, one of them had to have been adopted—or switched in the cradle. Morty Wendover was tall and svelte, with neatly combed brown hair, a white dress shirt, and a pinstripe suit. He held out his hand. "Ms. O'Dell?"

"Yes. Thanks for seeing me on such short notice." I shook his hand.

"My sympathy for your loss," he said.

"Thank you."

"Please have a seat."

I settled myself into a maroon leather chair as Morty sat behind his mahogany desk. "What can I do for you?"

"I understand that my uncle Jerome was in contact with your company about a document."

"Yes, I believe he emailed my brother Marshall. But nothing came of it. Every once in a while we get someone who cleans out an attic and thinks we're *Antiques Roadshow* and really just wants free information."

Was it significant that Marshall used the exact same phrase?

"I understand that my uncle, for some reason, never went ahead with the authentication. But now I want to proceed with the process."

Morty sat very still. "I see."

"Yes. I understand that the initial fee is a thousand dollars?"

"That's the retainer. It's deducted from the final cost of the authentication," he said.

"Would you do the authentication in this office?" I asked.

"Yes. We offer a whole range of services at this facility, from handwriting analysis and forgery identification to document authentication. Mostly we work with wills, deeds, arbitration agreements, that sort of thing, and, of course, historical documents."

Some of this sounded familiar from my research on the Internet.

"Authentication of historical documents is a two-pronged process. First, there is identifying the physical evidence such as the age and type of ink and the paper the document is printed on. The fiber, etc. The second part of the process is establishing the provenance of the document, that is, its history. Who owned it, sold it, transferred it in a will, say, to another individual." He paused. "Your uncle never discussed the details or provenance of the document. Do you have that information?"

"Some of it," I said.

"You have the document with you?" he asked.

"No, it's in a safe location."

"I would need to see it before we enter into an agreement. I can usually establish whether it is worth pursuing upon a quick inspection. If it is a fake, it saves time and money for both of us."

"I see. Could we arrange an appointment in Etonville? Given its value, I think I would feel more secure meeting there."

He looked at his calendar. "I'm available tomorrow afternoon if that suits."

"I'll call you later today to confirm the time and place."

"Of course." He reached for a business card. "Call my cell phone directly."

I took the card and stared at his number.

"Thank you, Mr. Wendover, for your consideration."

"Not at all, Ms. O'Dell. It's not every day someone comes into possession of a Lincoln letter." He escorted me to the door. "I look forward to hearing from you."

I forced myself to walk calmly to the elevator, my heart thumping. As I stepped into the revolving glass door in the lobby, I was struck by the size of the man entering the rotating door from the outside. He was enormous, his broad shoulders straining the seams of his suit jacket. He looked familiar. Our eyes met, mine wide and curious, his flat and uninterested.

I drove past Bill, giving him a thumbs-up. He followed me to the Creston café; it was becoming my home away from home and a haven from the snooping eyes of Etonville.

"We need to smoke 'em out," I said feverishly after our coffees came. "Morty referred to a 'Lincoln letter.' According to Marshall, Jerome never mentioned the specific document. He knows more than he's letting on."

Bill just shook his head wearily. "I appreciate your enthusiasm, but how do you know Jerome didn't mention that it was Lincoln's letter to Morty in a phone call?"

"Jerome corresponded with Marshall by email," I said. "He said they never talked on the phone."

"But maybe Morty and Jerome did."

We drank our coffee in silence.

"Any word on the license plate?" I asked.

"Not yet."

"I told Morty I'd call him this afternoon and set up a meeting. What have we got to lose?" I asked. "We get him to Etonville, we confront him with the document, and we see how he responds. Worst-case scenario, we get an initial evaluation of the letter that the library can hopefully take to the bank."

"Best case?" he asked.

I shrugged. "He incriminates himself by something he says or does? Who knows, maybe returning to the scene of the crime will trigger a confession?"

"In all my years of law enforcement, I've never seen *that* happen," Bill said glumly. "What do you mean 'returning to the scene of the crime'?"

"I think we should meet in the theater."

"The theater? Why?" Bill asked.

"Where else? We don't want to tip our hand, but we need privacy and security. That leaves out the Municipal Building or a restaurant or some isolated location. Our homes aren't safe if Morty thinks we have the letter stashed there. The theater is public, but not too public. It's empty in the afternoon before rehearsals. It has possibilities. I could hook up with Morty in the front row of the house, and you could still be somewhere on the premises watching it all, like from the light booth or backstage."

"That is the wackiest plan I've ever heard," he said.

"So you come up with a better one."

Bill drummed his fingers on the table.

In the end, Bill agreed to my calling Morty and inviting him to the theater tomorrow at five o'clock—on the pretext that I worked for the ELT and it was most convenient for me to connect there. Of course I would not have the actual document, just a photocopy that Morty could examine as a preliminary appraisal. Bill would take care of that. I'd call Lola to make sure that no last-minute afternoon meetings or crew work were added to the schedule, and Walter didn't show up until seven these days. That would give us two hours. Bill would be backstage, with a clear view of the front row. Suki would be on the street in an unmarked car just in case backup was needed. And Edna would be on dispatch. The plan seemed simple enough. I was wound up with the possibility of actually moving the murder investigation forward; Bill was skeptical but grudgingly willing to give it a try.

Chapter 26

B est laid plans. I didn't manage to call Morty until four-thirty because chaos had broken out at the Windjammer a couple of
hours earlier. Lunch had been fine, a decent crowd for a Wednesday,
and folks were scarfing down Henry's secret cheeseburgers, zucchini
frittata, and gazpacho. Then all hell broke loose. Enrico dropped a
pot of beef stock that Henry had planned to use for the evening's
stew; there was a quarter-inch slick of liquid and grease spread across
the kitchen floor. Luckily, no one was scalded. Gillian called in trau-
matized and crying because she had just broken up with her
boyfriend, again, and Pauli arrived with the final version of the website. Minus any publicity for the Windjammer's primary competitor.
For two cents, I'd have closed the place down for the night.

By the time I'd calmed Henry down and talked him into a simpler
dinner special, gotten Enrico calmed down enough to clean up the
kitchen, calmed Benny down and assured him I would cover Gillian
for the night, and calmed Pauli, guaranteeing him that Henry would
have already forgotten about the La Famiglia debacle and would still
pay him, I was frazzled and bushed. I had forgotten that my main
mission for the afternoon was to reach Morty. I tapped on his cell
phone number, and no one answered. I left a message for him to call
me and went back to work.

At seven, I deposited two dishes on a table for the Banger sisters,
who were on high alert.

"Dodie, how is the show going?" one of them asked.

"Just fine," I said. Then my cell phone rang. It was Mortimer. "I'm
sorry. I have to take this." I stepped to my back booth and tapped the
ANSWER button. "Hello, Mortimer?"

"Yes. Sorry I am just now getting back to you. It's been a hectic day."

I could identify with that. "I was calling to see if we could meet tomorrow afternoon. Around five?"

"Tomorrow is good, but it will need to be later. I'm booked all day. How is . . . eight? Eight-thirty?"

We hadn't counted on Morty's not being able to make it at five. I thought quickly: Walter had been starting rehearsal earlier and ending things by nine-thirty. "If we need to meet in the evening, nine-thirty would be better."

Morty agreed, and I went on to tell him that we would meet in the theater since I would be working there. He wasn't overly surprised; he probably was used to unusual meeting places with clients.

Bill, on the other hand, wasn't thrilled when I called him about the change in plans. Meeting at night didn't feel right to him.

Lola was equally dismayed when I caught her on a rehearsal break. "How are we going to get everyone out of the theater?"

"Rehearsals have been ending around that time anyway, right?"

"I'll do my best."

Benny flagged me down. "Dodie, can you give me a hand here—?"

"I'm coming," I said. "Talk to you later, Lola."

Now all I needed was a good night's sleep so that I would be at the top of my game.

I awoke at eight and yawned, stretching my arms over my head. Light flooded my bedroom and beckoned me into another day. I assessed the evening's upcoming events: the wheels were turning, the stage was set, and the players would be in place. I lingered over coffee, took a long hot shower, and dressed carefully, casual in black slacks and a pale green silk shirt that complemented my eyes.

I had to pick up the copy of the Lincoln letter that Bill had made and I offered to stop by the station after the lunch hour. I popped into the Municipal Building at three and caught him just as his squad car pulled into the space labeled CHIEF. His fierce blue eyes lasered through me.

"Are we all set for tonight?" he asked as he held the door for me.

"Yep," I said, more nonchalantly than I felt. In reality, I'd been jazzed all afternoon in anticipation of my big night.

"Look, this is probably going to be short and to-the-point. You let him take a look at the copy of the letter, you ask a few pertinent questions. . . . You do have pertinent questions ready, right?"

"Of course I do." I needed to get some pertinent questions ready.

He strode down the hallway, tossing his directive over his shoulder. "And you make a date for a next appointment, at which time you will bring him the actual document."

"Got it."

Edna looked up as we passed her window. She nodded knowingly, as though she knew something was up. "I'm on duty tonight so I'll miss rehearsal. Walter's doing Juliet's death scene. I think he's going to have Abby stand in for the Nurse."

"Better than standing in for Juliet."

Edna snorted and went back to work.

"Dodie?" Bill called out.

"Coming."

He handed me the copy of the Lincoln letter in a manila file like the one Mary had used for the original. "Remember, we don't have proof these guys have anything to do with Jerome's murder. All we know is that Jerome contacted them," he said seriously.

I nodded solemnly. "Bill, I've been thinking this through."

"Uh-oh, what now?" He moaned.

"What if the copy doesn't satisfy Morty? What if he won't talk without the original?"

"Then we call it off."

I paused. "We probably only have one shot with him. How about if I have the original as a backup?"

Bill raised his hands as if to ward off my idea. "No way."

"Hear me out. I won't show it to him unless I need to. But this is our big chance."

I saw hesitation and I pressed my advantage. "With you in the theater, no one is going to get away with anything. Right?"

He reluctantly nodded. "I'll bring it with me. If he wants it, you say that you need to retrieve it from a secure location. Like the office. Then you come backstage by way of the emergency corridor and get it from me." Then his tone softened and he gestured for me to sit while he perched on the edge of his desk, twelve inches away. "In the unlikely event someone tries to pull something, don't take any chances. Just get out of the way. I'll be watching, and Suki's on the street. Edna will always be able to reach me if for some reason we lose touch. Okay?"

I was staring into his eyes and got lost for a moment.

"Dodie? Okay?" he asked again.

"Uh-huh," I said quickly.

He leaned forward. "Be careful, you hear?"

Despite the impending episode with Morty Wendover, which might have proven a distraction to a lesser actor, Lola's Lady Capulet was in peak form, equal parts mother love and devious sexpot. For several weeks now, Abby had been both faithful dog and whining thespian, and rewarding her with the stand-in role for the night apparently seemed appropriate to Walter. The maternal, nurturing Nurse went out the window the minute Abby stepped into the scene. Walter had spent an hour on Juliet drinking the magical vial that would put her to sleep and then collapsing in terror and resignation on the platform bed. I was getting nervous. It was eight-thirty and Walter didn't look as though he had any intention of ending rehearsal soon.

Abby stood over Juliet, facing upstage. "*How sound asleep she is. I needs must wake her.*" Abby shook Juliet's shoulders so hard the poor girl's teeth clattered.

"Hey!" Juliet protested.

But Walter was busy signaling Lola that it was nearly time for her entrance. I also tried to catch Lola's eye and give her the universal signs for "hurry it up" and "cut it off."

Juliet lay back down.

Abby went back to work. "*Alas alas! Help help! My lady's dead.*" *Thwap.* She slapped Juliet across the face and caught her unawares.

"Stop it!" Juliet screamed.

"What?" Abby asked innocently.

I rose from my seat and headed down the aisle. If someone didn't stop Abby, we might have a real death scene. "Penny, go up there and stop Abby. She's going to kill Juliet."

Penny chuckled. "Juliet's already dead."

"Penny!"

"Haven't you ever heard of method acting?"

"Lola, love, move a little farther downstage," Walter called out.

Lady Capulet swept into Juliet's boudoir, lamenting at her death until Abby, just for good measure, picked the top half of Juliet off the platform, in pretended grief, then bounced her off the bed, yelling, "*She's dead, deceas'd', she's dead, alack the day!*"

"That's it," Juliet squawked and grabbed Abby's hair. She yanked hard and Abby's head snapped back. Abby reached for Juliet's throat.

Walter finally noticed what was going on and signaled for Penny. "Abby! Decorum!"

Penny had heaved herself out of her seat. "Cat fight," she said and dove between them.

"Get off me!" Abby squealed. "She doesn't know anything about acting. I should have been Juliet."

"Abby, please," Walter said. "This is not suitable behavior for rehearsal. We need to conduct ourselves as professionals," he pleaded.

"Conduct this," Abby roared, flipping Walter the bird, and flounced off the stage.

Penny grimaced. "That Abby's loopy. I told Walter to steer clear of her ever since she threw a tantrum over the casting for *Little Mary Sunshine*. As if she could carry a tune in a bucket."

"She's mad she didn't get my role," Juliet announced to everyone and sat in the first row.

I caught up with Lola and pointed to my watch. "Lola, we've got to get everyone out of here."

"I know," she said anxiously. "Walter agreed to stop at quarter to nine, but now with this disruption, and Juliet's upset . . . he says he wants to run it again."

"He can't do that," I wailed. "Morty Wendover is due here in thirty minutes."

Lola twisted her hands. "What should we do?"

"Can I help?"

We spun around and faced Elliot.

"Is there a problem?" he asked kindly.

I made a quick calculation. No one else was supposed to know about the meeting with Morty except Lola; but I needed help and Elliot was the most trusted person here next to us. "Elliot, we need to clear the stage, the theater really. Rehearsal has to end. Now," I said emphatically. "It's life or death," I added for good measure.

Elliot's quizzical expression could have triggered a lengthy explanation; instead, he nodded. He crossed to Walter, made a firm proclamation, and then gestured to Penny. Whatever he said worked, because in ten minutes the cast was packing up and splitting. Juliet was accompanied by two Ladies-in-Waiting, who commiserated mightily. Walter, with Lola's sympathy, swallowed two aspirins for his headache.

Penny tapped her clipboard. "I'm usually the last one out," she said meaningfully to me.

Elliot swept up the aisle, escorting Penny ahead of him. At the door to the theater he turned back and smiled at me. "Thanks," I said softly. It was nine-fifteen.

No sooner had Elliot exited into the lobby than Bill walked on stage.

"All set?" he asked.

"How did you—?" I gasped.

"I've been here for an hour. Your cast is pretty crazy." He checked his watch. "Stay alert." Then he went backstage again.

I sat in the first row of seats. The series of small spotlights that lit the house were distributed randomly across the ceiling and gave off just enough illumination for audience members to read their programs. The platforms and flexible cubes, that comprised the now-affordable *Romeo and Juliet* set, were covered in shadows, and the black curtains stage right and left looked ominous. Even though I knew Bill was standing guard, the atmosphere felt weird and haunted. I shuddered.

The door to the theater opened, and Morty stepped through it. "Ms. O'Dell?"

I was relieved to see his courteous face, atop a brown suit and tie. He looked so normal.

"Mr. Wendover? I'm down here."

He shaded his eyes, then walked slowly down the aisle. "I must confess, this is the most unusual spot I've ever conducted business in."

"I appreciate your coming here at such a late hour."

"So you work in the theater?" he asked, surveying the stage.

"Yes. I'm a production manager."

"Like uncle, like niece," he said.

I stared blankly at him. "I'm sorry?"

"Your uncle Jerome? He was a part of the theater, yes?"

My heart skipped a beat and my palms were damp. That was a weird comment. Had Jerome mentioned the ELT? "Yes, of course. He used to work the box office."

I steadied myself by leaning against the lip of the stage.

He smiled. "As we discussed, the usual first step is an examination of the document," he said politely and waited.

"Sure." I pulled the copy out of my bag and handed it to him.

Morty raised an eyebrow. "This is a reproduction."

"I thought maybe you could make an initial determination based on the handwriting."

He seemed to be weighing his options. "Ms. O'Dell, authenticating your uncle's document can only be done with the original. There are many excellent Lincoln forgeries. But the only way to validate a letter like this is through examining the paper and ink. I must see the original if you want an assessment. Do you have the letter with you?"

My silence told him what he needed to know.

"I understand your reluctance. You might have a fortune in your possession. Let's have a look. I might be able to save you time and money." He watched me consider his offer. "If you would be more comfortable in my office, we can arrange another meeting."

"No, we might as well do it now. If you can wait a minute, I'll get it. Just make yourself comfortable."

Morty smiled and sat down as I walked calmly up the aisle and into the lobby. I followed Bill's directions and opened an emergency door that led to a hallway. At the end of it, one could access the scene shop and backstage area.

Bill had been watching the entire exchange and was waiting for me.

"I'll be right here in case anything happens," he said softly, handing me the file.

My hands shook. "Thanks." I squared my shoulders and retraced my steps.

I walked back to the front row with the folder holding the Lincoln letter and prayed that this was not a mistake.

"Here it is." I flipped it open to show Morty the parchment paper in its plastic sleeve. He took a magnifying glass from an inside coat pocket and bent his head over the letter. I thought I heard a slight gasp, but I could have been wrong. He lifted his head, and the color seemed to have drained from his face, though his expression was as bland as it had been since his arrival.

"Well?" I said.

"It's fairly dark here. Is there somewhere else we could go?"

Leaving the house was not part of the plan. Walter's office would make the most sense, but Bill was backstage. I had to think fast.

"Somewhere with brighter incandescent light?" Morty said.

"Maybe a dressing room? Makeup mirrors are very bright."

Morty nodded. I took back the file and stashed the document in my bag. We climbed the steps house right. I took my time picking my way around the balcony/ladder, platform bed, and assorted square blocks that would serve as chairs, tables, and coffins. Morty was two steps behind me. And Bill was somewhere behind the black curtains.

"*Romeo and Juliet?*"

"Yes. Big challenge." I laughed to keep myself calm.

We entered the green room and I flicked on the fluorescent over-heads. I still had Lola's master key so I crossed to the women's dressing room and unlocked the door. Before I could withdraw the key from the lock, Morty had turned on the light bulbs that rimmed each actor's mirror. I blinked.

"This should do it," Morty said and sat in one of the makeup chairs.

I carefully placed the letter on the makeup counter, one hand still on the corner of the encased document. Morty took out his magnifying glass again and studied the text, the signature, and the paper fiber.

"The letter is promising," he said.

"That's good to hear." I could feel tension in my solar plexus. Every breath was like a knot being tied, then loosened.

"But of course I will need to do some lab tests."

"How long will that take?" I asked. I hoped Bill was close by, overhearing all of our conversation.

"It depends on the date of the document. The quality of the paper, the composition of the ink ..." He raised his hands as if in regret. "There's little else I can say at this point."

"Well, I'll come by your office tomorrow."

"I'm sorry Ms. O'Dell. ..." His polite smile had turned into a sneer. "Or whoever you are, but I cannot let this letter out of my possession."

"Excuse me?" I said.

He reached for the letter and I grasped it away from him. "Don't tear it!" he yelled and stood.

Suddenly I had the upper hand. "It's that valuable?"

"You have no idea what you are holding in your hand."

I eased back a couple of steps, guesstimating the distance to the door. "Worth half a million, huh?" I tried to release a nonchalant laugh, but the sound caught on the back of my throat. I sputtered. "No wonder you killed Jerome for it."

My accusation stopped him in his tracks. "I don't know what you are talking about."

"Jerome said he wouldn't pay your fee, so you tried to get access to it yourself. When he refused, you killed him."

Where was Bill?

"Jerome had no idea what he had found. Now I mean to have it."

Morty faltered for a split second. Sitting on the makeup table to my right was a stack of blouses and an iron. I used his hesitation to heave the iron at him. I clipped him on the left side of his head and he howled, then fell to the ground. I slammed my hand against the light switch and ran into the green room. If he got to his feet, he would be expecting me to run to the stage; a better option was lying low in the wardrobe room and trying to contact Bill. I reversed direction, sprinted down a short hallway off the green room, and plunged Lola's master key into the lock.

I pulled the door shut. My eyes adjusting to the faint light, I could see rows of costumes running parallel from one side of the room to the other. The closest racks would be devoted to *Romeo and Juliet*.

I whipped out my cell phone and punched in Bill's number. His voice mail came on. "Bill, I'm in the wardrobe room and Morty's in the women's dressing room." I clicked off.

I shook my head. I had to think straight. Bill had said Edna would be at dispatch if I couldn't reach him. I tapped on 911.

"Edna—" I hissed.

"Dodie, is that you?"

"I'm trapped in the wardrobe room at the theater. You've got to find Bill. He's not answering his cell."

"Hold on."

I could hear her sending a radio message. Maybe to Bill or to Suki. Please God not to Ralph. "It's a 240 and maybe a 217. But be prepared for a 207. . . . What? A twenty—oh, forget the code and just get to the theater, Ralph."

My heart sank. I heard a noise in the hallway and clicked off. I stooped down, crawling behind the first rack of costumes. The door handle turned slowly, and a figure was silhouetted in the entrance backlit by the light from the green room.

"Dodie?"

I nearly cried with relief. "Elliot?"

The wardrobe lights snapped on and my eyes closed instinctively to avoid the harsh glare of the fluorescents. I scrambled to my feet. "Elliot, am I glad to see you! There's a man in the women's dressing room and he—"

"Yes, I saw him."

"I was sorry I had to lob that iron."

Elliot chuckled. "I think you put him out of commission. What happened in there?"

"He wanted a letter . . . the valuable document that got Jerome murdered." My eyes slid to my bag, which rested underneath the clothing rack. Elliot's eyes followed mine.

"That's right," Elliot said smoothly.

Too smoothly. My skin crawled. "You know about . . . ?"

"The Lincoln letter? Yes. Jerome told me all about it."

Elliot pulled a gun from his pocket and pointed it at me.

"Elliot . . . ?" I froze. I could feel the sweat trickling down the inside of my silk blouse. "What are you doing?"

"Give me the letter."

My mind was reeling. I couldn't put together my image of the Elliot I had come to know the past few weeks with this man holding a gun on me.

"Don't waste my time," he said and waved the gun at me. "You don't want to end up like Jerome."

I gasped. "You, you . . . murdered . . . ?"

"Well, I didn't pull the trigger." He paused. "I was sorry, but he was obstinate. I couldn't reason with him." He waggled the gun and smiled. "Unlike you, I'm sure. I like you, Dodie, and I'd hate to have to do something we'd both regret."

I prayed that Bill would be here any minute. I had to keep him talking. "Elliot, how could you do that to your best friend?"

"Jerome was about to call the whole thing off. I couldn't have that. There was too much money at stake. Now hand it over."

My mind was racing. "Did Marshall know what Morty was up to?"

"Marshall couldn't find his way out of a paper bag. He had nothing to do with this."

"So Morty's the brains in the family. Wonderful company you keep, Elliot," I said, my voice shaky.

"We go way back."

Please, Bill, show up! "And you dumped Jerome's body on the loading dock? That seems stupid. Like you were telling the police where Jerome was murdered."

Elliot's mouth formed a tight line. "Jerome wasn't supposed to die. But afterwards, Morty panicked. It was getting close to dawn and he was afraid to be seen." Elliot shrugged. "It was the simplest solution." He took a threatening step toward me. "Enough talk."

I stood in his way.

"Move!" he said and gestured with his gun.

I eased a couple of steps to my right, and Elliot bent down to retrieve my bag. He took his eyes off me for one second, and I dashed for the entrance to the wardrobe room. Elliot whipped around just in time to see me collide with Bill in the doorway, his service pistol pointed at Elliot's head.

"Drop the gun."

Elliot complied.

Relief flooded through my veins like warm milk. The man was my hero.

Main Street was awash with flashing lights atop squad cars. Even though the station was just around the corner, the perpetrators were loaded into the back of two vehicles. Bill had placed Elliot in his patrol car, with the obligatory hand on the perp's head to foil inadvertent cranial damage, while Suki and Ralph handled Morty, who was groggy and disheveled, and the massive fellow I had seen coming into Morty's office building. He drove Morty in the black SUV. I remembered later that he was the mountain of flesh I had bumped into at Jerome's funeral. It turns out he and Morty were responsible for the break-ins. And while Morty and I had been doing business in the dressing room, he'd had a run-in with Bill. Literally.

Lola and I sipped from coffee containers.

She shook her head. "Jerome and Elliot were such good friends. At least, I thought they were."

"I think Jerome did, too. That's why he confided in Elliot about the letter."

"And took Elliot's advice about Forensic Document Services," she said.

"Jerome and Mary never needed the money as much as Elliot."

"I knew he spent a lot in Atlantic City. Even that he was in debt. But this?" Lola shook her head. "He never let on."

We'd learned later that Elliot's debts had provided motivation, and Morty, who was a forger and handwriting expert, had provided assistance. They were both high rollers who'd met in Atlantic City, where they'd plotted the theft. Jerome's murder was collateral damage. Elliot would have preferred not to have Jerome killed, as he'd said, but Jerome had smelled a rat and was about to tell Mary to turn the document over to the library. Elliot had to act fast because Jerome had intended to visit Mary the day after the auditions and end the whole business. *MR 4/16*. I was willing to bet that a diamond ring would have been part of that visit.

"I almost made a fool of myself over Elliot," Lola said sheepishly. "I feel like I don't know him after years of working together."

"We were all taken in. Myself included."

"But I should have been suspicious, the way he disappeared, then reappeared after Jerome died," Lola said.

The squad cars drove off, blue and red lights rotating. The crowd that had gathered was dispersing. Tomorrow morning, Etonville would be saturated with gossip and innuendo. But for once I didn't mind the prospect. I was beginning to think that Etonville's rumor mill was really just a testament to its community spirit. The town was feeling more and more like home.

Bill joined us, rubbing his head where Morty's hatchet man had delivered a glancing blow before Bill had knocked him out. "I've got to get to the station. It'll be a long night of paperwork. Good job, Dodie."

I smiled. "Thanks. How's your head?"

"I'll live."

"I'll check in with you tomorrow," I said.

"It's a deal."

Lola watched me watching Bill walk off. "Hmmm," she said.

Chapter 27

"One, please," a husky voice said.

I looked through the box office partition, ripped off a stub from my roll of tickets, and exchanged it for fifteen dollars. "Enjoy the show," I said to Mary.

"Thank you," she said and placed her hand on the lip of the window. Jerome's diamond ring sparkled in the lobby light. I thought, and Bill agreed, that there was no point in leaving it in the evidence locker. It didn't bear on the murder case, and Jerome would have been pleased to see her wearing it. The Lincoln letter, on the other hand, had been transferred to a legitimate authentication company by the Etonville Public Library. Whether it was worth half a million or not remained to be seen, but with the library probably coming into some big bucks, Mildred had coaxed Mary into taking up residence once again in the special collections. Luther, who claimed he couldn't trust Mary, had his doubts, but Mildred was persuasive—she threatened to resign. Besides Bill had convinced Luther that there was no point in pressing charges against Mary, now that the letter was safe.

Mary toddled off to the house and I began to close up the box office.

Behind me, Lola had slipped into the lobby from backstage. She was in full makeup, her hair in an updo, thanks to Carol, queen of the updos, and was wearing a dark purple dressing gown.

"What are you doing out here? It's nearly eight o'clock." Real time, according to Penny, but in theater time it was "places."

"I wanted to check the house," she said. "It looks like most of Etonville has turned out for opening night."

"I hope not. I'm counting on a big crowd tomorrow when we

debut our dinner-then-theater. We're going to set up an outdoor café."

After spending long hours deliberating about the theme for the *Romeo and Juliet* dinner, I had decided that, although the play seemed to be about passion, murder, poison, and the heat in Verona, it was also about reconciliation. The Jets and the Sharks, the Capulets and Montagues, the Windjammer and La Famiglia. I'd negotiated a truce between the two restaurants such that Henry made the entrees, La Famiglia provided several pasta dishes, and Georgette's Bakery—neutral territory—supplied desserts. Everyone was, well, if not exactly happy, at least talking.

I supposed reconciliation was in the air. JC replaced the balcony/ladder with a five-foot platform that cost less and didn't trigger Romeo's "angoraphobia," Abby was on probation with the Etonville Little Theatre for her lack of professionalism, and Walter had promised to keep his fingers out of the box office till. Lola was now the treasurer. With the murder wrapped up, Bill had let Walter off the hook with a stern warning and Walter's guarantee that he would repay the ELT funds.

Penny bounced into the lobby, head set in place and clipboard tucked under her arm, closely followed by Walter in a flowing shirt that revealed a little bulge at his belly.

"Lola, your public can't see you before the curtain rises." He tried to take her hand and kiss it. He'd been in an exceptionally good mood since Elliot had been removed from the show.

"Walter, stow it. I'm on my way now," Lola said firmly. Some relationship work needed to be done there.

"Lola, you should be backstage now. You're on." Penny pushed her glasses up her nose. "O'Dell, we go in five."

Carol stuck her head into the lobby. "I'm not finished," she said and waved a can of hair spray.

"Well, this is it," I said. I extended my hand and Lola took it. Carol laid hers on top. Penny got into it and clapped Carol's. Walter just looked at us blankly.

"Oh, come on, Walter. Live a little," Lola said.

Walter tentatively rested his hand on Penny's.

"Show time!" I snapped a group selfie.

"Let's do it," Penny said, and everyone darted off.

I closed the box-office window.

The lights were dimming as I entered the house and spotted my row, halfway down the aisle. Carol and her husband sat next to Pauli and his date, a young brunette who looked an awful lot like him. Carol was euphoric.

The pre-show music swelled and the main drape rose. I slipped into the second seat from the aisle and glanced at the empty one next to me. *Oh well*, I thought, and settled in. *He probably had an emergency. A 217 or a 450 or a 1098—*

"Hope I'm not too late," Bill said.

"Just in time," I whispered to Etonville's new hero. Since arresting Elliot for Jerome's murder, Bill had attained a new status in town. His photograph from an interview with the *Etonville Standard* was going up in the lobby of the Municipal Building right next to Bull Bennett and his thirty-pound bass.

The house went out and we sat in darkness for three seconds. Lights gradually came up on the company—Walter looked resplendent in Elizabethan velvet, Lola regal in blue satin. They stood on either side of the Prince, the formerly disgruntled Servant-Watchman-Guard who had gotten promoted since the first Prince was resting in the Episcopal cemetery and the second one was sitting in the county jail awaiting his day in court. The iambic pentameter rolled out of their mouths, Walter's head bobbing slightly.

I relaxed into the back of my seat. *Tonight's for you, Jerome*, I thought.

Unexpectedly, Bill squeezed my hand.

OMG.

ABOUT THE AUTHOR

Suzanne Trauth is a novelist, playwright, screenwriter, and a former university theater professor. She is a member of Mystery Writers of America, Sisters in Crime, and the Dramatists Guild. When she is not writing, Suzanne coaches actors and serves as a celebrant performing wedding ceremonies. She lives in Woodland Park, New Jersey. Readers can visit her website at www.suzannetrauth.com

Lightning Source UK Ltd.
Milton Keynes UK
UKOW04f1833271117
313459UK00001B/150/P